final
edit

final edit

robert a. carter

THE MYSTERIOUS PRESS

Published by Warner Books

A Time Warner Company

Mysterious Press books are published by Warner Books, Inc.,
1271 Avenue of the Americas, New York, NY 10020.

W A Time Warner Company

The Mysterious Press name and logo are registered trademarks of Warner Books, Inc.
Printed in the United States of America
First printing: July 1994

10 9 8 7 6 5 4 3 2 1

Library of Congress Cataloging-in-Publication Data

Carter, Robert A.
    Final edit / Robert A. Carter.
      p. cm.
    ISBN 0-89296-549-5
    1. Publishers and publishing—New York (N.Y.)—Fiction.
  I. Title.
    PS3553.A783F56 1994
    813'.54—dc20   94-5068
                                  CIP

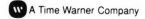

*This one is for Regula Noetzli,
my favorite literary agent*

ACKNOWLEDGMENTS

My thanks to Roger Bryant Hunting, former Judge of the New York Criminal Court, for helpful information; to my wife, Reade Johnson Carter, for her steadfast support; and to William Malloy and Justine Elias of Mysterious Press, for their invaluable editorial guidance.

Nothing in his life
became him like the leaving it; he died
as one that had been studied in his death
To throw away the dearest thing he ow'ed
As 'twere a careless trifle.

Macbeth, I, iv, 7–11

final
edit

Prologue

The murder of Parker Foxcroft sent shock waves through the book publishing community that would easily have registered 7.5 on the Richter scale.

This is the how the *New York Times* obituary writer eulogized him:

> Not since the legendary Max Perkins has an editor inspired so much devotion among his authors and colleagues. The words "A Parker Foxcroft Book" were a hallmark of quality and literary distinction. Foxcroft did in fact have his own imprint at Barlow & Company, a small, prestigious, family-owned Manhattan firm. During the course of his twenty-two-year career, Foxcroft edited the works of two Nobel laureates, several Pulitzer Prize winners, and at least five National Book Award winners and nominees. Among his authors were . . .

This song of praise was followed by laudatory comments from several of Foxcroft's authors, a brace of literary agents, and three editors from other houses. Conspicuous by his absence from this outpouring of esteem was the publisher of Barlow & Company, Nicholas Barlow. Many wondered at the time about his silence.

Chapter 1

If ever a man was cut out to be a murder victim, it was certainly Parker Foxcroft. Arrogant, ruthless, manipulative, a womanizer and a rampant literary snob, he was notoriously devious, vicious at times—even for the book business.

I ought to know; he worked for me. As the president and publisher of Barlow & Company, I hired Parker as a senior editor and gave him his own imprint three years ago. I was within a nanominute of firing him, too, when someone with a stronger motive than I *iced* him, as the mobsters put it in the crime novels I so happily and successfully publish. Or is the word now *whacked*? *Offed,* perhaps? At any rate, there may soon be almost as many synonyms for "killed" as there are for "drunk" (357 at last count, beginning with "bagged" and ending with "zonked").

I can't say I was surprised when Parker turned up dead, but I was certainly inconvenienced, in more ways than one. You see, *I* was the one who found his body, not long after we had a violent shouting match.

*   *   *

It was at the ABA Convention that I realized something would have to be done about Parker.

Like the Trobriand Islanders or the Benevolent and Protective Order of Elks, we book publishers have our peculiar and arcane tribal rites. One is the Frankfurt Book Fair; another is the American Booksellers Association Convention. Frankfurt, however, is a global affair, an *Oktoberfest* held in four cavernous convention halls a third of a mile west of the *Bahnhof,* Frankfurt's rail station, while the ABA—it is never referred to formally—is a moveable feast, convened each year in a different locale. There are only a handful of cities in America with convention centers large enough to hold it, for it is a mighty gathering of the clans: some 25,000 to 30,000 people attending—5,000 or 6,000 of whom are actually booksellers—and there are 1,200 or more exhibitors, most of them book publishers. At the ABA, publishers launch their new lists and push their established titles; booksellers come to see, to buy, to attend seminars, and to meet old friends.

All of which explains why I found myself in Washington, D.C., on Friday, May 28, the Memorial Day weekend. The choice of this holiday for the ABA is also part of the ritual. It is one of the cruelest bits of scheduling I know: to keep the publishers away from the beaches, the tennis courts, and the golf links, so that the booksellers—who would normally close their shops on this weekend—can enjoy their moment in the sun.

And sun was what hit me when I got off the shuttle at Washington National, collected my bag, and stepped out of the terminal. Hit me with tropical force. Here it was, only the tag end of May, and already ninety in the shade.

I turned to Sidney Leopold, the editor in chief of my

publishing house, who had accompanied me on the flight down.

"*God*, Sidney, the heat. 'Summer is icumen in,' no? 'Lhude sing cuccu!' "

"Ice-cream weather all right, Nuh-Nick," he said.

"I was thinking vodka and tonic myself."

"Do you know, Nick," said Sidney, "that Hä-Häagen-Dazs has come out with a new line called 'Exträas'—wu-with an umlaut, of course."

"Oh?"

"A thousand cuh-calories more than their regular—*flavors*."

It was enough to turn me ashen. I must explain that ice cream, all kinds and varieties of it, is Sidney's ruling passion. Were I to consume as much of it as he packs away in an ordinary month, I would probably weigh in at 50 pounds over my fighting weight, which is 225 or 230, give or take a few pounds. Nicholas Barlow, *Homo giganticus*. No thank you. As it is, I can hardly open a menu these days, or pass by a bakery, without gaining weight—or so it would seem. Sidney, meanwhile, remains slim and flat-bellied through it all.

A cab, mercifully air-conditioned, pulled up just then and rescued us from the heat. And the humidity. Washington is world-famous for both.

Fond as I am of our nation's capital, I've always appreciated John F. Kennedy's quip at its expense. "Washington," JFK said, "is a city of southern efficiency and northern charm." Still, you must agree that a city that will not allow any building to rise higher than ninety feet—so as not to block anyone's view of the Capitol, I believe—certainly has its architectural priorities straight.

We checked in at the Shoreham Hotel shortly after noon.

I know there are more luxurious hotels in town; the Shoreham is a trifle shabby-genteel, but I like it, and there is a great deal of nostalgia connected with the place, for me at least. When I was still an undergraduate at Princeton, I attended a couple of ABAs with my father. In those days, the convention was held every year in Washington—I suspect because the association had some kind of sweetheart deal with the hotel—and the exhibits were all set up in the basement garage of the Shoreham. People usually stayed either at the Shoreham or at the Park-Sheraton, now the Sheraton Washington, across the street.

And what memories I have . . .

Wandering the halls of the hotel in the small hours of the morning, looking for parties. We found them by following the roars of laughter and boisterous conversation coming from the open doors of hospitality suites, or the sound of a guitar and someone singing a folk song . . . The nights then seemed to be one long, continuous party . . . and the mornings one long hangover. Vodka stingers and brandy Alexanders were high on our list of preferred drinks. So, like the chain-smokers of long ago who were unwittingly writing their death certificates every day that passed, we were heedless in our haste to wreak a similar havoc on our livers . . .

Lest you think I'm some kind of Mrs. Grundy, I hasten to add that I still smoke an occasional cigar, if it's a good one, and feel quite comfortable with a glass in my hand, if that glass is filled with the precise mixture of Absolut and Noilly Prat. I drink, frankly, whenever the spirit moves me.

Diving into the pool one morning, I spotted something white and shining at the bottom. It was a convention badge, of all things. When I fished it out, I discovered that it was my *badge, though I hadn't the faintest idea how it got there . . .*

There was always at least one poker game, a dollar and five dollars, in one hotel room or another, blue with smoke and reeking of malt. It was a democratic game: publishers sat facing their sales reps, and the reps went head-to-head with booksellers. The game was stag, of course . . .

Pleasant memories, to be sure. The year has never quite been complete for me without an ABA. And as much as they grouse about the expense of it, and claim that it's really not worth it ("Nobody does any business there" is the common refrain), I suspect that most of my fellow publishers feel the same way, even if they go because it would be imprudent to stay away. If it's an orgy, at least it's our very own orgy.

Chapter 2

As soon as we had unpacked, Sidney and I headed for the Convention Center, this time in an unair-conditioned cab.

We found our booth quickly enough, and in it Mary Sunday, our sales manager, wearing the most woeful expression I had seen on her face since our star sales rep defected to Simon & Schuster.

"Oh, Nick," she wailed, "the *books* haven't come. That buggerall exhibitor's service has fucked us up for fair." Not for Mary the ladylike euphemisms.

I made an effort to cheer her up. "Well, at least the posters are here."

Some of the exhibitors at the ABA still make it a practice to show off actual books; others display only oversize posters or the jackets of their forthcoming titles. Barlow & Company does both, though the books somehow seem superfluous, since almost no one takes the time to browse through them. I once calculated that if a person were to visit every booth at the ABA at least once in the three and a half days of the convention, each booth would receive exactly forty-five seconds of one's attention. No, the best we could hope for is that passersby would be attracted by the posters and stop in so we could talk up our forthcoming list. The whole point of the exercise is to show our new stuff—best foot forward, and all that.

"But the *catalogs* haven't shown up, either," said Mary Sunday. "And our location is terrible. *Terrible*. It sucks."

"I duh-don't know," said Sidney. "We're not too fuh-far from the cuh-concession stands. Could be worse." I knew that Sidney, once again, was thinking ice cream.

But Mary was inconsolable. "I wish they'd let us pick our own space the way they used to, instead of assigning booths by lottery," she said. "Here we are with a greeting-card company on one side of us and a university press on the other."

Two of our sales reps were with us in the booth (actually we had splurged and taken *three* booths, and at considerable expense. Though small, we're a proud company, in my humble opinion the best publisher of mysteries and thrillers in the business, among our other achievements). The reps were stacking up order forms in the hope that when the booksellers did come around tomorrow, they would really want to place orders. One of the reps, Chezna Newman, a comely young woman with a distinctive New York accent, chimed in with: "What's wrong"—the word came out "wrong-uh"—"with a univoisity press?" Chezna also had a distressing habit of chewing gum with her mouth open. Those two imperfections aside, she was damned good at pushing books out into the marketplace.

"I don't know, the proximity of all that high-toned schol-arship might give us even more class than we already have."

This came from the other sales rep in the booth, Toby Finn, a veteran of more than twenty years in the business.

Small, shrewd, and glib, Toby had been flown into D.C. from Chicago as a reward for an especially good year.

"Outside of no books and no catalogs, are we ready to go?" I put the question to Mary, who sighed and nodded. Chezna grinned, and Toby Finn gave me the thumbs-up sign.

Things were heating up on the exhibition floor by now. Forklifts moving down the aisles with huge cartons, crates, and skids of books. Carpets were being laid and nailed into place; banners were being strung; electric wires and spotlights put up. It was bedlam, din, and confusion throughout the hall, and quite incredible to think that by tomorrow morning it would all be ready.

"In that case," I said, "I think I'll hit the pool. Coming, Sidney?"

"Shuh-shuh-*sure.*"

"I'll see you all later in the hospitality suite." The suite was another extravagance, but useful for entertaining booksellers, foreign publishers, and sundry media people. It boasted a bar, always open, and the bedroom was shared by Mary Sunday and Chezna Newman, which made the extra expense bearable.

"The suite is ready, I take it?"

"Fully stocked," said Sunday. "Plenty of booze, beer, soda, nibbles, and ice."

"Good show." And with that, Sidney and I headed for the Shoreham, leaving Mary and company to finish the work.

When I got back to the hotel, I found a message in my box: "Call M. Mandelbaum ASAP." Up in my room, I dialed the office and asked for my controller.

"Mort? It's Nick."

"Oh, Nick, good, thanks for calling back. How's the weather in Washington?"

I knew Mort Mandelbaum hadn't called me long-distance just for a weather report, so I cut him short. "What's up?"

"Bad news, Nick. The bank is threatening to reduce our line of credit. Just when we're facing heavy print bills for the fall list."

"Serious cuts?"

"Serious enough. Any reduction right now will hurt."

"Do you think I ought to go to the bank and remind them of auld lang syne?" We had been banking with Federal Trust ever since my parents had started Barlow & Company. It had been an altogether satisfactory union, if a relationship based entirely on money can be compared to a marriage. Why, then, were they giving us a problem now?

"That might be a good idea, Nick," said Mandelbaum. "As soon as you can? Please?"

"Or we might ask the printers to extend us more credit."

"What? Surely you joke."

"That's right. Joke."

"And maybe you could arrange to come back from the ABA with a best-seller under your arm. To pay for all those money-losers Parker Foxcroft brings in? Please?"

"Parker's books give us prestige, Mort. They give us great visibility in the trade."

A sigh. "Who can pay the printers with prestige? Not Mortimer Mandelbaum."

"I'll be back in the office on Tuesday morning. We'll deal with the bank then."

"Okay, Nick." He still sounded miserable, so I added:

"Cheer up, Morty. Remember my motto."

"How could I forget? It's in a frame on your desk. 'Something will turn up.' The picture of the guy with the noose around his neck? Right?"

"Right. Dr. Samuel Johnson. Also Mr. Micawber." And we rang off.

I spent the balance of the afternoon floundering in the hotel pool and basking in the shade, a cold vodka and tonic in hand, while admiring the bathing beauties reclining around the pool. Not for me the drudgery of setting up an exhibit. Rank, after all, does have its privileges.

When the cocktail hour rolled around, I showered, changed into what I thought was the right outfit for the occasion: dove-gray cotton slacks, lightweight navy-blue blazer, white shirt, and my favorite club tie—a number from The Players on Gramercy Park: silver masks of comedy and tragedy on a maroon field—and Gucci loafers. Summer is as summer does.

At the hospitality suite, I found Mary Sunday and Toby Finn tending bar, and Chezna Newman chatting with a bookseller. Sidney Leopold was sipping a soda in a corner of the room, looking intently into the eyes of one of his authors.

"Nick," Mary sang out. "Good news!"

"Let me guess. The books came."

"Yeah, finally! Also the catalogs."

I heaved a sigh of relief. All was now well at the Barlow & Company booth. I had learned at ABAs past that nothing can demoralize an exhibitor more than missing the crucial elements of the exhibit. I remember one year coming on a friend of mine sitting in a folding chair in the midst of . . . nothing, absolutely nothing—except a hand-lettered sign giving the name of his company and the number of his booth. When he saw me, he smiled wanly, and when I put the question to him, he raised his hands in mute supplication. "Shoulda stayed home, Nick," he said with a sigh. I was tempted to offer him part of our booth—we had too many books out, anyway—but thought he might feel I was making fun of him. The poor devil's booth never did show up, so after waiting a day he returned home, a loser however you look at it.

Just then Parker Foxcroft entered the suite. He proceeded to the bar, where he accepted a drink from Mary. Leaning over, he whispered something in her ear. She giggled, and Parker joined in with his distinctive whoop of laughter. Parker's laugh is more a bray, which I have always thought he affects. When he is really amused, it comes out as a snort: huah . . . huah . . . HUAH!

Spotting me, he approached, all six feet three of him. Parker is the only member of my staff who can look me straight in the eye. Lanky frame; you'd call him slim if you fancied the look, skinny if you did not. (No, I am not at all envious.) His hair is rather thin, too, long strands combed from the side of his head across his pate to cover the bald spot—the kind of coiffure I think would be perilous in a high wind. I was reminded of something my father told me years ago, when I had commented on an actor whose toupee I thought was rather improbable. "Just remember," said my father, "that not everyone in this world is as well feathered as we are." That was long before my father's golden fleece, too, became only a distant memory.

When Parker laughs, his ordinarily pale complexion reddens as though exposed too long in the sun. By the time he reached me, his guffaws had subsided to a stray chuckle or two, though his cheeks remained a bright red. I could not understand why so many women apparently found him irresistible; yet he was seldom seen without one beauty or another on his arm, and his social life was spoken of in the office with genuine awe. But then, there is no mystery so insoluble as human sexuality. Perhaps it is better to leave it unsolved. As Mae West said of the Kinsey report: it takes all the fun out of sex.

"Nick," said Parker in a near shout. "I *love* the booth." The look on his face was infuriatingly complacent, however—a smirk, in fact.

I braced myself.

"But where is the poster for *A Wind from the South?*"

This was Parker's lead title on the fall list. He had refused to concede, after any amount of opposition from the reps at our sales conference, that there might not be great enthusiasm for a historical novel set in Philadelphia in 1790 during a yellow fever epidemic—except perhaps in Philadelphia. "It has Pulitzer Prize written all over it," he protested. I could imagine that award, literally written in Parker's own hand on the jacket. And when Parker said, as he often did, that one of his books would "get a good press," I visualized the book clamped tightly in a vise, oozing printer's ink.

"Mary is in charge of the exhibit," I said. "Did you ask her?"

"She said you had the final say."

"Only if there is a deadlock of some kind."

"Nevertheless," he said, pointing his index finger in the general direction of my chest, and staring at me with those pinkish eyes of his, "the buck stops here."

I shrugged. "We can't feature every book on the list." A lame excuse, but the best I could come up with on the spur of the moment.

"You seem to have gone all out for that private-dick novel," said Parker, putting a good deal of weight on the word "dick." I do not allow anyone to make light of Barlow & Company mysteries; they're not only my bread and butter, they're also my champagne and caviar.

"*Say It with Bullets,*" I said, "will probably pay both your salary and mine this year." Set in Buffalo, my lead fall mystery starred P.I. Homer Blank, plodding through the snowdrifts in search of a computer hack who had broken the entry codes of a local bank and was robbing it silly. To kick off the promotion for the book, we had brought not only a poster to the ABA but also a special convention edition in paperback, with a personal message on the back cover from yours truly—a gesture I make only once a year, so as not to water my own stock.

"Perhaps *I* ought to think of acquiring a mystery," said Foxcroft.

"Stick to your last, Parker," I said.

If it seems odd that I put up with such impertinence from one of my own employees, which I suppose no one in the cloak-and-suit or tool-and-dye business would do, look at it this way: Parker Foxcroft has the *touch.* Authors come to him eagerly, hoping to be anointed. Critics for the *New Statesman, The Times Literary Supplement,* and other high-toned journals turn cartwheels to praise the books he edits, season after season. I am frequently tempted to fire him, but how can I, as long as he has the touch?

Still, I found it inexplicably irritating that in addition to his other abrasive qualities, the man bore the names of *two* private schools.

Parker drifted off, and I sidled over to Sidney, who was standing alone by the window.

"Has Harry arrived yet, do you know?"

"Bunter?" said Sidney. "I don't know."

"I hope so," I said. "We're due at the *New Yorker* party this evening. How about you?"

Harry Bunter is my subsidiary rights director, a job well worth a vice-presidency and a handsome salary. As the saying goes, it's the pigs closest to the trough who get the most to eat, and those who bring in revenue who enjoy the highest salaries. When the fiscal year is over, a rights director like Harry Bunter is often solely responsible for the difference between red ink and black.

"You don't mind if I skip the party scene tonight, do you, Nick?" said Sidney. "I'd rather curl up with a good manuscript."

"Absolutely not," I said, patting him on the shoulder. He looked startled. "That is, I absolutely do *not* mind. Whatever you like, Sidney. You may have more fun than any of us."

There being no other guests in sight, it seemed time to close up the hospitality suite and get ready for the parties. Mary and Chezna offered to tidy up, as well they might, since it was their living room.

"Until later," I said. "We'll reopen for business after dinner," and took off for the hotel.

Chapter 3

Back in my room, I thought about my phone conversation with Mort Mandelbaum. I was reminded once again, as I have been so often in my years as a publisher, how precarious the business is. The bankers are right to be skeptical about our financial health. No matter how I diddle with the figures, it always works out that at least thirty percent of the books I publish lose money, forty percent of them break even, and another thirty make money—if I'm lucky. And the margin of profit is seldom more than ten percent, often as low as five. Who would go into a business with those odds? A gambler. A hopeless optimist. Someone who loves making books more than making money—but would be deliriously happy making both.

The phone interrupted my reverie, which, as is true so often when I think about finances, was without resolution.

"Nick? It's Harry."

"Harry, you're here. Good."

"I'm downstairs, Nick."

"I'll be right down."

*   *   *

Party-giving at the ABA has changed over the years. The wide-open hospitality of long ago has gone by the board, along with the freeloading. Most of the parties worth attending are by invitation only, and the invitations are given out sparingly, especially in hard economic times. Some of the publishers have even gone so far as to set up cash bars and eliminate food. The *New Yorker* party, however, is always popular, because it is usually held in an exotic location, and is well catered. Not for Si Newhouse your routine hotel suite. This year's party was to be a moonlight cruise on a boat, *The Queen of the Potomac,* and invitations were much in demand. Barlow & Company had been rationed two.

I picked up Harry Bunter in the lobby. If Harry were selling real estate instead of intellectual property rights, he'd be a member of the Five Million Dollar Club, and they'd put his name and picture in an ad: "Harry Bunter, Salesman of the Month," that sort of thing. What he does, he does incomparably well.

Not that you'd know it to look at him. Today, as usual, Harry was wearing a light gray suit that looked as though it hadn't felt the kiss of an iron in months. His collar was open, necktie hanging loosely down over his substantial gut. Harry has what is commonly called a "corporation." The heat of the day had not treated him kindly, either: sweat glistened on his neck and face, and his thinning auburn hair was plastered across his forehead. As usual, he was enveloped in a blue haze of tobacco smoke, his cigarette in a plastic holder, which, despite all evidence to the contrary, he firmly believed would protect him from lung cancer. And also as usual, the shoulders of his suit were sprinkled with ashes. Joe Camel himself.

The odd part of it is that Harry is married to one of the

most beautiful women I know. Claire Lindsay Bunter is one of Parker Foxcroft's distinguished authors, and as soignée as Harry is rumpled. Perhaps opposites do attract, after all.

"Jesus, Nick," Bunter said. "You look dressed for . . . for a reception at Buckingham Palace, for chrissake."

To my outfit at the hospitality suite, I had added a broad-brimmed panama hat and a malacca cane. Just before leaving the suite, I had pinched a carnation from the flower arrangement on the coffee table; it was now planted in my buttonhole. Even so, I hardly felt overdressed—except alongside Harry.

We took a cab through Rock Creek Park, its trees prodigal with green leaves shimmering in the setting sun, to the Harry T. Thompson Boat Center, the designated point of departure in the *New Yorker* invitation. Quite a crowd had already gathered at the dock, although we were at least half an hour early. Once the barrier was lifted and the ramp was clear, we went on board.

The Queen of the Potomac reminded me of the Circle Line boats that ply the waters of the Hudson and East rivers around Manhattan, only tonier by any standard. A full-size cutout of Eustace Tilley greeted us at the first two bars; a rock group with a strong calypso beat was playing in the bow; I recognized Arrow's "Hot Hot Hot"—as appropriate for Washington, D.C., as it was for the Caribbean.

"Upper or lower deck?" I said to Harry.

"Lower's fine," he replied. "Let's hope I don't get seasick."

I ordered a Stolichnaya martini; Harry settled for a bottle of Amstel Light. As we sipped, we looked around to see who we might fraternize with.

"Nick," Harry said, coming up for air and wiping foam

from his lips, "I've got news that will improve your appetite. As well as your disposition."

"Nothing wrong with my appetite, alas," I said. "Shoot."

"Well," he began, "a certain best-selling author . . . excuse me, Nick . . ." At this he pulled a cigarette from a rumpled pack, lit it, and stuffed it into his holder. All this took a deal of time, as Mark Twain might say, and I felt fidgety, wondering if the cigarette shtick was merely Harry's way of heightening the suspense.

"Come on, Harry," I said. "What best-selling author?"

He ignored my remark, and after a puff or two, continued. "As I was saying . . . you've heard of Herbert Poole, Nick." It was not a question.

"Everybody on this tub has heard of him," I said. "The author of the number one best-seller on the *Times Book Review* list?"

Pan at Twilight. A novel at once erotic and elegantly crafted, but accessible even to the great unread. A masterpiece, some reviewers had called it—but that word is so grossly overworked, I distrust its use. Herbert Poole had, however, been favorably compared to D. H. Lawrence, among other poets of the carnal. I hadn't read the book myself. It probably wouldn't surprise anybody to learn that we publishers read few books—only those we *have* to read, usually. And we buy even fewer. Instead, we scrounge them from fellow publishers.

I recall once asking Charles Scribner the elder for one of his books, promising in return to send him any one of mine he might covet. I forget what book it was I wanted: probably a Hemingway volume, one of the many published since his death. In fact, more Hemingway books have turned up since his suicide than were published in his lifetime. Posthumous

Hemingway has been a growth industry for the Scribners and Hemingway's widow, Mary.

"I don't approve of the practice," Charlie sniffed, "but in your case, I'll make an exception."

"So," I said to Bunter, "what about Herbert Poole?"

"Well," said Harry, "I've heard via the grapevine—actually a friend of mine at Random House told me, well . . . that Poole might . . . just *might* be interested in writing a mystery for his next book."

"Ahhh."

"And who better to publish him than the great Nicholas Barlow, master of mystery, high-muck-a-muck of the thriller?"

I haven't blushed in years. And didn't blush then, either.

"No doubt he's heard of your triumph last year in the murder of Jordan Walker."

"It was really my brother, Tim, who solved that one." Nor could I forget that the book we finally got out of it didn't exactly burn up the charts. If you don't have a live celebrity to tour, a Graham Farrar . . . well, forget publishing a celebrity tell-all.

Almost imperceptibly, *The Queen of the Potomac* slipped away from the dock and headed upriver.

I turned again to Harry, who by now had another bottle of beer in his hand.

"How do you suggest we proceed, Harry? What modus operandi? Directly to Poole? Or through his agent? Who is his agent, by the way?"

He mulled that over a moment. Bypassing the glass on the bar in front of him, Harry took a deep swig of his beer straight from the bottle, sighed, and said: "Poole will be here tomorrow signing autographs, which you would know if you read your convention program or the *Show Daily*."

"I can barely manage to keep up with my *Times*."

"And his agent, the lovely Kay McIntire, will also be here."

By now the line at the bar was two or three deep. I edged away from it toward the rail, beckoning Harry to follow me.

"You really have made me the happiest of men, Harry."

"It would be a coup, wouldn't it? Every major publisher in town is probably after Poole—including all those who turned down *Pan at Twilight*."

"I'm sure."

"But—"

"But what?"

"It's probably gonna cost you, Nick."

"We'll have to discuss that with Mort Mandelbaum when we get back to the city. Can you hold up your end?"

"I'd expect a bidding situation with the book clubs, and a paperback floor of, say, a quarter," said Harry. Like the Richard Condon/*Prizzi's Honor*/Jack Nicholson gimmick, Harry liked saying "five" when he meant "five thousand," "fifty" for "fifty thousand," and so on. "A quarter" was a quarter of a million. Or maybe "250 big ones." The habit is contagious.

We glided up the Potomac past the Tidal Basin, built from land reclaimed from the river—so that the symmetry that inspired L'Enfant in his master plan for Washington could be maintained. As we moved along, the moon rose, swollen and phosphorescent in its brilliance, lending its glow to the floodlights shining on the Jefferson Memorial, that columned rotunda modeled after the Pantheon in Rome, which Jefferson so admired that he designed the University of Virginia in its style as well.

"A lovely evening," I said. Harry nodded.

"Not half-bad," he said, "as evenings go."

Just then I heard that familiar bray of laughter. Parker Foxcroft had somehow wangled an invitation, or had crashed the party, and was fast approaching.

"Parker!" I called out. "Over here, Parker!"

He was not alone. On his arm was one of those rare beauties that every once in a long while turn up in book publishing—when, if they knew better, they would go into fashion modeling or acting. Blonde, slender, and, I could see when she drew near, with a figure that was at once full-bodied and elegant. She was wearing light blue cotton jeans and a white button-down man's shirt—from the Gap, I supposed, or was it Banana Republic? I whistled silently. *Parker Foxcroft does it again,* I thought. As Parker came near, Harry Bunter moved off, rather abruptly, it seemed to me.

"Nick," said Foxcroft, "I'd like you to meet Susan Markham. Assistant editor at Little, Brown. Susan, this is my boss, the well-known eponymous head of Barlow and Company."

I extended my hand. She took and pressed it gently, but firmly enough to generate the smallest amount of electricity.

"You're with an excellent house," I said.

"You're quite a house yourself." *My God,* I thought, *is it that bad? I must consider a diet.*

"Susan almost worked for us," said Parker.

"Oh?"

"But you turned her down when she applied for a job," he said.

I turned to Susan Markham. "And just why did I do that?"

"Because all I could do at that time was type, file, and answer the phone," she said. "And apparently you didn't need a typist, a file clerk, or a receptionist. I, on the other hand, aspired to be an editorial assistant—and I guess you didn't need one of those, either."

When young, newly graduated college students arrive at our office looking for a job every fall, any job, at entry level, we put them through an inevitable rite of passage. They must submit to being underpaid, given menial tasks to perform, and forced to wait months or even a year or two for advancement. And why? Because everyone else entering publishing had to go through the same kind of initiation. Which, of course, is no reason at all. Still, the only people who are allowed to skip "boot camp" are those who inherit a place in the industry, like me.

"Obviously, Little, Brown saw something in you I did not," I said. "Color me obtuse. Anyway, you've clearly moved well along past the typing, filing, and telephoning stage."

"Still," she said, "I was disappointed you didn't hire me. I would have done practically anything to get a job at Barlow and Company."

I smiled, for I was fresh out of anything else to say. Not for me to fall into the false-modesty trap.

"Shall we sample the food?" said Parker to Susan Markham. And without waiting for an answer, he drew her away. And just when I was beginning to enjoy the conversation! It was to weep. Clearly the only consolation *was* food. I followed Parker and his companion to the stern, where the buffet tables had been set up. There were oysters on the half shell with a pungent sauce, succulent fat shrimp, a decent *pâté de campagne,* pigs in blankets, and tiny, extremely hot pizzas smoking away in chafing dishes. There were even crudités and a dip, which I ignored, in favor of white and yellow cubes of cheese speared with toothpicks. Consolation was quick, and highly satisfying. When I had a plateful heaped high and a glass of white wine, I looked around for a friendly tablemate. Parker and Susan Markham had seated themselves on the port side of the boat; spotting Harry Bunter starboard, I joined him.

"Ah, I see you're stoking up, Nick," he said. There was a sour note in his voice, as though he were reprimanding me somehow, the way a small boy might be scolded for stuffing himself with too much cake and ice cream.

"So what's it with you, Harry?"

"Oh *shit,*" he said softly. "That goddamn *son of a bitch.*"

"Which one?"

"Parker Foxcroft," he said, putting a spin of contempt in every syllable of the great editor's name.

"What about Parker?"

"That poor girl," Harry said. "I feel sorry for her, mixed up with that lousy bastard."

"I don't know," I said. "She looks as though she can take care of herself. And she certainly is of age. What's the problem?"

"He spoils every woman he touches," said Bunter. I'm not often shocked these days; book publishers, like movie and television producers, are exposed to every kind of depravity—secondhand. But Harry's vehemence did startle me. Then I remembered there had been rumors around the office that Parker had been having an affair with Harry's wife, Claire. Usually I ignore the local quidnuncs, but if the report was true . . .

"I don't know how he gets away with it," Bunter said, "but someday, someday—somebody is going to fix that prick for good."

Time to change the subject. I asked Harry how things were going on the rights front. He brightened. "A good

season," he said. "You really brought us some lovely proper-
ties."

And he began to rattle off his recent string of sales, large
and small, to this reprint house and that book club or
magazine. I listened happily to his soothing litany while
looking over the rail at the flickering lights of Georgetown.
For by now we had reversed course and were heading down-
river. I leaned back in my chair, content to enjoy the night
air and the moonlight and the largesse of *The New Yorker.*
It wasn't such a bad kickoff for the ABA, after all.

Chapter 4

Saturday morning, the first day the trade fair opens to convention-goers. I had breakfast in my room: eggs Benedict, by no means up to the standards set by my treasured cook, Pepita, but satisfactory; coffee, piping hot, a welcome improvement on most hotel room service; and both the *Times* and the *Washington Post*. Neither paper had any coverage of the ABA.

At the Convention Center, I headed straight for the Barlow & Company booth. It was a few minutes before nine. All hands were there, including Harry Bunter. Harry had a pair of dark half-moons under his eyes; I wondered if it was a hangover, or just a sleepless night.

"All set, folks?" I said. Mary Sunday and Chezna Newman smiled and nodded; Toby Finn gave me the thumbs-up sign. Harry shrugged and said: "As ready as I'll ever be." The cigarette holder in his hand shook slightly as he raised it to his lips, for the last few puffs before the crowd arrived. The ABA is strictly a nonsmoking affair.

For rights directors like Harry, the ABA has become a must. Though the ostensible purpose of the convention is to sell books to the trade, and to launch one's new list, there are agents there as well as booksellers, and foreign publishers by the score; which means that there are deals being made, both on the floor and in hotel suites, at breakfast, lunch, and dinner. Harry was there to see what he could sell, primarily, but also what we might buy.

Herbert Poole's next book, for example. I had to do something about that.

Now the doors opened, and the booksellers rushed into the exhibit hall. It was rather like the running of the bulls at Pamplona. Here they came, people of all sizes, shapes, and colors. I have never been able to find a common denominator for the breed of person who opens a bookstore, no *genus librarium,* so to speak—though I have often reflected that only wine or flower merchants could claim to trade in stuff as precious as do the booksellers.

And what a motley assortment of costumes I saw among them: Hawaiian sport shirts, tee-shirts in every color of the rainbow and bearing every conceivable brand name or slogan; elderly gents in shorts and white socks with black shoes; baseball caps and straw hats; women pushing strollers or bearing infants on their backs like papooses. And there were shopping carts and wheeled luggage carriers, the better for those pushing or pulling them to collect all the loot the publishers were giving away in their booths.

What were we handing out so liberally? Shopping bags in paper and in cloth; calendars; posters; buttons with our company name or the title of a book on them; free reading copies; candy; coffee; balloons; catalogs; flyers; occasionally even food. *Chotchkes* of all kinds. The trade show had all the panache and calculated frenzy of a carnival.

As I watched the parade go past, I was struck by how much like the ABAs of years past this all was. Only the booths were more elaborate and much costlier; this convention was different in scale but not in kind from all the others. Some of the "booths" manned by major publishers were the size of New York City studio apartments, complete with couches, chairs, and elaborate bookcases. There were also huge illuminated signs, and TV sets endlessly showing the same videos of book jackets and grimly smiling authors. Bigger and better displays to draw in the booksellers, who, as always, were outnumbered by the publishers.

"Good morning, Nick Barlow." I turned, startled by a silvery voice, coming from right behind me. It was Parker Foxcroft's companion from the party last evening—what was her name? Susan—

"Susan Markham, right?" I said.

"You have a good memory, Mr. Barlow."

"Only when somebody—or something—is memorable," I said. "And call me Nick, by all means."

She smiled. A lovely smile, quick and bright and altogether winning—and stunning aquamarine eyes. Today she was wearing black spandex pants and a matching top. I looked at her again, this time without benefit of a vodka martini. She was even more beautiful than I had remembered.

"You're not in your booth?" I said.

"I'm not officially on duty," she replied. "I was sent here more to learn what happens at ABA, and possibly as a reward for good conduct."

"You're lucky," I said. "Most of us would be happy if we could treat this as a holiday."

"But surely you can keep whatever schedule you like, Nick."

"Sure. But I still have to show the flag from time to time. Is this your first visit to Washington?"

She nodded.

"Then you ought to go sight-seeing."

"It would be more fun," she said, looking at me directly, and speaking in measured tones, "if I had a knowledgeable guide to show me around."

For a moment I stood perfectly still, without a word to say. I realized that I was being offered an invitation by this beautiful young woman; I was both touched and flattered. But—

"I only wish *I* could oblige you," I said, shrugging. "Unfortunately—"

"You're tied up."

"Yes. I am."

"Too bad," she said. "I guess I'll have to resort to a guide-book." And she strolled off down the aisle.

I knew I had rejected an overture that would not be made to me again. Why? I wondered. Because I no longer believed in casual encounters? Because I did not wish to be involved, even in a fleeting liaison, a flirtation? It wasn't that I felt too old for Susan Markham, not at all. Then what was it that held me back?

The passage of time, I suppose. ABAs past and ABAs present.

At ABAs past, I somehow felt that a successful seduction was almost obligatory, whether it was a conquest or simply a matter of serendipity.

Elaine, for one . . . she hadn't been sent to Washington by her publisher, but had come on her own, and had no room at the hotel, so she spent the night in mine . . . Though she was determined to be chaste, her resolve weakened before the night was over and she cast off the slip she was wearing, cried out: "This isn't fair to you!" and mounted me, taking me into her willing young body . . .

Vicki, for another . . . she had worked at Barlow & Company for a time, but then moved to another firm. We happened to be alone in an elevator at the Shoreham . . . she having come from the pool, still in her bathing suit with a towel over her shoulders . . . When she dropped her room key on the floor of the elevator, I picked it up, and when we got to her floor, I left the elevator with her, the key still in my hand, and when we reached the door of her room, I unlocked it and went in with her . . . Bless you, dear Vicki . . .

Then there was Martha . . . I invited her to my room for drinks before going out to the Jockey Club for dinner . . . We had the drinks but forgot about the dinner and ordered from room service . . . later she said: "I didn't plan to go to bed with you, Nick . . . yes, I did; I wore my prettiest underwear." *We had planned to make love in the bathtub, but forgot about that, too, left the water running and flooded the bathroom floor . . .*

There were others, of course, all of them fondly remembered; and some who found me resistible, or found other men more attractive, or just weren't there for me. Failure can often be as poignant in recollection as success, and far more instructive.

During the lunch break I called Margo Richmond, hoping her voice would relieve the somewhat sour taste of the self-restraint I had experienced in refusing Susan Markham's invitation to show her Washington.

Though I half expected an answering machine when I called her apartment—we talk to more machines on the phone these days than people—Margo was there.

"Nick," she said, "it's good to hear from you."

Margo and I have discussed, off and on, the possibility of living together—just the possibility—and not marriage, certainly. "We tried that, and it didn't work for either of us," said she, and I couldn't disagree. Marriage, as someone once remarked, is a romance in which the hero dies in the first act.

"Are you having fun?"

"No," I said, "but I won't bore you with the details."

"No little fling?"

"I am saving myself for you, my love."

"Is that irony I detect in your voice, Nicky?"

"There is no one in New York I miss but you, darling, and that's the truth."

She was silent for a moment. "You mustn't depend on me too much, my dear. I'm not cut out to be a support system for the male ego."

"But you have been a pal," I said, "and more."

"And also less," she said softly.

Before ringing off, we agreed to have dinner one evening soon after I got back from Washington. It is never easy living in the world of the liberated woman, but it is certainly always exciting.

That afternoon Parker Foxcroft showed up in our booth. Only Mary Sunday, Harry Bunter, and I were there at the time. Parker walked over to Bunter, who was replenishing our supply of catalogs. He had his empty cigarette holder clamped between his teeth, suffering, I suspected, from nicotine withdrawal. At any rate, he seemed in no mood for small talk when Foxcroft confronted him by saying, in stentorian tones: "I called the office yesterday, *Bunter.*"

Harry looked up, took the cigarette holder out of his mouth, and said mildly, "So?"

"I spoke to your secretary."

At this Harry visibly bristled. "What the hell for?" he demanded.

"I wanted to know if you'd sent the galleys of *Rainbow Territory* to the book clubs." *Rainbow Territory* was one of Parker's strongest contenders for—what else?—next year's

National Book Award for fiction. "She told me you had not, although you promised to do so last week."

"Listen, Foxcroft," said Harry, "you let me run my office my own way, and I'll let you run yours."

"Well, I took the liberty of *telling* her myself to send the galleys out."

At this, Harry blew, nor could I blame him. "You meddling son of a bitch," he said. "*I* decide when the galleys go out, and when they don't."

Parker stepped back a pace. "No need to get abusive," he said.

"Don't you ever pull a stunt like that again, or I'll—"

"You'll what?" said Parker, Mr. Cool himself.

"Oh, go to hell," said Harry. I stepped in, thinking it was about time somebody broke up the combatants, but Harry would have none of the peacemaking process. He shoved the catalogs he was holding into their carton and stalked off, all the way back to New York, as it later turned out, probably to change the locks on his office. It occurred to me while watching this little scene unfold that it was probably quite true that his wife had been having an affair with Parker Foxcroft. Nothing else, not even Parker's interference in Harry's office, would account for his anger and his bitterness.

Chapter 5

Sunday morning. "Complacencies of the peignoir, and late coffee and oranges in a sunny chair," wrote Wallace Stevens in his magnificent poem. Not for me those pleasures. For Sunday is the same as any other day at the ABA. The publishers are in their booths; the booksellers roam the halls again in search of enlightenment, or at least in search of freebies, most of which are gone by the second day of the convention. In other words, business as usual. I doubt anyone here much thinks of worship or even of playing golf—well, worship anyway. I'm sure things are different at the Christian Booksellers Association Convention, which is usually held somewhere in the Bible Belt, but I've never attended one of those. Barlow & Company, thank God, has no religious list. I am a firm believer in the separation of church and state—and literature. While I respect those publishers who deal in denominational titles, I am convinced that religious differences, along with nationalism, have been responsible for most of the world's worst calamities and much of its human misery.

I put in some time at the booth again, listening to a few

complaints from booksellers who had received books with defective jackets, or whose credit had been suspended for one reason or another, chatting up visitors on the merits of my fall list, and patrolling the corridors myself, to see what the competition was up to.

Then I headed for the autographing tables in the rear of the hall, looking for Herbert Poole.

I found him busy signing copies of his book fed to him one after another by a young woman from his publishing house and by his agent, Kay McIntire. A long line of booksellers had formed in front of the Poole table.

When I caught Kay McIntire's eye, I waved at her. She waved back, and motioned me to move to the side of the room, where she joined me shortly afterward.

"Good morning, Nick," she said. "I don't suppose you're looking for an autograph, are you?"

I smiled—coyly, I hope. "Only on a contract," I said. "Oh?"

"I've heard that Poole might want to write a mystery. If that is true, I'd like to talk deal with you, Kay."

Kay McIntire is one of the most honest and straightforward agents I know, and surely the most attractive. We've known each other for years, and but for the presence of Margo in my life, I would certainly have thought of her in romantic terms. Once, when the three of us were having dinner at The Players, Hartley Reed, the advertising genius and one of my authors, approached our table, took Kay's hand in his, and said: "You're the most beautiful woman in this room, and I'm dying to know your name."

Later, down in the Grill Room of the Club, when I was ordering after-dinner drinks, Reed came up to me and asked—nay, demanded—to meet her again. "Arrange a lunch for the three of us. Pick any restaurant you like," he said. "How about La Grenouille?"

I knew that Hartley was much married—thirty years or more, I figured. "You're thinking of leaving the reservation, are you?" I said.

"My friend," he replied in a deep, solemn voice, "I have never been *on* the reservation."

The lunch, however, did not take place because—but that's another story. At the moment, I was thinking of Kay only as an agent.

"How about it, Kay? Is Mr. Poole ready to jump ship?"

"You know I wouldn't encourage an author to leave his publisher for somebody else," she said, "unless his publisher was somehow wrong for him."

"But if he wants to write a mystery—"

"I'm not recommending that, either," said Kay, considering her words with great care. "I'm not so sure it's a good idea for him to break step quite so sharply. Readers will expect him to follow *Pan at Twilight* with—well, *Pan at Twilight Two,* I suppose."

"I'm mistaken in my assumption, then?"

"Mmm," she said, "not entirely. But it's certainly premature to think about a contract, Nick. Much too soon."

I looked again at the autographing table. Poole was still signing, smiling frequently, leaning forward to pick up a signee's name, murmuring an occasional comment. He looked younger than I had expected: full head of curly blond hair, a tanned, lean face, the kind of author who would photograph or televise well, and who could expect to be regarded as a sex object in his own right, leaving aside the kind of books he wrote.

As I watched, he continued to work the line of autograph

seekers, most of whom were women—looking as though there was no place in all the world he would rather be than right here, scribbling away, risking writer's cramp to satisfy his loyal fans. One young woman in shorts and a tee-shirt was carrying a small baby. Poole leaned over the table, and I thought—*My God, do you suppose he's going to kiss it?*—but he only tickled the child under the chin.

"I understand," I said. "Any chance of the three of us dining tonight?"

She shook her head. "We have movie interest, and the interested party is here in Washington"—she named a well-known Hollywood producer—"but I'll let you know if or when we're ready to talk to you. You know I admire Barlow and Company, Nick."

"I appreciate that."

"And you're not so bad yourself," she added, "for a Leo."

I found it diverting that an agent as canny as Kay would be hooked on astrology and the New Age, but she was, to a surprising extent. She had once charted a horoscope for me, finding my future full of delightful treats—one of which I now hoped might be Herbert Poole.

With one last glance at Poole, still bent to his labors, I took my leave of Kay and went back to the hotel for my afternoon siesta.

There was a message in my box at the Shoreham that my mother had called, so before dozing off I dialed her home number in Weston, Connecticut.

"Mother," I said, "you called?"

"Indeed I did. Nicholas—"

"Yes, Mother?" When she used my full Christian name, I knew I was in for it, so I assumed the most comfortable position I could find, which was supine, on my bed.

"Nicholas, I've spoken to your Mr. Mandelbaum," she said, "and he tells me that there's a problem at the bank—"

Morty was now *my* Mr. Mandelbaum, despite her having approved hiring him. You see, while I am CEO and COO of the company, my mother is the major shareholder, and still controls the purse strings, which makes the tie that binds more of an umbilicus than anything else.

We talked at some length about the problem with the bank, and I ended by assuring her I would deal with it first thing I got back to New York.

"I should hope so," she said. "Here you are off in Washington when you ought to be back home."

"Mother," I reminded her, as patiently as I could, "there is nothing I could do about it on a Sunday, now, is there?"

"But Washington—"

"I am *not* down here to have a good time, Mother. The ABA, as you will remember, is work. Work, not play. I would just as soon be back home, to tell you the truth."

"Well," she said finally, "be sure to take care of yourself. Don't go to too many parties, and don't drink too much."

"Yes, Mother," I sighed. "Now, would you put Tim on?"

Tim is my younger brother—my brilliant, bedridden brother. I can say of my brother Tim what Sherlock Holmes said of his brother Mycroft in *The Adventure of the Bruce-Partington Plans*: "He has the tidiest and most orderly brain, with the greatest capacity for storing facts, of any man living."

"Nick," he said when he came on the phone, "what's the news?" His voice was strong and vibrant, which cheered me enormously. It meant he was having one of his better days.

I could never be sure what kind of mood I would find him in. If it weren't that he had good reason for his mood swings, I would have characterized my brother as a manic-depressive, but when you're paralyzed from the waist down—

"The news is . . . promising," I said—and then I told him about Herbert Poole. Even though I hadn't really gotten anywhere with Kay, I knew it would cheer him up to know there might be the prospect of another best-seller—and a mystery at that.

When I showed up again at our booth the next day, Mary Sunday and our two reps were handling the booksellers, and Parker Foxcroft was deep in a heated conversation with a man I recognized as Andrew Phelps, a reviewer for the *Washington Post*.

"Now, wait just a damn minute—" I heard Phelps say. "I don't—"

"You *know* that I'm right!" Parker's voice had risen to a threatening pitch. "You're biased as hell, and everybody in the trade knows it."

What the holy *hell* was going on here? I knew that Phelps was not a particularly good friend of Barlow & Company, and he had savaged a few of our books in what I thought was an excessively harsh fashion, but still—

"Look here, Foxcroft—"

"You look here. I've a good mind to write your publisher and complain."

"Okay, *okay*," said Phelps. "I'm sorry I ever stopped by your booth in the first place. I was only trying—"

At this I stepped forward. The whole thing, in my opinion, had gone far enough. "Mr. Phelps," I said, "I'm Nicholas Barlow and—"

Which was as far as I got. Phelps emitted something between a snort and a snarl, turned his back on me, and stalked off.

"Parker," I said with as much civility as I could muster, "what the hell was that all about?"

Foxcroft drew himself up to his full height and said: "I told Mr. Phelps what I thought of his reviews."

"You *what?*" I was on the verge of shouting. "Don't you *know* that nothing hurts us more than slamming a reviewer? Someone who is in a position to do us real injury? For Christ's sake, Parker—"

"Nick," said Foxcroft. He sounded somehow hurt, as though I was on Phelps's side. "Phelps has trashed my books—and more than once."

"Well, if he hasn't done you in so far, he sure as hell will now—and probably all the rest of our books as well."

"Oh, come *on,* Nick—"

Now I realized that I *was* shouting. And that people nearby were hanging on my every word. Mary Sunday just stood there, openmouthed. As for Parker Foxcroft, his face turned even a deeper red than usual.

I brought my voice down, almost to a whisper. "If you ever do a thing like that again—"

"Look, Nick—"

"Just stay away from reviewers, understand, Parker? Leave it to the publicity department. *Don't fuck us up.*"

And that was it. For what it was worth, the high point of the ABA. I had had enough of Parker Foxcroft, and I am sure he had had enough of me. There was nothing left but to head for Washington National and catch a USAir shuttle back to New York.

*   *   *

Though I didn't feel especially bright-eyed, I thought I'd better check into the office, primarily to empty my in-box into the circular file.

To my astonishment, I found the office closed and locked. Where was everybody?

I had completely forgotten that it was a legal holiday. I had no choice but to go home. What a lovely choice.

Chapter 6

I devoted the morning after I got back from Washington to emptying my in-box into my circular file; by afternoon I was ready to deal with whatever problems were waiting for me.

There were two—or so I thought. The first was the bank. I called in Mortimer Mandelbaum and asked him to set up a meeting with Clifford Franklin, the loan officer at our bank.

"As soon as possible, Mort," I said. "We've got to keep our line of credit wide open." And then I told Mandelbaum about the possibility of signing Herbert Poole for a mystery.

He fairly beamed. "So you did land a best-seller in Washington," he said.

"Not yet. And suppose Kay McIntire and Poole decide to auction his next book off? Could we afford to take part in an auction?"

"Probably not."

Auctions for potential best-sellers are a fact of life in book publishing these days, and a small house like Barlow & Company is ill prepared to take part in them. First, we do not have the deep pockets of the major houses. And second, we do not own a paperback reprint house, which means that we cannot offer what is called a hard-soft contract, with one advance covering both the hardcover and the paperback editions. Agents prefer hard-soft deals because they and their clients get to keep the entire advance, unlike a deal covering hardcover rights only. In that case the hardcover publisher sells the paperback rights to a reprint house and keeps a share—sometimes as much as half—of the reprint money.

No, we had to hope we could persuade Herbert Poole that we were the best house to publish his mystery, on our merits alone.

If he decides to write a mystery, that is.

If if if . . . if I don't have an ulcer, it is only because of the genes that gave me a cast-iron stomach.

The second problem arrived in my office shortly after lunch, in the person of Lester Crispin, the company's art director. As always, Crispin knocked sharply on my door, and when I bade him come in, went at once to the couch on the far wall and slumped rather than sat down on it. He began to stroke his beard, a black bristly affair, so fearsome it gives him the air of a pirate. Added to that is the physique of a wrestler and hands that would do credit to a bricklayer. Today he was wearing a shirt open to the breastbone, revealing a thatch of curly black chest hair.

"Nick," he said. "Goddamn it, Nick."

"What is it, Les?"

He started drumming the meaty fingers of his left hand on the arm of the couch. "Shit, man," he said finally. "That's all I can say, *shit*."

"Let me guess," I said. "Parker Foxcroft."

He sat up straight and stared at me. "How the hell did

you know that?" he said. "You're a fucking mind reader, Nick."

"Just a stab." As though Parker hadn't been the source of most of my irritation these past few days . . .

"Has he been in to see you? About me, I mean."

"No, he hasn't. Why should he have?"

"*Son* of a bitch."

"Are you speaking about Parker, or is that just a general son of a bitch?"

"Both." He shook his head as though to clear it of whatever he was thinking, perhaps to clear it of the image of Parker Foxcroft. I had frequently done the same thing.

"Specifically, what about Parker?" I asked Crispin.

"As you may know, Nick, he's a hard man to satisfy."

I nodded. "Go on," I said.

"I can't seem to satisfy the bastard at all. Ever. It's bitch bitch bitch, one bitch after another. 'The colors are all wrong,' he says. Or 'Why don't you hire a better designer?' Or 'I could do better art than that myself, and you can't draw a straight line.' *Jesus,* Nick—"

"I'm aware," I said, "of some of his complaints. Not all of them. If I haven't reacted to them, it's because I thought you had the situation well under control. You are, after all, the best art director in the business. In my humble opinion." I meant it, too; Crispin not only turned out beautiful books and splendid jackets; he had brought home several firsts in American Institute of Graphic Arts competitions.

"Yeah yeah." He waved his hand. "That's all well and good, but—well, I'm damn sick and tired of it. For three years, the man has nagged at me, thrown first-rate jackets back in my face. I've had two top designers tell me they won't work on a Parker Foxcroft book again. And now I just lost my assistant. She quit because Parker Foxcroft screamed and swore at her. How much am I supposed to put up with, Nick, I ask you, goddamn it."

"What do you suggest I do?"

"Fire the bastard."

"You mean that?"

"I do. Either you fire him, Nick, or you'll have my resignation on your desk tomorrow morning."

I sat back in my chair and, as I often do when I have something on my mind, made a steeple of my fingertips. This was rather more of a problem than I had expected. *Of course you've thought of firing Parker yourself, haven't you? Yeah, sure, but I can't say that to Crispin, now can I?*

"You don't think if I talk to Parker—" I said.

"No damn good, Nick. Forget it."

"Even so—" Common fairness demanded that I give Parker a chance. *A chance to what? To explain? To mend his ways? Forget it! . . . All right, then, a chance to apologize and start afresh. He does, after all, have that goddamned touch . . . He also has an iron-clad contract . . . How the hell can I fire him without eating that? . . .*

I was brought abruptly back from my thoughts by Crispin, who pushed himself out of my couch, planted himself in front of my desk, his hands making fists, as though he was about to box with me, and said: "Obviously, you're not about to fire him. Okay, so be it. I've got no choice but to pack it in."

"Come on, Les, be reasonable." I said that even as I realized that reason had nothing to do with it, that I was somehow hoping that this problem would be resolved without my needing to fire Parker. But how? By divine intervention, perhaps? Damn it all, anyway!

I knew even as Crispin turned and headed toward the

door that I had just lost the best art director the firm had ever had. I hoped to God that giving Parker the benefit of the doubt wasn't the biggest mistake I'd made all day.

All day, hell—all year.

My last hope, and a faint one at best, was that I might still persuade Parker to make peace with Crispin.

Blessed are the peacemakers, for they shall be caught in the cross fire of the antagonists!

I buzzed Hannah Stein on the intercom.

"Hannah," I said, "see if you can track down Parker Foxcroft."

When my secretary buzzed me back, it was to report that Foxcroft was not in his office.

"Try him at home," I said. "It may be one of his editing days." One of the peculiar realities of the publishing business is that virtually no editing is done in editorial offices. The editors are all too busy at meetings, handling administrative details, dealing with agents and authors—anything and everything but editing books. For the most part, they must do that at home, or whenever and wherever they can find the time. Like so many of his breed, Parker had an unlisted home phone number so he could work undisturbed by anyone but me.

"No answer," said Hannah.

Damn, I thought. *Where could he be? Certainly he's not still at the ABA . . .*

Aloud: "Leave a message in his office, please, Hannah—that I want to talk to him as soon as possible, no matter what the hour may be—night or day."

I had no plans for that evening, so I thought I'd stop by The Players for a drink and a bite to eat in the Grill Room.

The Club is only a block away from my town house at 2 Gramercy Park, which makes it my second home—and a beautiful one.

Only a few members were in the Grill when I walked in. Two women sat chatting at one of the small round tables. A young man I did not recognize sat at the long common table; he was wearing an open red-checked sport shirt and a safari jacket. Dress in the Grill Room is considerably less formal than dress upstairs in the Howard Lindsay Dining Room, mainly to accommodate actors who come to the Club wearing rehearsal clothes. Nor are they the only ones to dress casually. An older man standing at the bar was also tieless, and carried his coat slung over his arm. It was Frederick Drew. I knew him slightly, and knew also that despite a familiar theatrical last name, he was not an actor but a poet. The Players is a much-loved haven not only for people in the theater but also for writers, artists, publishers, patrons of the arts, even doctors and lawyers.

Drew was staring down at the drink he held cupped in his left hand when I walked up to the bar.

"Hello, Fred," I said, "how's the Muse?"

He looked up at me and smiled. It was the wryest and saddest of smiles. He had a deeply lined face, huge dark eyes sunk back in their sockets, under bushy black brows; his steel-gray hair looked as though he'd combed it with his fingers.

"Erato?" he replied. "The lady is still alive—in the cross-word puzzles, at least."

Barlow & Company does not publish much poetry— perhaps one or two volumes a year—not merely because it doesn't sell, except to other poets, but because I want only first-rate poets on my list, and there aren't many of those. Frederick Drew was one of them—but as far as I knew, he hadn't brought out a new collection in years. Rumor had it that he was an alcoholic; I wouldn't be surprised; I'd certainly seen him at this bar often enough.

"You know the saying, of course," he went on. "There's no money in poetry, but then there's no poetry in money, either."

"I have your *Selected Poems* on my bedside table," I said. "I must bring it round one of these days for you to sign."

"That's kind of you." He didn't sound all that appreciative, however. I knew that he lived on the income from a teaching job he had at the Alexander Hamilton Institute, a school of continuing education in Westchester.

He raised the glass to his lips and drained it in one swallow.

"A refill?" I said. "On me, of course." I signaled to the barman. "And while you're at it, Juan," I said to him, "would you mix me an Absolut martini? A walker, please." A walker at the Club is a drink and a half, served in a miniature carafe.

"What's the matter?" said Drew. "You think I can't afford to buy my own liquor?"

I started to move away. If there's one thing I dislike, it's a belligerent drunk, and The Players has had its share of them.

"Don't leave on my account, Nick. Please." I moved back again. "I'm sorry," said Drew. "I'm not myself this evening."

"I'm sorry to hear that, Fred." In general, I do not encourage alcoholic confessions, but Drew was a highly respected poet, after all, and a Player, and—well, I was feeling rather mellow. I often do feel that way at the Club.

"What's going on?" I said.

"I've lost my job."

I murmured something unintelligible, just sounds meant to be consoling.

"You know I am an adjunct lecturer at Hamilton," he said. I nodded. "Was, I ought to say. I've just been replaced. Found out about it this afternoon, y'know? And y'know why they dumped me? Found out about that, too. I'll tell you why, Nick. Yes." The last word came out "yesh."

Just then the concierge came down the stairs and called to me. "Telephone, Mr. Barlow—a Mr. Foxcroft. Extension four."

"Thanks, Eric." A timely interruption, I thought; Drew was threatening to become maudlin. I went to the phone booth near the men's room, shutting the glass door behind me as I switched on the light and picked up the phone. "Hello?"

"Hello, Nick."

"Parker," I said. "Where have you been? I looked for you today. You weren't at the office and you weren't at home, either."

A brief silence. Then: "Important appointments, Nick."

"I'd like to talk with you, Parker."

"Go ahead."

"Not on the phone, in person."

"Can't it wait until tomorrow?"

"I think not."

"Okay, fine by me. I'm in the office."

I thought for a moment and then decided that dinner could wait.

"I'll be over shortly," I said, and hung up the phone.

When I returned to the bar to reclaim my martini, I found that I was now alone. Frederick Drew hadn't waited to tell me why he had been fired.

Chapter 7

It was after eight o'clock before I left the Club and headed for the office. I had changed my mind about dinner, and decided to have a sandwich and a glass of beer to carry me through the evening. While I was still in the Grill an old friend, a literary agent named Bruno Wiley, stopped by the bar, and we schmoozed for a while.

"Interested in a biography?" said Wiley.

"Bruno, you know we're not supposed to talk business in the Club." A Players rule, it is true, but I suspect one honored more in the breach than in the observance.

"*Ha*. A biography of—" He dropped the name of a prominent businessman.

"What makes you think a book like that would sell?" I asked him.

"Remember *Iacocca*?"

"That was a fluke, Bruno." Who could forget the autobiography that caused the leveling of at least one entire forest? "The timing was perfect for Lee Iacocca," I continued. "People were looking for a hero, preferably a businessman, an automobile manufacturer if possible. The same book published today would sink without a trace. The autobiography of a prominent businesswoman would have a better chance."

"Ah," Bruno said, lowering his voice and moving closer to me, "but there will be *subvention.*"

"That's different. Tell me more."

Subvention is a form—how shall I put it?—of subsidy for a book by outside interests, either individuals or companies with a strong desire to see that book published. Rather like vanity publishing, you say? Not quite. The book will carry the imprint of a reputable house, not that of a vanity publisher, and money will be forthcoming to pay for the book's production and distribution costs, or somebody will guarantee to buy enough copies to make the project worthwhile.

Has Barlow & Company ever indulged in this practice? Not officially—but virtually every other major house has.

At any rate, there was no harm in *listening* to Bruno Wiley; after all, we were in something of a financial bind. So I listened. And some time passed, until I finally remembered that Parker Foxcroft was expecting me.

I said good night to Bruno and stepped out into one of those rare June nights—the first—when the skies are clear and the air is fresh and cool, and our thoughts turn to the beach and the deep green woods. In my case, to the woods around Weston, Connecticut. I was not looking forward to my impending discussion with Parker, for, like most males of my upbringing, I dislike altercations of all kinds, and avoid them wherever possible.

When I reached the office, I pulled out my key ring and fumbled around with the keys until I realized that the office door was unlocked. *How odd,* I thought. *Inexcusable lapse of security, really.* Though the building has a night watchman, I've always urged any of our people who might be working late to lock themselves in. You can't be too careful; I myself was once surprised after hours by an intruder.

Walking down the hall toward my own office, I saw a light under Parker Foxcroft's door. I stopped and took hold of the doorknob, then hesitated. It struck me that our confrontation, for that is what I meant it to be, would be more successful if it took place in my office not his, giving me the psychological edge. So I decided to call him in on the intercom.

"Parker?"

A grunted acknowledgment.

"Nick. Would you come into my office, please?"

Another grunt, this one of assent. Then the connection was broken.

While waiting, I picked up several files on my desk that had long been lying there, begging for attention and receiving none. They received none now, either; I simply leafed through them, killing time, not looking for inspiration. After a few minutes passed with no Parker, I punched the intercom again. This time he did not answer.

"Hell," I muttered. *I may have to go to his office, after all . . .*

I stepped out into the hall and made one last attempt to summon him. "Parker!" I bellowed. "Where are you?" Silence. *Strange,* I thought. *The light under his door has gone out.* I strode down the hall, wondering if he'd skipped out on me. *Damn Parker, anyway!*

Just as I opened his door, I heard the sound of footsteps behind me. As I started to turn, I felt a sharp, vicious blow on the back of my neck. Startled, I reeled forward and smashed into Parker's door, stumbled and almost fell.

"Who's there?" I cried out. "What's this?"

When I finally turned around, I saw a dark figure move swiftly through the shadows of the foyer. The front door clicked open and then slammed shut, too quickly for me to move or call out, still less to see who had gone out.

Stepping into Parker's office, still somewhat dazed by the blow I'd been struck, I groped for the light switch. When I pressed it, two lamps went on—a floor lamp next to his couch and a fluorescent lamp which threw a wide swath of light across the desk. In the center of that swath lay the head and shoulders of Parker Foxcroft. His arms hung limply behind him, along the sides of his chair.

There was no doubt in my mind that he was dead; a large dark gout of blood had already soaked into his desk blotter. The thin blond hair on the back of his head was matted with blood. He would edit no more—at least not in this world.

I stood over his body for a moment, wishing I had not stayed so long at The Players. If I'd come sooner, Parker might still be alive . . . or—my God, what a chilling thought—would we *both* be lying here dead?

I shuddered as I reached for the phone on Parker's desk.

Chapter 8

An hour later, I was still in the office. Only now it was a crime scene. With me were two detectives from the Thirteenth Precinct. The lieutenant, a short, stocky man with a brush cut—about thirty-five, I guessed—introduced himself as Robert Hatcher. With his splayed ears and the pleat in his nose, he resembled a light-heavyweight, or a man who could once have played tackle for the New York Giants. His partner, Sergeant Lawrence Falco, on the other hand, was rather spindly, and wore a sweatshirt, jeans, and a royal-blue poplin jacket with a Mets insignia on the right breast pocket. A baseball cap completed his outfit. Falco's taut, swarthy face was riddled with acne scars. He held a much-chewed yellow pencil in one hand and a small Handi-Notes pad in the other. It was Hatcher who led the questioning.

"You say you got here about eight o'clock?"

"As near eight as I could tell," I said. "I didn't look at my watch."

"And you think Foxcroft was alive when you arrived?"

"I thought so at the time, but now—"

"Now what?"

"I'm not sure. I didn't actually hear him say anything."
I had told Hatcher and Falco about the way I'd been hit,
and about the figure I saw slipping out the office door. Was
it a man or a woman? I couldn't tell in the dark.

"How many people have keys to this office?" asked
Hatcher.

All my key people, I was about to say, when it occurred to
me that this might sound flip; and if there's one thing I've
learned, it's that you do not crack wise with the police. So
I began to list them. "Sidney Leopold, my editor in chief.
Lester Crispin, my art director. Harry Bunter, rights director. Mary Sunday, our sales manager . . ."

Hatcher took this in stride. Publishing isn't the only
equal opportunity employer, after all; so is the police force.
"Who else?" he said.

Falco was busy writing in his notebook while Hatcher
walked over to the window and stood looking out, hands
behind his back, which was turned toward me.

"Mortimer Mandelbaum, of course. My controller. And
my secretary, Hannah Stein."

"And Foxcroft?"

"Naturally."

"Nobody else?"

"That's the lot." I sighed. "But the door was left unlocked. Anyone could have come in."

"I'll want to talk to everybody tomorrow morning,"
Hatcher said, turning to face me. "Tell me, did the victim
have any enemies you know of?"

"Well . . ." I hesitated just long enough for Hatcher's
eyes to narrow. He raised his head and stared directly at me.
"So he *did* have enemies."

"I suppose so," I said. " 'Enemies' may be too strong a

word, though, Lieutenant. Let's say he didn't have many friends."

"Names?"

"Just about everyone in the office."

"Including you, Mr. Barlow?" Hatcher had gray eyes, gray lightly flecked with blue, and they were fixed on mine. His ears went up slightly, and two sharp furrows appeared on his forehead. I had the feeling I was looking at a proper bulldog. Ought I to tell him about my recent quarrel with Parker? Let him find out for himself—he would, soon enough. I merely nodded.

Hatcher turned to Falco. "The weapon, Sergeant?"

Falco put away his notebook and produced a plastic Ziploc bag. Inside it I saw what appeared to be a small-caliber gun.

Hatcher held up the bag. "Recognize this?" he said.

"No, should I?"

"It's a cheap .25-caliber semiautomatic, otherwise known as a Saturday night special. Anyone could pick up one on the street for seventy-five or a hundred dollars. It's the amateur's weapon of choice. Foxcroft was shot in the right temple at close range with this little baby. Except for its weight, you might think it was a water gun."

"Any chance he might have committed suicide?" I asked, knowing the answer ahead of time. Parker was too much under his own intoxicating spell to quit this mortal coil untimely.

"None," said Falco, joining the conversation for the first time. Or was it an interrogation? More an interview, I supposed.

"I think that's all for now," said Hatcher. "As soon as the crime scene boys are finished, and the M.E.'s men take the body away, you can go home. Needless to say—"

"I'm not planning to go anywhere. I'll be available whenever you want me." I rose from my chair and crossed to the door. When I opened it, I could see light pouring out of Parker's office down the hall, punctuated by a camera flashing, and I could hear the sound of men moving around inside.

"I appreciate your time," Hatcher said. "I know this must have been a shock to you. Finding the body and all, that is."

I'll say it has, I thought. *The only dead bodies I'm used to around here are all between the covers of books. Or on the pages of manuscripts.*

When the police finally packed up their gear, and Parker had been trundled off in a body bag strapped to a gurney (as though he might have wanted to get up and move around), I got up myself and left the office.

Outside, a coroner's vehicle waited, roof light flashing, and several police cars, drawing a few curious bystanders with their bright red beacons. A slam of the ambulance back door, and Parker was gone, whisked off to an inhospitable morgue I had visited once and dreaded entering ever again.

A line of Donne's came into my mind: "Any man's *death* diminishes *me,* because I am involved in *Mankind."* That was rather how I felt at this moment: smaller somehow, and more vulnerable. *It could have happened to me.* And Parker Foxcroft was surely not just *any* man; in his own way, at what he did best, he was a genius. But what kind of *man* was he? It occurred to me that although I had worked with Parker for almost three years, I knew him hardly at all. We did not socialize, Parker and I. I had never set foot in his apartment, nor had he ever been in my house. He was not a Player, so I never ran into him at 16 Gramercy Park. He was, like so many of the people we work with, a stranger.

* * *

I did not feel quite like going home to bed, although it was getting late, so I strolled back to The Players, breathing deeply of the flower-steeped air when I passed by Gramercy Park.

I was not surprised to find Frederick Drew in the Grill Room, leaning on the bar and in earnest conversation with Juan, the barman. When he saw me, his face brightened into what was for him almost a smile. I did not expect to find him any more sober than when I had seen him last, nor was he.

"Nick," he murmured. "Well met by distilled waters."

"*Arsenic and Old Lace,*" I said. Drew nodded. Howard Lindsay, who had more than a hand in that particular play, was president of the Club back in the fifties, and often concluded his master of ceremonies role at a Players Pipe Night—these are formal Club entertainments of one kind or another—with the same line: "Let me lead you beside distilled waters," as he directed the audience to quit the dining room and descend to the Grill.

"Fred," I said, "I'm glad to see you." A lie, but I was curious about one thing. "When we were talking earlier this evening . . ."

"Yes?"

"Excuse me a moment, Fred. I turned to the barman. "Juan—please. A Rémy Martin."

When I had the brandy snifter well in hand, and had inhaled deeply of the glorious smoky aroma of Rémy, I said: "You were about to tell me how you lost your teaching job when I was called to the phone. By the time I got back you were gone."

"Yeah," he said. " 'Nature her custom holds, Let shame say what it will.' " I recognized the Shakespearean line inscribed over the urinals in the Club's men's room. "Piss call."

"What happened, Fred? Tell me."

He drew himself up, leaned toward me, coming so close I thought for a moment he was going to seize me by the lapels. When he spoke, his face turned a choleric red, and his voice could have been heard all through the room. Even the barman stiffened. As for me, I shrank back from the full force of his anger.

"That *fucking* Parker *fucking* Foxcroft *fucked* me but good!"

It was hard for me to know what to say. "Parker? How?" A lame response, but the only one I could come up with.

"You know I was teaching creative writing—and what a crock of shit that is, as though anybody could teach anybody else how to write creatively—at the Hamilton Institute, right?"

I nodded.

"Well, your man Foxcroft is apparently a bosom buddy—asshole buddy, I should say—of the head of the English Department at Hamilton, a guy named Larry Peterson. What did Foxcroft do? He persuaded Peterson to drop me from the faculty and give my courses to a young protégé of Foxcroft's." He shook his head as though to clear it; I could see tears forming in his eyes. He named a short-story writer who had been published widely and was enjoying a vogue.

"I'm sorry to hear that, Fred—damned sorry, in fact."

"Dead in the water," he said, his voice now so soft I could barely hear him. "Killed by a cocksucker named Parker god-*damned* Foxcroft."

I wondered if I ought to tell him that he was speaking of the *late* Parker Foxcroft. Perhaps it would cheer him up, even if it wouldn't get him his job back. For some reason even I didn't understand, I remained silent.

"Nick," said Drew, tears now streaming down his cheeks, "I depended on that job to put food on my table. And I've got two other mouths to feed. My wife can't work . . . and . . . well, *shit*, man, what am I supposed to do?"

Few things, I think, are harder to bear than the sight of a grown man weeping—and if that man is less than a friend, the experience is more painful still. I had every reason to sympathize with Frederick Drew and none to mourn Parker Foxcroft, but the men of my generation and class—if that word doesn't sound too pompous—were raised as young Stoics. To muffle the sobs, suppress the tears, take the agony inside oneself, quite as a Spartan warrior, it is said, was expected to let a fox gnaw at his entrails without showing any evidence of pain.

Drew pulled a handkerchief out of his back pocket and wiped his eyes. "Someday—somehow—Foxcroft will get his," he said.

Amen, I said to myself. *Selah—whatever that means.*

Chapter 9

"Other sins only speak," wrote John Webster in *The Duchess of Malfi*, "murder shrieks out."

I would have to agree. When one of my mystery authors delivers a book in which there *is* no murder, I begin to worry at once. Readers expect murders in their mysteries; no other crime is quite as popular or as intriguing. In short, murder sells books.

But when the murder is in my own backyard, in effect, I could do with less shrieking all the way round.

The morning after Parker's body was discovered, the first problem I had to deal with was the press. Ordinarily I welcome publicity, as long as it is favorable, or at least not invidious. In this instance, I decided to shut my office door to the reporters and the television cameramen who milled around the Barlow & Company anteroom, hoping for an interview. I declined. Hannah Stein, my secretary, was instructed to tell everyone who asked that I had no comment. I somehow could not summon up the crocodile tears that were probably called for in the circumstances. Though I did not care much for Parker, really, I cared for hypocrisy even less. Let them think his death had left me speechless.

Of course the police were also present, and I'm sure the reporters converged on them, and like good public servants, they were happy to oblige the television people as well. For myself, as soon as I could, I sent for Sidney Leopold. He popped in through the private entrance to my office, bright-eyed as always, his frizzy brown curls even more tousled than usual.

"Nick," he said, raising one hand and waving it in a kind of greeting, "what's guh-going on around here? Puh-people all over the place . . . cameras . . . puh-police?"

I gave him the bad news. "Oh, my Guh-God," he said, slumping into the visitor's chair. "Oh, my *God.*"

"Don't worry, Sidney, I'm sure you can account for your whereabouts last evening."

He turned a shade paler. "Actually I was at huh-home alone at the time."

"Then you *don't* have an alibi."

"Hey, Nick, sh-surely you don't think that I—that I—"

"Certainly not, Sidney. You had no reason to wish Parker dead, had you?"

"I th-thought he was a son of a buh-bitch, but if I started kuh-killing every SOB I know, I'd have to buh-be a serial killer."

"My sentiments exactly."

The buzzer on my desk rang softly. I picked up the phone. "Yes, Hannah?"

"Lieutenant Hatcher would like to see you, Nick."

"Not as presentable as Joe Scanlon, is he?" Scanlon was an NYPD detective, now on leave to write a book for Barlow & Company.

"Really, Nick! I'd rather not say."

"Send him in, by all means."

Hatcher came in briskly, all business, and got to the point at once. Hannah was right behind him. She turned to go, but I motioned her to stay.

"I'm going to need to talk to the members of your staff, Mr. Barlow. Could you—?"

"There's a conference room down the hall, Lieutenant. Hannah, will you show Lieutenant Hatcher where it is? He may also want to ask you a few questions."

"Right," said Hatcher. "Then I'll want to see the others, one by one."

"Hannah will bring them to you." I turned to Sidney. "You don't mind leading the pack, do you?"

He shrugged.

I had a feeling little work was going to be done in the office this day. I flipped open the pages of my desk calendar to Wednesday, June 2. "2:00 BANK," it read. I groaned silently, impaled on the horns of a dilemma. Lifting the phone, I dialed Mort Mandelbaum's extension.

"The bank date, Morty," I said.

"Two o'clock, right, Nick?"

"You'll have to reschedule that appointment."

"What? But—it's an emergency."

"I realize that. However, there's the matter of Parker Foxcroft's murder. I think the police ought to have first call on our attention. And, Morty?"

"Yes?"

"How's your alibi?"

A shocked silence, a bit of sputtering, and the phone went dead.

My turn with the inquisitors came just after lunch.

"The lieutenant would like to see you now, Nick," Hannah informed me. I cursed under my breath, straightened my tie, and headed for the conference room. Hatcher, appearing quite morose, was sitting at the head of the conference table, his chin resting on one hand, in the other a pencil poised over his notebook. He squinted up at me.

"Mr. Barlow."

"Yes, Lieutenant?"

"You sure you've been completely candid with me?"

"I certainly thought so."

"Isn't it true that you were involved in a heated discussion with the deceased at"—he glanced at his notebook—"the ABA . . . the American Booksellers Association?"

"Yes, that's correct."

"And isn't it also true that you were . . . well, un*happy* about Mr. Foxcroft's situation at your firm?"

"Yes, I suppose I was."

"Why didn't you mention this before?"

"I didn't think it was important."

Hatcher rose from his chair and took a turn around the room. When he returned, he did not resume his chair, but positioned himself on the edge of the conference table. Moments passed.

"Mr. Barlow," he said at last, "what was your business arrangement with Foxcroft? Your financial arrangement, I mean."

"As an imprint publisher, he was under contract to me. Perhaps I ought to explain what an imprint publisher is . . ."

"Yeah," said Hatcher. "Do. *If* you please."

I gave him beady-eyed stare for beady-eyed stare. "I'll do my best. An imprint publisher, as the name implies, has his own imprint—his own name on the books he brings in. Arrangements vary from house to house, of course."

"I'm only interested in *your* house, and in *his* imprint."

"Parker Foxcroft acquired and signed up his own authors and his own books. I financed his operation, provided the money he paid his authors in advances, and paid for the costs of manufacturing and marketing his books. In turn I gave him a drawing account—a salary, in effect—and performance bonuses when his books did well."

Hatcher closed his notebook and rose from his chair. "Wait a *minute*," he said. "Hold it there. It looks to me like you took all the risks and Foxcroft made out like a bandit."

"Not quite," I said. "There was no distribution of earnings on his books until his drawing account had been earned out. In effect, he was still an employee of my company, despite his imprint. He was not a partner, and he had no equity. If his books didn't make money, neither did he. If his books lost money, well . . ."

"But you said he had a contract." Hatcher was a bulldog, all right, and with a bone he wasn't going to let go of. "And you couldn't exactly fire him if his books didn't earn money."

I admitted it would be difficult.

"How long did his contract have to run?"

I hesitated, remembering how queasy I had felt about the possibility of having to buy Parker out. Hatcher waited me out, impassive, to me inscrutable. I only wished I could say the same for myself.

"A year and a half, Lieutenant."

"A year and a half. Getting rid of him could have been costly, right?"

"Right." I couldn't have agreed more.

"Just *how* costly?"

"I'd rather not say."

Hatcher's eyebrows rose. "Oh?"

"That's privileged information," I said.

Hatcher squared his shoulders and tucked his notebook in his inside jacket pocket. Apparently my interview was over.

"Lieutenant . . ."

"What, Mr. Barlow?"

"Did you learn anything from questioning the other members of my staff? If you don't mind telling me, that is."

"Sure, I learned a few things."

"Like?"

"You were right, nobody cared much for the victim. The question is . . ."

"Yes?"

"Who didn't care for him to go on publishing books?"

Having no answer to this, I fell back on the typical Irish response to a question: another question. "Is that all, Lieutenant?"

"Not quite. I've been fingerprinting all the members of your staff. I'd also appreciate yours."

"Mine? Is that necessary? My prints are on file with the FBI." Again the raised-eyebrows response. "I was in Air Force Intelligence in Washington a number of years ago, and I needed a security clearance."

"That's fine—but it would be more convenient if we could get them again now."

"Oh, very well—if I must, I must." I made sure that Hatcher took careful note of my displeasure. As it turned out, it was Sergeant Falco who did the dirty work of taking my prints. Once I'd cleaned up, I returned to the conference room and said to Hatcher: "*Now* is that all?"

"For now."

Dismissed from my own conference room, for God's sweet sake, that was one hell of a note!

I was quite certain now that this was going to be a day when little or no business would be done in the offices of Barlow & Company.

However, I didn't reckon on the tenacity, the fierce concentration, of my editor in chief. Not long after I returned to my office, slammed the door, and lay back on my couch, hands locked behind my head, I heard a soft knock from the adjoining office.

"Come in, Sidney."

He peered around the edge of the door, hesitating to come all the way in. "You're sh-sure you duh-don't mind, Nick?"

"I don't mind, Sidney. Not you, anyway."

"It's hell having the cuh-cuh-cops all over the place, no?"

I did not feel his question needed a reply. Sidney had always been sensitive to my changes of temper and forgiving of my occasional moodiness. He merely nodded and pressed on.

"I've guh-got something that might interest you, Nuh-Nick."

"What is it, Sidney?" I said, sounding, I supposed, rather like Eeyore conversing with Christopher Robin.

"A promising nuh-new author," he said. "Nick, it's your cup of tea, not muh-mine. A puh-private eye. Fuh-female."

I brightened instantly, as though I had been confronted with a balance sheet showing nothing but black ink. Female P.I.'s were, at the moment, at least, highly fungible. I didn't have one, how I would love to have one. *Yes, yes, yes.*

"Tell me more, Sidney."

"Well, Nick, it cuh-came over the fuh-fucking . . . over the fuh-fucking . . ."

"Transom?"

"Right!"

That meant it was submitted by the author directly, and

not through an agent. Better and better. One of my colleagues has a sampler behind his desk which reads: "An
agent to a publisher is as a knife to the throat." I think most
of us in the trade would applaud that sentiment.

"Who's the author?" I said.

"A wuh-woman—"

"I would hope so."

He ignored my feeble jest. "—nuh-named Sarah Goodall."

"What do we have, Sidney? Outline and chapters? A
complete manuscript?"

"Muh-manuscript," he said with a deep sigh. For Sidney,
speaking at any length must be like what running a marathon would be for most of us. And I know for a fact that
Sidney *has* run the New York Marathon.

"Give it to me, please, Sidney," I said, "before I break
down and cry."

He did, and I didn't. Instead, I packed a manuscript of
comforting heft into my attaché case and headed for home,
knowing I would not want for bedtime reading.

Hope lived once again in my mercenary publisher's heart.

Chapter 10

Home for me is a town house, number 2 Gramercy Park. The house is located on the western side of the park. The block is not altogether pristine, that is, not all the houses are original historic landmark buildings, but mine certainly is, built sometime around 1885. Walking there from my office, I stopped again outside to admire its lines. The front stoop that I'm sure once fronted the street has been replaced by a recessed entryway, but the rest of the façade remains as it originally was; I know this because I have seen early photographs. Like The Players, number 2 was designed by Stanford White of McKim, Mead & White fame. The façade is limestone, peach in color, with two large windows on the second floor, two on the third, and an oxeye on the top story, where there is also a small terrace. The roof I altered by adding a deck for sunbathing and for cocktails or brunch in fine weather. Despite the naysayers, there *are* glorious days in New York City. Someone once wrote that if it had not been such a superb natural seaport, consequently a center of trade and commerce, the climate might have made Manhattan Island a playground on the order of Hilton Head or

Fire Island. Alas, there are days when it is windier than Chicago ever was, rendering my rooftop aerie unusable.

Inside, I also find much to admire, beginning with a long hallway covered with white-and-black-checked ceramic tile, a steep hardwood staircase, the original white brick wall on the left, and immediately on the right, a long, wide, high-ceilinged living room. This room I created when I bought the house, by having a wall knocked down between two nineteenth-century parlors, one no doubt for the gentlemen, in which they could smoke their cigars, sip their brandy, and talk politics, and the other for the ladies, to gossip and do needlepoint or whatever nineteenth-century ladies did. Two sliding doors led into a large formal dining room, which, like the living room, has a wood-burning fireplace. Then comes the kitchen—completely contemporary, of course, but with brass plumbing, a butcher-block carving table in the center, with copper pots hanging overhead, two deep ovens, and a microwave. Here my cook, Pepita, holds sway, her wonders to perform. Out back a walled-in formal garden with a fountain, a pool stocked with Japanese carp and goldfish, and a sundial. Upstairs . . . well, the upstairs rooms are what might be expected: bedrooms, a suite for Pepita and her husband, Oscar, a sitting room, bathrooms, the usual.

I realize that all this might sound pretentious, even ostentatious, but it is not, really. I have been in Manhattan town houses that are equipped with gymnasiums, movie theaters, and indoor swimming pools; me, I prefer a dwelling place that might have survived untouched from the Victorian period, fine antiques and all, except with all the modern conveniences.

Oscar, my houseman cum chauffeur, met me at the door and relieved me of my hat and stick. In a brass salver on a side table in the hallway were several messages Oscar or Pepita had collected for me. I pocketed them and headed upstairs.

Once I had changed into slacks and a sport shirt, I buzzed Oscar and asked him to bring me a vodka and tonic. When that had been safely placed on the coffee table in my sitting room, along with a wedge of Camembert and rice crackers, I leafed through the messages.

Neither Oscar nor Pepita is an adept of our mother tongue, and their interpretations of my callers' names in particular were somewhat garbled; however, I was able to make out all but one; and for that one I would have to rely on the phone number. One of the messages was from Margo. I decided to call her first.

"Nick," she said when I got her on the line, "are you all right?"

"Absolutely. After all, murder is an everyday affair around my office."

"You must be serious, Nick."

"When was I ever otherwise?"

I had not spoken to Margo since my call from Washington, and I suddenly felt a compelling need to see her again.

"Margo . . ."

"Yes?"

"I feel a compelling need to see you."

"When?"

"Tonight." Realizing that I might sound somewhat peremptory, I added: "If you're not otherwise occupied, that is."

"Well . . ."

"Yes?"

"Come on over, Nick. I'll whip up something—an omelet and a salad, maybe. Bring something from your cellar, okay?"

"I'll be there within the hour," I said, and hung up.

The second message was from my brother, Tim, and his calls were infrequent and almost always important. He picked up his phone almost before it had started to ring.

"Nick," he said. "Buddy. I thought you ought to know. Mother has been carrying on something ferocious."

"Oh?"

"Yeah, it's your man Mandelbaum. He's got Gertrude convinced that you're on the verge of bankruptcy. Not you, I mean Barlow and Company."

"Oh, beautiful. Just what I need. Shit! *Sheeit.*"

"I hope you're planning a trip out to Weston this weekend."

"I wasn't, but—"

"You will."

"I will indeed."

"Some excitement, isn't there?"

"I see you watch the five o'clock news," I said.

"Faithfully. The outside of your office building is quite photogenic, you know, Nick?"

"So is the interior. Anyway, no matter what they say, I didn't do it."

"I want to hear all about it."

I bet you do, I thought. Tim is the nearest thing I know to an armchair detective. In his case the armchair has wheels, it is true, but in it, he reigns like a monarch of the cerebral, seldom more than a few paces from his Macintosh and his modem, his library of several thousand volumes, his fax machine. I do believe that if Tim reads something once, he will remember it for at least a year, and if he reads it twice, he will remember it forever.

"Do your best to calm Mother down," I said, "and I'll see you on Friday evening."

"*D'accord.*"

My last message was the one I couldn't decipher, so I dialed the number.

"Seven eight seven four two hundred," a voice chirped. If there's one telephone practice I detest, it is hearing someone answer with a number instead of a name. *I know the number I'm calling, damn it, I just don't know whose number it is!*

It was a struggle to keep my tone of voice civil, but I did my best. "Whom have I reached, please?"

"Kay McIntire and Associates."

"This is Nicholas Barlow. I believe Ms. McIntire called and left a message for me."

"Just a moment, Mr. Barlow." I waited while vaguely symphonic music played tinnily in my ear. I continue to wonder why people resort to telephone music, which is merely elevator music of poorer sound quality, when silence is so much simpler and more soothing to the ear. I realize I sound like a curmudgeon, but then, that is precisely the reputation I have and must steadfastly uphold.

"Hello, Nick. Thanks for getting back so promptly." The voice of Kay McIntire was the real telephone music: husky and warm.

"You're working late, aren't you, Kay?"

"An agent's day is never done."

"Or a publisher's, either. You called."

"Yes. I have pleasant news for you."

"Oh? I'm glad. It's been only unpleasant since yesterday evening."

"I know. I heard about Parker on 'Good Day, New York.' What can we say, Nick?"

"Only that now he knows something we don't know."

Her laugh, like her voice, was throaty and soft. "You never liked him much, did you?"

"I liked his credits," I said. "But it's too soon to figure out what his epitaph ought to be, isn't it?"

"The editor's editor?"

"Surely," I hastened to say, "you didn't call to praise Parker?"

"No, you're right. Nor to bury him, either. I called to tell you that Herbert Poole wants to talk book with you. Mystery novel."

"That's welcome news indeed, Kay. Like when?"

"Can you fit him in this week?"

"Lunch on Friday, perhaps? Just the three of us."

"Let me look." I waited with my own pocket diary at the ready. She was back almost immediately. "That'll be fine. You say where."

"The Century," I suggested. "Twelve-thirty." We murmured our goodbyes and rang off.

Herbert Poole, best-selling author, I said to myself. *He had written three losers and then, with his fourth novel,* Big Casino! *Welcome to Barlow and Company, Herbert—I hope.* My motto had proved out again, hadn't it? "Something will turn up."

With two bottles of 1990 Nuits-St.-Georges in a canvas book bag with the inscription "TEMPUS VITA LIBRI" on its flank—a souvenir of the recent ABA Convention—I cabbed to Margo's apartment on the Upper East Side. The doorman greeted me by name, which startled me slightly, because I had not been there all that often; Margo cherishes her privacy rather more than I do mine. "Evening, Henry," I said, and headed for the elevator.

The apartment is listed as a semi-duplex. The rent, which

is stabilized, is somewhere in the neighborhood of two thousand dollars a month, I believe. It is almost, but not quite, on Sutton Place.

The door was slightly ajar when I arrived at her floor, so I walked in and down a flight of seven steps leading from the entrance gallery to the living room, which has high chalk-white walls and a powder-blue ceiling, a somewhat ecclesiastical window, leaded and fourteen feet high, and a lot of furniture covered with chintz, white with giant cabbage roses. A grand piano with the top slanted up made a splendid silhouette against the windows, which looked down on a fashionable, urban view of the Queensboro Bridge, with the wastes of Yorkville reaching northward and the white stone monolith of the Cornell Medical Center standing out in the night like a fresh bandage on dirty skin. Car lights flashed across the bridge and there were hundreds of golden squares of light on the sheer apartment-house walls. The stars, as always in Manhattan, were blotted out by the lights of the city, and there was no moon in the sky.

Margo called out from the kitchen. "Come on in, Nick. Fix yourself a drink."

I went straight to Margo's bar, switched on the fluorescent light, and proceeded to build myself a dry Absolut martini, straight up, with an olive—ice-cold, of course, and stirred, not shaken.

Margo joined me as I sat on a barstool, sipping away, contented as a pig in clover, though I would not wish anyone but me to apply that metaphor to myself. She was wearing a black silk cocktail dress, cut low and square in the bodice, and rustling slightly as she moved. There was an apron in her hand, which she tossed on a nearby chair, just before reaching up and kissing me.

"Nick," she said, beaming at me with her cat-green eyes and flashing her tiny, perfectly shaped white teeth, "we have a lot to catch up on, starting with murder and working backward to the ABA."

Margo and I have gotten along much better since we divorced than we did in the last year or so of our five-year marriage, and I still find her the most alluring woman I know. Unfortunately she does not necessarily find me always the pick of my gender. Ah well, I keep making the manly seductive effort. I lifted my glass in a silent toast.

"May I fix you something?" I said after a liquid pause.

"I'll wait for the wine. I'm sure it's superb."

"It ought to be. The 1990 Bordeaux were the best vintages for red burgundy in over thirty years."

"So you say."

"So says Robert Parker. The wine authority, not the creator of Spenser and Hawk."

"Shall we get more comfortable?" Margo led the way into the center of the living room, where she occupied a couch and I settled in an overstuffed chair. We sat for a while in a companionable silence, while I sipped my drink.

"I hope you aren't expecting a three- or four-course dinner," said Margo. "I have something left over to warm up—nothing fancy."

"I have never gone hungry in your company," I said.

What Margo had left over was a penne with fresh, uncooked tomato sauce, made from ripe red tomatoes, with lots of garlic, hot green chiles, pepper flakes, basil, and several kinds of cheese, along with hot Italian bread and a crisp Caesar salad, one of the few salads I eat with gusto.

"This wine *is* superb," said she, holding a glass of it up to the flickering candles on the dining room table.

"I've often wondered," I said, "which of several indulgences I would miss most if I were deprived of it."

She drained her wineglass and held it out for me to fill. "Such as?"

"Food, drink, and sex, in about that order, I believe."

"But isn't there something sexual about eating?" Margo said. "And drinking?"

I raised my own wineglass and stroked it, while I thought a moment. Only then did I sip it. "You're thinking of *Tom Jones,*" I said. "But I've always believed that when a man and a woman sit down together to eat, it is almost as intimate an experience as making love."

"Almost?"

"Well—not *quite* as intimate."

Margo set her glass down on the table with a sharp *click.* "Nick Barlow," she said, "are you attempting to seduce me?"

"Is that so unusual?"

"I thought you'd know better by now."

At that instant, I did not know what to say, but I knew exactly what Margo meant. Our last romantic interlude— some weeks ago by now—and any others in recent years had all followed the same pattern. It was Margo who initiated them. Margo who had always been in complete control of the event. And it was I who had been the more than willing acolyte in the venereal ceremony. I had only thought I was seducing her; it was she who led me—every step of the way. Did I wish to continue to be he who must obey—or ought I to change partners and dance with somebody else? Maybe it was time to move on.

But I knew without any reservation—or any misgiving, either—that I would go to bed tonight alone. And chaste.

"Still," I said, "there's still food and drink. May I have some more of that bracing pasta?"

"Of course," said Margo, smiling her Da Vinci smile, "if you'll pour some more of that extraordinary wine."

We finally did get around to discussing the ABA, which, in the way conventions have, was fast fading out of mind. She wanted to know if any of the parties had been fun, so I told her about the one I'd attended at the Library of Congress. The party was given in the huge and majestic foyer of the library. Marble underfoot and all around me, Italian mosaics on the floor, ornamental cornucopias, ribbons and vines galore. We were served plump oysters on the half shell, champagne, and sweet fresh strawberries on ice.

"I felt more at home in this building than in any other in the capital," I told Margo. There was the world's largest library, the home of all knowledge, and the home as well of the Copyright Office, a publisher's best friend.

The contentment I exuded must have been visible to any of the partygoers in my vicinity, because one of them came up and said, "Nick, you look like you just swallowed an agent whole."

It was Bernie Rath, the executive director of the American Booksellers Association, and the master of all its revels. Short, stocky, bearded Bernie is a transplanted Canadian, and a warm supporter of the written and printed word, as well as a sworn enemy of censorship. I have always liked him.

"What news on the Rialto, Bernie?" I said. "How's the convention going?"

"Setting new records for attendance," he said.

"What are people talking about?" Usually there is one book or author that sets everyone at the ABA to talking. I have always hoped it would be one of my books; it usually turns out to be the new Norman Mailer novel or the sequel to *Gone with the Wind.*

"As a matter of fact," Bernie said, "they're talking mostly about the new multimedia."

The new electronic developments—they're quite something. They are the specter haunting everyone in book publishing. In a world where a device held in one's hand can communicate with a computer thousands of miles away, where databases containing hundreds of volumes of text, sound transcriptions, and color photographs can be accessed night and day within seconds, how is intellectual property to be protected? How are publishers to know what to charge for what they *think* they own, and who is to police the computer pirates? No wonder we are all trembling at the thought of these wondrous innovations in microchip storage, and reluctant to jump on the Japanese bandwagon; they threaten to put us all out of business.

Sober thoughts, but appropriate in the home of the Copyright Office. And just like that my mood altered, from euphoria in the presence of so much grandeur, to gloom at the prospect of becoming irrelevant, superfluous, a dinosaur of print in an electronic universe.

I am not sure how much of what I felt I was able to convey to Bernie Rath, who nodded sagely and drifted off— or to Margo, in her lamplit living room; it didn't seem to matter too much.

The murder of Parker Foxcroft, however, was something else. That kept us going until my bedtime.

"What was it like finding him, Nick? How did you feel?"

I had no doubt that the memory of that moment would never leave me. How did I feel? I answered Margo's first question first.

"There was the unmistakable odor of death in Parker's

office when I walked in," I said. "The odors of blood and excretions. After a visit to the morgue, and a fleeting sojourn at one of our recent undeclared wars, I didn't *need* to see his body to know. How did I feel? I was shocked, certainly, and rather frightened. The murder must have taken place shortly before I arrived—the murderer was still there, for God's sake . . . and despite reports to the contrary, I still haven't got used to being around corpses."

"Who would want to kill Parker Foxcroft? Have you any ideas?"

"That's what the police wanted to know. The answer is . . ."

She finished the sentence for me. "Anybody."

"Precisely."

I went home after dinner without complaint, feeling pleasantly satisfied—and not all that disappointed. After a day like this one, I wasn't altogether sure that I would have been up to Margo, who at her best has more than once kept me awake and virile a good part of the night. And I was confident there would be other nights, somewhere along the way. And if not, well . . .

Since my divorce, I have found that there are substantial rewards in the single state. For example: curling up in bed with the cushions plumped up, the night-light on, a snifter of Courvoisier in hand, and the manuscript Sidney had given me on my bedside table.

I picked up the first few pages of the manuscript. *Iceman*. Okay, nice title. "By Sarah Goodall." Never heard of her, but it was probably a first effort. Where, I wondered, would the setting be? California? Sue Grafton had staked out the southern part of the state. Chicago? Sara Paretsky territory. Forget Richmond—Kay Scarpetta had central Virginia in her medical bag, thanks to Patricia D. Cornwell. It was getting hard these days to find a city that some P.I., male or female, hasn't already laid claim to. There are at least two in Boston and half a dozen or more in New York City. And isn't there one in San Francisco? A gay sleuth, I believe.

I read on.

St. Paul, Minnesota, on a cold December night is about as cheerful as the Ramsey County Morgue. Only a fool or a private investigator working a case, as I was, would be over on the South Side in weather like this. Even with the temperature at twelve above, I could still smell the stockyards. Sleet whipped against my cheeks, and stung my eyes until they watered, almost blinding me.

I'm P. V. Knudsen, and I'm a licensed freelance investigator. You can call me a private cop. The "P" stands for Paula, a name I don't much like, and the "V" for Violet, which I like even less. I'm thirty-five and holding. I've been married twice. My first husband ran off with my best friend, and I threw the second one out when I caught him pushing PCP in the Groveland Park schoolyard. As you might expect, after two Mr. Wrongs, I don't have a lot of faith in the male of the species. I hear there are birds that manage to remain monogamous, however, and maybe they're what the whole thing is for.

Although I was bundled up in my heaviest parka, the wind still whipped at my arms, and I could tell that the gloves I wore weren't going to stave off frostbite. I slapped my right hand under my left shoulder, where

I could feel the comforting bulge of my shoulder holster. I was packing a .380 Beretta. What I like about this gun is its grip, which feels perfect for my hand. Also, it takes a thirteen-round staggered magazine. I like to go with a friend of mine on the force to the target range in Minneapolis for practice, at least once a month. At thirty yards, I can group my shots perfectly, right in the center of the targets. You never know when the target is going to be a baddie aiming at you.

I wouldn't have had the gun with me, except that I was on a tail, in the darkest, loneliest part of town. The case I was on this time was industrial espionage.

It all started when a man named Edgar Ayres came to see me. It was just after Thanksgiving and I couldn't help but notice that my bank account was as weak as a busted flush.

So, when Ayres called me, I was ready to listen to any good offer, as long as it was legitimate . . .

I was intrigued enough to read on. I would love to have a good female P.I. series, and this one looked promising. Why is this genre popular? Ask the Sisters in Crime. All I know is that men and women readers both seem to like the idea of a woman packing a gun and getting off a karate chop with the best of them—the more hard-boiled, the better.

To paraphrase Raymond Chandler: "Down these mean streets a woman must go who is not herself mean, who is neither tarnished nor afraid. She must be a complete woman and a common woman and yet an unusual woman. She must be the best woman in her world, and a good enough woman for any world." Anyway, that's the general idea.

When at last I fell asleep, it was not because I had lost

interest in the manuscript. It was simply "Nature's soft nurse," as Shakespeare put it, brushing my eyes with her healing touch.

In the morning . . . I'll read some more . . . in the . . . morning . . .

Chapter 11

The weather was pleasant enough for me to have breakfast on the roof deck, where I finished reading the *Iceman* manuscript. I have wondered why so many people seem to find their first meal of the day boring, and why they so often eat the same thing day after day. Traveling abroad, I have had some quite exotic breakfasts, everything from *pâté de campagne* and toast points in Paris to gluten bread and elderberries with clotted cream in Frankfurt. This morning I feasted on kippered herring and Pepita's French toast— made with day-old sourdough bread, slathered with maple syrup and garnished with fresh blueberries.

As I sat drinking my second cup of Juan Valdez's coffee, Oscar appeared with the portable phone in his hand. "Miz Reechmon," he announced.

"So nice to hear from you," I murmured before Margo had the chance to drop her bombshell.

"Nick," she said, "I wanted to say I'm sorry about last night. I know you were disappointed . . ."

"Disappointment is never fatal, my dear," I said. "And not even final."

"I've been thinking . . ."

"Go ahead."

"I don't think we ought to see each other for a while."

I felt a sharp stab in the vicinity of my chest which I knew *was* certainly disappointment. "But why?"

"Let's just say I think we need some distance between us, and perhaps some time to decide where we stand—and also where we're going."

"That's quite rational of you, Margo. I wish I felt the same way."

"That's the problem, Nick. You seem to be emotionally involved, and I am not—not in the same way. Oh, I like you well enough . . ."

"Thanks for small favors."

"And anyway you know your business always comes ahead of everything else."

When I'm not involved in the murder of one of my editors, that is.

There didn't appear to be much more for me to say; clearly Margo's mind was made up, and she was not to be persuaded otherwise—not by my oratory, at any rate. I muttered something about being sorry, and she said something about getting in touch with me at some later date, and then we both hung up. It occurred to me that I was probably far less satisfied with this conversation than Margo was. Margo, Margo . . . why? The author of the only book on astrology I have ever published (and that with tongue firmly in cheek) would say that she was simply being a true Gemini—and perhaps in this case astrology did have the correct answer.

By this time, my second helping of French toast had cooled off, and so had my ardor. If I didn't have another woman in my life for some time to come, it would *not* be a hardship at all.

I would miss Margo's companionship, of course. And what about the second ticket I had for the Philharmonic's Mostly Mozart? It was our custom, Margo and I, to have an early dinner at one of our favorite restaurants, Pierre au Tunnel, perhaps, Le Quercy, or Sfuzzi, and then stroll in a leisurely fashion up to what Margo, to my delight, insists on calling Eddie Fisher Hall.

Now I would just have to find another music lover.

Once back at the office, I sent for Sidney and gave him my considered editorial report on his new discovery.

"It needs work, Sidney."

"Duh-don't they all, though?"

I have long dreamt of the day when a manuscript would cross my desk in such perfect array that I could not imagine changing a word of it, not even adding or eliminating a comma—a masterpiece, like some rare diamond fresh from the cutter's bench. I am still waiting, and I strongly suspect my dream will never come true.

"However, Sidney—*Iceman* is, even in its imperfect state, well worth a contract and a modest advance—say, ten thousand dollars. The usual split."

"Fuh-five on signing and the rest on acceptance?"

I nodded. "And I'd like to meet the author as soon as you can arrange it," I said.

"That muh-may be hard. She lives in Muh-muh . . ."

He clenched his right fist tightly and grimaced.

"Minneapolis?"

"Right."

"Well, then, whenever."

Sidney returned to his office, and I turned to the day's mail, which consisted largely of magazines and flyers, assorted press clippings, and a couple of invitations to press parties. The invitations come from fellow publishers and are issued not so much in the spirit of bonhomie as of curiosity, to find out what I'm up to. I go to them in the same spirit and to pick up any gossip I can.

I withdrew the current issue of *Publishers Weekly* from the pile and was about to open it when my eye was caught by a distinctively feminine light green envelope—addressed to me and marked "Personal." I slit it open with a sudden sense of anticipation and read:

> Dear Nick Barlow:
>   I have just learned about the terrible thing that has happened to Parker Foxcroft. I am shocked beyond measure by his murder, and I know you must be too. How could such a thing have happened?
>   If there is any way I can help, I hope you will call on me.
>
> Sincerely,

It was signed "Susan Markham," and included both a home address and a phone number.

Sitting back in my chair, I put the note away in my inside coat pocket, not without first rereading it and giving it some thought. Susan Markham . . . I had not expected to hear from her after the ABA, not after the cavalier way I had rebuffed her overtures, if "overtures" wasn't too strong a word to describe her conversation with me. It occurred to me that it might be useful—informative, perhaps—to follow up on her offer to help.

Just then Hannah buzzed me.

"Lieutenant Hatcher is on the phone," she said.

I picked up. "Yes, Lieutenant?"

"Mr. Barlow," he said in the clipped, uninflected way he had of speaking, "we'd like you to come over to headquarters for further questioning. If you don't mind."

"Well . . ."

"You're free to bring your attorney, of course." I got the distinct impression that he thought bringing a lawyer would be a good idea.

"I thought I'd told you all I know," I said in a futile appeal to Hatcher's better nature.

He waited a couple of beats before replying. "There are still some . . . loose ends? You know . . . to tie up."

I looked at my watch. "When would you like me to stop in?"

"How about eleven o'clock?"

"I'll see if my attorney can meet me there, and let you know."

"That'll be fine."

I got Alex Margolies on the line as quickly as Hannah could find him. Alex is both my lawyer and a friend; he has also been trained as a CPA, which makes him useful on many fronts. Much as I rely on the good Mortimer Mandelbaum, I would not dream of filing taxes without having the forms vetted by Alex.

"You're lucky, Nick," he said. "I was supposed to be in court this morning, but we got a postponement."

"So you'll meet me at the Thirteenth Precinct."

"Sure thing."

I gave him the address, hung up, and sat there, swearing under my breath. The last thing I needed was another of what Hatcher called "interviews" and I was beginning to think of as inquisitions.

I asked Hannah to confirm my appointment with Lieutenant Hatcher and picked up the *Publishers Weekly* again. The first thing I turned to was the best-seller list, and I was gratified to see that Herbert Poole's *Pan at Twilight,* like Abou Ben Adam, still headed the list.

I met Alex Margolies in the anteroom of the Thirteenth Precinct house shortly before eleven. We looked around, taking in the general shabbiness and congestion of the place. There were three sergeants at the reception counter—two male, one female—and half a dozen assorted citizens either at the counter or seated on benches nearby.

I didn't need to fill Alex in on why were there; he is as avid a reader of the crime reports as I am.

"Other than your finding the corpus delicti," he said to me, pitching his voice lower than usual, "what reason have the cops to suspect you?"

I told him about the quarrel and about my decision to get rid of Parker.

"But I didn't mean to get rid of him *that* way."

"Well," he said, "we'll see what this Lieutenant Hatcher has to say for himself."

Suddenly, as though summoned by the mere mention of his name, Hatcher appeared, virtually at my elbow.

"Mr. Barlow," he said, "I appreciate your coming." He turned to Alex. "And you're . . ."

"Alexander Margolies, attorney-at-law."

Hatcher nodded. "Pleased to meet you, Counselor. Won't you both come in my office?"

We followed meekly after him, through a hallway with a water fountain and a pay phone, both in use at the moment by uniformed patrolpeople. There were also posters on a bulletin board—the ten most wanted, perhaps? The walls were painted in what we call "men's-room green," a shade both bilious and antiseptic.

Hatcher's office was private if not what I would call

inviting. His desk and chair; a couple of well-worn visitors' chairs; several file cabinets; a computer terminal and printer; and nothing hanging on the walls but a Sierra Club calendar. I don't know what I expected Hatcher's desk to look like; it was actually rather neat: an in-box, an out-box, a blotter, and a phone—nothing else except a file folder, which he now opened. Alex and I took our seats and waited. After a long few moments of leafing through the file, he finally arrived at what appeared to be my dossier; at least, I assumed that's what it was.

"A few routine questions, Mr. Barlow," was his opening line. I braced myself. Is there anything routine about a murder investigation? Yes, I suppose so. And yet every murder is different, and every murderer. There are an infinite number of changes to be rung on the original crime, which started, after all, with Cain and Abel.

"For starters," said Hatcher, "I'd like to know more about your relationship with the victim."

"I've already told you what our business arrangement was."

Hatcher sighed with evident weariness. "I mean how did you get along?"

"Well enough to work together," I said.

"Yet I've learned from interviewing your staff that you have had a number of run-ins with Foxcroft. That doesn't sound to me like you were able to work with him all that well, does it?"

He apparently expected an answer to his question; I merely shrugged.

"You were thinking about getting rid of him, weren't you?"

"That would give Foxcroft more reason to kill me than the other way around, Lieutenant."

"Just what kind of financial troubles is your company having, Mr. Barlow?"

I looked at Alex Margolies, who shook his head. "That's privileged information, Lieutenant, and I'm advising my client not to answer your question."

"Okay," said Hatcher, visibly shifting gears. "Do you own a gun, Mr. Barlow?"

"No, I do not." I was going to add that I despise guns and the havoc they wreak in our society, that if I could wipe them all off the face of the earth by a wave of my hand, I would do it in an instant, and while I was being godlike, I would also dissolve the National Rifle Association, like this: *Bang! You're dead.* However, looking at the police special in Hatcher's shoulder holster, I thought it better to keep my opinions to myself.

"But you are familiar with firearms."

"Only what I read in mysteries and crime novels, Lieutenant. And as I've already told you, I was in Air Force Intelligence, so of course I had to know how to handle a forty-five."

Hatcher pressed on, looking occasionally at his file. What did I know of Foxcroft's relationships with other members of the firm? With this Harry Bunter, for example? With Lester Crispin? With Sidney Leopold? I was noncommittal in every instance.

Finally Alex rose to his feet and said: "Lieutenant, I'm going to advise my client not to answer any further questions, especially those concerning other members of his firm. Those questions are not relevant. I assume," he added, "that my client is not being charged with any offense?"

"Not at this time," said Hatcher, also rising from his chair.

Not at this time? I thought. *Why, you son of a bitch!*

"Anyway," Hatcher added, "have a nice day."

I might have known his tag line would be that dreary cliché.

Once Alex and I were free of the cozy atmosphere of the station house, I turned to him and said: "He's not going to let up on me, is he?"

Alex nodded. "It would appear that at the moment, you're the only suspect he has."

I knew what I was going to do when I got back to the office. Call Joe Scanlon with an SOS.

Chapter 12

"Look, Nick—I don't know if I can help you or not."

Lieutenant Joseph Scanlon opened his hands in the classic gesture of "coming up empty." He had been in my office that Friday morning for almost an hour, while I had run through everything I could tell him about Parker Foxcroft and the events leading up to Parker's murder. He leaned forward in his chair, hunching his shoulders, his forehead creased in a frown that quickly slipped into a wicked grin.

"Here you go again, Nick, as a recent president was fond of saying."

"Hey, Joe—man, this is definitely *not* the way I like to spend my time—or yours. I didn't choose to be mixed up in this business. But I do need help." Did I protest too much? I don't think so. I *was* beginning to feel beset, even paranoid. But as Sam Spade would have said if he'd been in the book business, when someone kills your editor, a publisher's supposed to do something about it . . .

"I can see that. However, I can't really stick my nose into a murder in another precinct than my own. Especially when I'm on leave."

"Isn't there anything you can do?"

He was silent for a few moments. Then: "Well, maybe I can get some information for you, if that would help. Sergeant Falco was with me at the Police Academy, and I've sort of kept in touch. Given him a call every so often—had a drink with him once in a while—that sort of thing. He might be willing to share what he knows. After all, I'm still more of a cop than a civilian."

"Make that 'author,' Joe."

"If you say so, Nick. And I suppose I might do a bit of digging into the life and times of Parker Foxcroft, if that would help."

I felt an immediate surge of relief. It seemed to me that if not home free, at least I was no longer alone, I had help. And I couldn't help but also feel elated that I was once again faced with a real mystery, and not just another paper puzzle.

"By the way, Joe—have you done anything about getting representation?"

"No, not yet." I had suggested more than once, since Scanlon had turned in the first draft of his book, that he ought to have an agent. I know—even Shakespeare had something to say about them: "Let every eye negotiate for itself and trust no agent." However, when it comes to the publishing business, I cannot help but think of Joe Scanlon as a naïf among rogues, a true babe in the woods. I am not implying that *I* would cheat him, heaven forfend—but I want him to make as much money from his book as possible, and that means a whopping paperback reprint deal, movie and television sales—all beyond my power to generate, but always possible with an accomplished agent.

"Have you got anyone in mind?" Scanlon said.

"Yes. Kay McIntire." Actually I didn't have anyone in mind, but hers was the first name that popped into my mind, I suppose because I had a lunch date with her in two hours. "I'll speak to Kay about representing you."

"I'd appreciate it, Nick."

God, how wonderful! Scanlon was still appreciative. That is because publication—and possibly fame—still awaited him. In this virginal state, authors are almost always grateful for whatever favors are done them, and so they should be. After all, no one *asked* them or any other author to write their first novel. As Thomas Wolfe put it: "Nobody discovered me. I discovered myself."

Scanlon and I parted with his promise to report to me as soon as he had information from Falco—though not before I reminded him that his revised manuscript was due on the first of August.

"I'm on schedule, Nick," he said.

I took his elbow and steered him toward the door. "Good man," I said.

Some observers of the publishing scene have argued that lunch is the most important part of anyone's day, and that nothing either preceding or following the midday meal is of any consequence. I have myself divided publishing folk into two types: those who must be pressed for decisions before they have gone to lunch, and those who are best approached *after* lunch. Which type am I? Definitely the former. After the wine has been poured, I do not trust myself to be a hardheaded businessman.

Lunch that Friday, however, was an exception. After it was over, I could hardly wait to get Herbert Poole to ink a contract.

The three of us—Poole, Kay McIntire, and I—met in the waiting room off the front door of the Century—more exactly, the Century Association. The club was given its name because its progenitors, in the year 1847, invited an even hundred gentlemen engaged in or interested in letters and the fine arts to join; forty-two accepted and became Founders; another forty-six joined during the first year. Nowadays there are many times one hundred—up to twelve hundred, to be exact—on the membership roster.

If The Players is my second home, my pit stop, so to speak, then the Century is where I hold court. I am a member as my father was a member, and probably for that reason; it was his favorite haunt. It is everything, I suppose, that people who don't care for private clubs, the populists, would despise. An imposing Stanford White building hardly two blocks from Grand Central Station. A great many overstuffed leather chairs, in which occasionally a member may be found sleeping. A security system at the door as good as any, probably, in the halls of government. Uniformed servitors, most of them African-American, who seem to have been there since the Crash of 1929. It does not have bedrooms, like the Yale and Harvard clubs, though there is a basement with a few billiard and pool tables—hardly any of them ever used these days—and a splendid library. The service is prompt, efficient, and unobtrusive. I am not aware of any scandal connected with the club, and publicity is shunned like a carrier of the HIV, although one brouhaha over the club's sale of a $2-million painting in order to pay for much-needed renovations did make the local papers, and the original refusal to admit one of my publishing colleagues—a woman—as a member broke into print as well, along with a few very proper names.

We climbed the marble stairs to the spacious second floor, and soon were seated around a low coffee table in a large foyer adjoining the Member's Bar and facing the spacious

East Room, me with the usual vodka martini, Kay with a margarita, and Poole contenting himself with a club soda and lime. I can be comfortable lunching with an abstainer, but I do prefer to feel that my guests, like me, are enjoying the quiet satisfaction brought by that first drink of the day.

I was eager to get down to business, but mindful of the courtesies I owed my two guests, I made small talk for a while. Anyway, the Century, like The Players, frowns on business discussions, which of course go on there all the time. As a consequence, the club has had to admit women members, after a century of gentlemanly discrimination, though it had to be practically dragooned into doing so. The sole ladies' before "liberation" was on the ground floor somewhere near the coatroom. Several others have since been constructed.

"Kay," I said, "I have an author who's looking for an agent, and I've already recommended you." I told her then about Joe Scanlon.

"Well," she said, "I do have a fairly full stable of writers just now . . ."

"Couldn't you squeeze in one more?"

"But, I was going to say, your man sounds interesting."

"He is that, all right—and a good writer."

"I'll meet with him anyhow, and we'll see what happens."

While we were talking, I took the opportunity of looking over Herbert Poole, who showed a polite interest in the conversation Kay and I were having. I made Poole out to be in his early or mid-thirties, just shy of six feet, lean, and good-looking in a fashion-model way, the kind of looks I usually don't pay much attention to. I like a face that shows more wear and tear, a face that has been around the block a few times. His voice was deep and rather grave—with just a touch of the Old Dominion in it—pleasing to my ear.

"Working with a real cop must be interesting for you," he remarked when there was a brief silence.

"It is that," I admitted, but I was thinking of Parker Foxcroft, not of Joe Scanlon's book.

"It's a novel?" said Poole.

"Yes, but not what you'd expect, a police procedural. It's a novel about a criminal lawyer whose client is accused of murder—rather like a latter-day Perry Mason."

"As Kay has told you, Mr. Barlow," Poole said, leaning in her direction, "I'm intrigued by the idea of writing a mystery."

"It never ceases to amaze me how many mainstream writers are," I said. "How many writers, period. What do you suppose the fascination of the genre is?"

"I rather think that it's the satisfaction of writing about something outside themselves and their egos, their ordinary or extraordinary problems." It was Kay who spoke, and I nodded in agreement. "In the straight novel, character is all-important; in the mystery it's story. There's always a story, usually a strong one. It must always have a beginning, a middle, and an end—and in the end, the criminal is caught, and the crime is solved. Q.E.D. Everyone is satisfied, the reader as well as the writer."

"That's not to say that character isn't important in a mystery," I said. "What character in fiction is more memorable than Sherlock Holmes, for example?"

"I wonder," said Poole, "if anyone has ever written a mystery in which the criminal is *not* caught, and the crime has not been solved."

"It's been done," I said, "and there are crime novels in which the criminal is sympathetic—the hero, in fact. Patricia Highsmith's hero Ripley, for one. Donald Westlake's Dortmunder, for another. But it would probably prove frustrating for the reader in most cases. I speak as one myself. I don't like loose ends; I want things neatly tied up."

"I'm not saying I'm going to write one like that," Poole said in his limpid drawl. "Like most authors, I write of what I know best."

"In the case of your current best-seller," I said, "sex."

Poole smiled. "I prefer to think of it as love, Mr. Barlow."

"Please—call me Nick. And I stand corrected. *Love*, certainly."

At this point Kay interrupted us. "Herbert has an idea which I think may appeal to you, Nick."

"Go ahead," I said.

"What I would like to do," Poole said, "is spend some time in your office, like a fly on the wall, so to speak. I'd like to meet and talk with your Joe Scanlon, for one—and any other mystery writers who might show up. I'd like to know how you managed to crack the Jordan Walker murder case, too."

"Well . . ."

"I promise I won't get in your way, or interfere with any of your normal business days. When you want me out of the way, I'll make myself scarce. And meanwhile I'll be making notes and writing."

Kay was wrong; I did not cotton to the idea. I like authors well enough—in their place. In mine, however, only when necessary. "Well . . ." I said, doing my best to think of a way to soften my refusal, "at the moment . . ."

"You'd rather not," Poole suggested.

"Precisely."

"Perhaps at a later date?" said Kay.

"We'll see."

Meanwhile, as I reminded Kay, there was the little matter of the contract.

"Ordinarily we'd go to auction, Nick, but this is quite unusual. We'll take into account the fact that Herbert has never written a mystery, and will need editorial guidance and help from you. The advance I'll ask for is lower than we'd usually expect to see. However, we'll want ninety percent of the paperback rights as well as the usual foreign and domestic rights."

I knew what Kay meant by that. One hundred percent of the performing rights, first and second serial rights, book club edition, large-print edition, library edition, abridgment, condensation, digest—

"Data storage transmission and retrieval," I said aloud.

"And electronic publishing in the teletext, video text, or any other form whether now in existence or hereafter developed." Kay finished the sentence for me. We both spoke the language of contract fluently.

"Only ten percent of the paperback money," I said. "I wonder if I'll be able to live with that."

"Tell you what," said Kay. "You go back to your office and figure out what you would expect to make from hardcover sales alone, and give me *your* suggested advance figure based on that number—and a straight fifteen percent royalty from the sale of the first copy."

"Fair enough, Kay."

"We ought to be able to come up with a mutually satisfactory offer by this afternoon."

"I would like that." I glanced down at the three empty glasses on the table. "Another round?"

"Not for me," said Poole, and Kay also shook her head.

"Then let's lunch," I said, and led the way through a set of double doors into what is called the Library Dining Room. The walls are, in fact, lined with books of all kinds, vintages,

and imprints—rather like what you would expect to find in
the library of a well-stocked country house.

We put in our orders; all three of us chose the fish of the
day, which was blackened catfish. The sommelier brought
a bottle of a good Montrachet, and while we wined and
dined, Herbert Poole enlightened me on how it felt to go
from obscurity to fame in one giant leap.

It felt, he said, "like winning the lottery. I don't think
any of my earlier books ever sold more than five or six
thousand copies. The first one sold even fewer than that."

"But this one—?"

"Is completely different in style and subject matter—and
that has apparently made all the difference."

I raised my wineglass. "I congratulate you," I said. We
touched glasses lightly and drank.

"To the muse of mystery," said Poole, and we toasted
that as well.

Nor was Herbert Poole displeased when at least two of
the members recognized him on the way out—whether from
his jacket photograph or an appearance he had put in on the
"Today" show, we did not know.

Kay proved to be right. What we came up with later that
day was an advance Barlow & Company could live with, and
one that Herbert Poole would not be ashamed to see on his
income tax forms.

And I could go out to Connecticut for the weekend with
a modest triumph to my name as well as a disaster. Scratch
Parker Foxcroft and add Herbert Poole.

Chapter 13

I know of few places I would rather be on a summer weekend than Connecticut—more precisely, Weston, Connecticut, where my family has lived for at least six generations. Before that, the Barlows were Virginians, and before that—well, like everyone else, I have a family history, and even a family tree, but I'm firmly convinced that if patriotism is the last refuge of a scoundrel, as Samuel Johnson observed, then ancestor worship is the last refuge of a snob—and I refuse to indulge in it.

Refuge, however, is not a bad way to describe the Casa Barlow in Weston. It is where I go to recharge my batteries, as well as to touch base. By now I think I've made my point: nothing is more satisfying after a week or two in New York City than to get the hell out of town.

I've been asked why I don't live in Connecticut full time and commute to New York; many of my colleagues do it without too much complaint. Certainly my father did it for years—but I have always felt that he who is tired of Manhattan is tired of life, to paraphrase the good Doctor Sam once more. Forgive me if I sound like *Bartlett's Quotations*.

I sometimes have Oscar drive me out to the country, but I usually take the Metro North train from Grand Central, that fabulous cathedral for wayfarers. First I pick up a *New York Post,* to find out what is going on in the underbelly of the city. "Headless Corpse in Topless Bar." No one will ever top that famous old *Post* headline. There is a bar car available, and I usually get one for the road. Sometimes I have company, sometimes I travel alone.

This trip I was startled to run into Harry Bunter on the train. There he was, slouched on an aisle seat, one of those seats that have no headrest, looking quite miserable. He was clutching a paper cup filled with what I assumed was Scotch.

"Harry," I said, "what are you doing here?"

"I suppose I'm taking a fucking train ride," he replied. "Isn't that what you're doing?"

"I mean, Harry, what brings you to Connecticut?" I knew that Harry and his wife, Claire, lived on Jane Street, in Greenwich Village.

"I've moved to Stamford."

"Since when?"

"Oh, couple of weeks now." He began to fidget, shifting back and forth in his seat. He appeared desperate for a cigarette, which of course is a no-no these days on Metro North. Gone, thank God, are the days when certain smoke-filled cars took on the aroma of army latrines, although I admit to being nostalgic for the occasional good panatela.

I looked at him with inquiry written in my features; he had used the singular noun in describing his relocation. What about Claire?

He read my inquiring look and said: "Claire and I have separated."

"I'm sorry to hear that, Harry. Want to talk about it?"

He shrugged. "Not particularly." He apparently felt that he might have hurt my feelings, because he quickly added: "Well, why not? You've been a good friend, Nick."

I'd known Harry Bunter for more than ten years, even longer than he'd worked for me. In fact, I wooed him away from William Morrow because I had seen him in action at Frankfurt, and knew how good a salesman he was.

"Let's see if we can find a seat built for two," I said, and led the way up the aisle, toward the doors at the end of the car, past the customary assortment of homebound travelers, some reading, others sleeping, not a few staring into space with expressions void of any interest in the passing parade. There were bags galore in the overhead racks, bags in the aisle and stacked in front of the doors in the center of the car—all the impedimenta and confusion of a Friday rush hour. Meanwhile, the conductor threaded his way through the hapless standees, uttering his familiar mantra, "Tickets, please. Tickets?"

We finally found an empty double, several cars forward, and just past Mount Vernon. Harry's cup was pretty well drained by now, and I was somewhat surprised to see him rattle the ice cubes and then pull a couple of miniatures out of his pocket and replenish it.

"Okay, Harry, give."

The intimate confidences of men who are estranged from their wives are all too familiar these days, are usually couched in threadbare phrases and marred by obvious omissions. Harry's tale of woe was no exception, but because of auld lang syne, I felt sympathy for him. I understand well enough the pain of a man who still loves a woman who has fallen out of love with him. This was Harry's plight, compounded by her having fallen in love with someone else.

"Parker Foxcroft?" I said.

Harry snorted, raised his cup to his lips, and drained it. "Foxcroft was only the last one," he said.

"You're sure?" I found this picture of Claire Bunter hard to credit. I had met her perhaps half a dozen times, no more, but I had always thought of her as a straightforward woman, reserved but not unfriendly, and certainly not promiscuous—not in appearance, at any rate. I have met beautiful women who make their sexual interest in a man known quite frankly, whether anyone is watching them or not. I would have sworn that Claire was a woman who would have been difficult to seduce; moreover, that she would have had to be seduced; that she would never have made the first overtures. Still, I had to assume that Harry knew what he was talking about—or else he was paranoid.

Theirs was a marriage, I knew, of two working people, two dedicated publishing people. I would have suspected that they took their respective manuscripts to bed with them—Claire those she was writing, and Harry those he was reading. Their marriage, like so many of that nature, was childless, but I had always thought it close-knit. Until the rumors started—and now Harry had confirmed them.

"What are you planning to do?" I asked.

"Divorce, I suppose," Harry grunted. Out came another pair of miniatures.

"Does Claire agree?"

"She'd better," he said, lowering his voice almost to a whisper. It was though he was talking only to himself now—that I was no longer really there.

And then he said the strangest thing of all: "Claire is capable . . . of *anything*."

Of Parker Foxcroft he said only: "I'm glad the son of a bitch is dead," which hardly surprised me. After this remark, he lapsed into a silence which lasted until the train reached Stamford, where he rose unsteadily, hoisted his briefcase, and left the train with a murmured good-bye.

Home again, home again, riggety-jiggety, as my father used to say whenever the family Cadillac approached the driveway of our spread on Kellogg Hill Road. Harry Dennehy, my mother's factotum, met me at the Westport station and drove me home with his customary skill and tact. After a brief and not unfriendly greeting, he kept his own counsel on the way.

When I arrived, it was almost seven o'clock, time only for a dry Rob Roy and a few crackers spread with Roquefort cheese dip, and then dinner. My younger brother, Tim, who has been paralyzed from the waist down since an accident some fifteen years ago, glided into the dining room in his wheelchair. My mother, Gertrude, as usual presided over the feast. There were no guests, which I found a relief, since I didn't really feel up to company, least of all anyone I didn't already know. We started off with raw oysters (I've never paid much attention to that superstition about months with "r's" in them), followed by roasted guinea hens with new potatoes and carrots in a light gravy, washed down with a fine, crisp Sancerre. When Mother's cook had cleared away the empty dishes and platters, I sighed in contentment, dabbed my mouth with my napkin, and prepared to rise. Mother motioned me to stay seated.

"Yes, Mother?" Although I am old enough to be lord of the manor myself, I defer to her, grande dame that she is, as though I were still a schoolboy.

"Nicholas," she said, rather brusquely, I thought, "I would like us to have a conference."

"Now?" Visions of a warm brandy snifter danced in my head, and faded away.

"*Now.*"

The truth is, when Mother, Tim, and I sit down at a table, it's the same thing as a stockholders' meeting of Barlow & Company. Mother owns fifty-one percent of the shares, I own thirty-four percent, and Tim fifteen percent. Although I am president and chief executive officer of the firm, as well as chief operating officer, Mother retains the title of chairman, and Tim is vice-president and secretary, and our controller, Mortimer Mandelbaum, is treasurer. We have thought of going public now and then, but either the economic climate has not been right for a stock issue or we have been reluctant to let the outside world in on our deliberations. I would not wish to have some elderly gent from New Jersey or a middle-aged lady from Miami Beach second-guessing my publishing decisions. Not that they are always perfect, not by any means. Still . . . I like to make my own mistakes and to be accountable for them only to my family.

"We must discuss the matter of the bank line of credit," Mother announced.

I was prepared for this, and reported on my meeting with the officer of the bank, which Mandelbaum had rescheduled for Friday afternoon, after my lunch at the Century with Kay McIntire and Herbert Poole.

The bank officer, a young man named Clifford Franklin, had been solicitous but firm. Yes, he understood our situation. He was aware that we were publishers of both Warren Dallas, the dean of military-hardware thrillers, and Prudence Henderson Harte ("What is she really *like,* Mr. Barlow? My wife loves her books"), the American Agatha Christie, as she has often been called. Actually Franklin hardly looked old enough to have a wife. It always disgruntles me to deal

with someone in authority who looks younger than I—
policemen, for example. However, I smiled and smiled, and
nodded and nodded, and hoped for the best, which was that
young Franklin would come to our rescue. For the sake of
American literature, of course.

"I must arrange to have a copy of Miss Harte's next book
autographed for your wife, Mr. Franklin," I said. He beamed
at me, while locking his hands behind his head and, figura-
tively, the door to the bank vault as well.

"Come, come, Nicholas," said my mother, "get to the
point."

"That's just it," I replied. "The point."

"I don't under*stand*."

"He restored our line of credit—"

"Good," she said.

"—but we must pay another percentage point in interest."

"What?"

"And that could of course wipe out our profit for this
fiscal year—unless we get lucky."

Tim, who had said nothing up to now—finance was
not his strongest suit, although if he had chosen to be an
economist, he could have given Alan Greenspan a run for
his money, I'm sure—murmured: "Something will turn
up."

I grinned at him and gave him the high sign. Mother
looked, as I'm sure she felt, as though she had eaten something indigestible. "A point," she said. *"Dear me."*

That was Friday evening. Saturday the three of us got on
the subject of Parker Foxcroft's murder.

"Lay it out for us, Nick," said my brother. "What does
it look like at this stage?"

If Tim had not brought it up, I certainly would have, because I was eager to have his opinion on the case.

"Suspects," I said. "After me, of course, there is—"

My mother was shocked to her roots. "Nicholas! How can you *possibly* think of yourself as a suspect?"

"I don't, but the police obviously do."

"Who else?" said Tim.

"First off, there is Harry Bunter. Also Lester Crispin." I explained what had happened at the ABA and the scene with Crispin in my office. "Harry looks to be the most likely prospect."

"Why?" asked my mother.

"I would say because he seemed to have the most resentment against Parker. I'd even go so far as to say he was enraged—fairly off his conk on the subject."

"Oh yes," I added, "and there's also Frederick Drew."

Tim did a double take. "The poet?"

"Yes. Parker cost him his job. He was both drunk and angry that night. Drunk for sure, but angry most of all." I described the scene in The Players.

"I don't see how he could have known that Mr. Foxcroft was in his office," said Mother.

I reconstructed the events before the murder in my mind. "Suppose," I said, "that he overheard the concierge tell me that Parker was on the phone. While I went back to the phone booth, he could have lifted up the extension on the bar and listened in on our conversation. When I got back to the bar, he was gone, ostensibly to the men's room. But suppose he actually left the club and headed for my office . . ."

"Yeah," said Tim, "that all makes sense. I think I like the case against Drew right now. Very much."

"But he's a poet," I said. "Not a violent man. And where would he come by a gun?"

"We don't have all the answers yet," said Tim. "Which means we go on asking the questions."

Like old times, I thought. *Just like playing Clue.*

On Sunday morning, I visited my brother in his room. It was one of his bad days; he was depressed, understandably rather bitter, and obviously in pain. His face was heavily lined and dreadfully pale. I found him lying in bed covered with a light cotton blanket, his head turned to the wall. Under that blanket and under the robe he was wearing lay his legs, withered and useless. "Tim," I said.

He looked up at me, unsmiling. "Shitty world, isn't it?" he said.

Once again I realized how fragile both he and his hold on life were, and how tragic the loss of his mobility. "Sometimes."

"*Often*times," he corrected me.

I picked up the book on his end table. *The Art of the Mystery Story,* a classic anthology edited by Howard Haycraft. I leafed through it, skipping over essays by G. K. Chesterton, E. M. Wrong, and Willard Huntington Wright (that was an interesting juxtaposition, Wrong and Wright), Dorothy L. Sayers. Tim had stuck his bookmark in the middle of an essay by Edmund Wilson called "Who Cares Who Killed Roger Ackroyd?"

"Wilson didn't care much for the genre, presumably," I said.

Tim snorted. " 'Reading them,' Wilson said, 'is like looking for a rusty nail in a crate of straw.' "

"Pretty harsh."

"Anyway," said Tim, "we know he never read *The Murder of Roger Ackroyd,* or he would certainly not have picked the title he did for his essay."

We sat in silence for some time. I decided to let Tim pick a subject. "Nick," he said after a while, "you haven't said much about the ABA."

"There isn't much to say."

"Don't tell me you didn't do anything out of the ordinary."

Out of the ordinary? What had I done out of the ordinary? I do not do much sight-seeing at ABAs; there's not really time for it, but I did make an exception for Washington. There were two places I felt I ought to visit, as pilgrimages, so to speak.

The first was the Lincoln Memorial. Inside that massive Doric temple is what many consider one of the great sculptures of the modern world, Daniel Chester French's statue of the seated, contemplative Lincoln. One can only stand in silence before it, and marvel—if there are not too many busloads of rambunctious children around; unfortunately this day there were. Much better to visit it at night, when it is floodlit and spectral. "He was a mountain in grandeur of the soul," wrote Walt Whitman. "He was a sea in deep undervoice of mystic loneliness, he was a star in steadfast purity of purpose and service, and he abides."

That might be a touch hagiolatrous, but still . . . I have always admired Abe Lincoln, not least because he wrote one of the best and most succinct book reviews ever published. It was one sentence long. "For those who like this kind of book," he observed, "this is the kind of book they will like."

"I went to the Lincoln Memorial," I said to Tim.

"And?"

"And afterward I walked the short distance northwest to the Vietnam Veterans Memorial." At least three of the more than 58,000 names inscribed on those two long black-granite walls were friends of mine—classmates at Princeton.

"What a sad and futile waste of the young that war was!" I said.

"Sad, all right. Futile, sure. Even more futile . . ." He let out his breath in a sigh that was almost a moan. I could read Tim's thoughts in his face. *Even more futile and sad than to be crippled for life in a stupid accident.* The tree Tim fell from while attempting to climb it had long since been cut down, but neither of us would ever forget it. One day Tim walked and ran and swam and rode horseback; the next day he was a paraplegic. He was right; at times it is a shitty world.

Yet, as I reminded Tim, every visitor to Washington ought to see the memorial, I feel, to run their fingers along those walls, to remember and honor those dead. The walls are enough; the statue of the three soldiers and the three women at the entrance plaza, even the flag flying nearby— in my prejudiced opinion—are superfluous. No, the walls are enough.

"Both those memorials commemorate wars," I said, "for after all, Lincoln was only a wartime president. The tragedy is that he was never given the chance to govern in a time of peace."

Tim nodded. "How different our history might have been," he said.

"That son of a bitch John Wilkes Booth. I've never forgiven him."

"Or Lee Harvey Oswald. Or Sirhan Sirhan."

The solitary killer, I thought. *Always striking without warning. Like whoever murdered Parker.*

Sunday afternoon was bright and clear, and there was a breeze just soft enough to ruffle the deepening grass in our meadow. I walked out with Bonnie and Zachary, our two Labs, who romped happily through their own green pastures, barking, sniffing the wild timothy, and chasing in vain after the resident birds. Summer in Connecticut is a season of incomparable small pleasures: fresh berries, cool running streams, the shade of towering oak trees, and the occasional glimpse of a deer straying out of the forest to nibble on our bushes and trees.

Yes, I find summer in Connecticut a source of considerable satisfaction. As is spring in Connecticut. And fall. And while we're at it, there's a little something to enjoy about winter, too, although I'm not quite sure what it is, if you don't ski, go ice-skating—or shovel snow.

As usual, I was storing up sensations as one absorbs sounds and odors, fleeting memories that would strengthen me against whatever pressures or obligations the coming week would bring.

To begin with, Parker Foxcroft's funeral tomorrow.

Chapter 14

The Foxcroft obsequies were scheduled for eleven o'clock in the Church of the Transfiguration on East 29th Street. I arrived at my office at half past nine, as usual. I had no sooner settled in than Hannah buzzed, and told me that Lester Crispin wanted to see me.

"Send him in," I said.

Crispin wasted no time with small talk, not even bothering to greet me. He made himself at home on my couch, crossed his legs, cleared his throat, and said: "Nick, I know I got upset and quit last Tuesday—"

"Upset?"

"You mean you don't remember?" He shook his head and sighed.

"Well, with so much going on around here . . ." I couldn't blame him for being annoyed. It's true, I had forgotten, but it's possible I didn't believe he really meant to quit. "I assume you've changed your mind now that Parker"—I leaned forward and drew my forefinger across my throat—" is no longer with us."

I could swear Crispin blushed, at least with that part of his face that wasn't hidden behind his beard.

"Well, yeah, as a matter of fact, I have changed my mind."

"I'm glad. I'd hate to lose you." I meant it, too; Crispin was a damn fine art director.

"I came back as soon as I heard the news."

"In time to be grilled by the police, I suppose."

He nodded. "Nick, I know I said some pretty harsh things about Foxcroft—"

"So you did." That part of the episode I did remember.

"Well, hey, whatever I may have threatened to do, I wouldn't have gone so far as to kill the son of a bitch, you know that."

"Yes, I do know." I was lying; I knew no such thing, but it seemed a matter of politesse to agree with him.

I got to my feet, expecting Crispin to follow suit, but he remained seated.

"Something else?" I said.

"Yeah. Do you happen to know if the cops have any suspects?"

"I'm as much in the dark as you are."

He grunted. "All the same, I'd rather no one knew how much I disliked Foxcroft."

"I don't see how that can be kept a secret. Somebody's bound to mention it. However, they certainly won't find out about it from me."

"I appreciate that."

"Incidentally, Les," I said, "I know it's none of my business—but I'm sure you got asked this, anyway, just as a matter of routine—where were you last Tuesday evening?"

"I was here at the office until almost seven, packing my

stuff in cartons so I could have it shipped to my apartment. After that I had dinner. At home. Alone. Why?"

"Did you see Parker while you were here at the office?"

"No, I didn't. But I heard *someone* come in, and I thought it might be him, so I decided to avoid the bastard."

"I see."

Crispin rose from the couch. "If there's nothing else, I'll get back to work."

My next visitor was Mary Sunday. The word for my sales manager is "diminutive"—or better perhaps, "dynamic." This morning she wore a frown, which masked the cheerful face she usually displayed to the world—at least that part of it concerned with Barlow & Company books.

"Bad news, Nick," she said.

"I know."

"Huh?"

"It's self-evident, Mary."

"I didn't know I was so transparent. Anyhow—" She crossed to the couch and plunked herself down. "Anyhow, Nick, the problem is Jerry Hart."

Jerry was one of our top sales reps, as well as one of the most loyal, and he had been working the southern territory out of Miami for twenty years. I couldn't imagine him causing trouble, not in this millennium.

"It's his wife, *el jefe*," said Mary. "The Big C."

"Oh my God, what a hell of a shame." Jerry's wife, Ellen, I knew, was as much company as he was. They'd been married at least forty years.

"Jerry wants to be taken off the road," Mary continued. "He doesn't want to be away from home overnight anymore. I think we're going to have to let him retire or resign."

"But *hell,* Jerry's been with the company since my father was running it. He's probably one of the few employees we have who *remember* my father."

"I know, but what can I do? I don't have a slot open in New York or Connecticut. New Jersey, either."

"Well, we've got to do *something,*" I said. "Is Jerry in town?"

"Yes, he is. He came back to put Ellen in the hospital for chemotherapy."

"Tell him to come and see me sometime this afternoon."

"What are you going to do, Nick?"

"I don't know, Mary—I'll think of something. Christ, after all these years . . . Jerry gone? I just can't see it."

"I'll tell him. But right now I'll start looking for a replacement, okay?"

"You do that, Mary."

As I sat there thinking of what I could do about Jerry Hart, Hannah notified me that the clock was inching toward eleven, and I'd better move myself northward. *Get me to the church,* I'd told her, *be sure and get me to the church on time.*

Most people call the Church of the Transfiguration "the Little Church Around the Corner." There's a story in that, a story that visitors to the church are usually told by anyone who knows the place. The church, which was built in 1848, was never completed. Only one wing of the transept was built. The transept is that lateral aisle crossing the nave of the church just before the apse, creating the cross-shaped plan that has been standard for many Christian churches since the Middle Ages. In any event, the good fathers of the Church of the Transfiguration built beautifully, but ran out of money before they could complete the cruciform, and they ultimately had to sell the ground on which the other part of the transept was to be constructed.

Anyhow, the story. The church was not especially fashionable in Victorian New York. The high-toned ladies and gentlemen of the period patronized another, much larger establishment on nearby Madison Avenue and 30th Street. To that other church—long since torn down—came Joseph Jefferson, the great actor and theater manager, one day. A leading man in his company had died, and Jefferson was there to request that the church conduct a funeral service for him. "Oh dear me, no," clucked the rector. "We couldn't hold services for an *actor*. Why don't you try the little church around the corner? I'm sure they'll oblige you."

At which point Jefferson said: "Then God bless the little church around the corner." The story spread; the church became so popular with theater people that it was also soon known as "the actors' church." One of the stained-glass windows portrays Jefferson playing his favorite role, Rip Van Winkle; another window in the part of the transept they finished shows Edwin Booth as Hamlet. While there may be more imposing Episcopal houses of worship in the city, the Little Church is certainly one of the loveliest. My father and mother were married in it, and so was I. It wasn't the church's fault my marriage didn't last.

We (I wasn't the only Barlow & Company staffer present: Mary Sunday and Mortimer Mandelbaum accompanied me) got to the church a few minutes short of the appointed hour, to find it almost packed. Parker would have been pleased to see the turnout, which reminded me of the old Hollywood story about Harry Cohn's funeral. Few producers, apparently, were as cordially despised as Cohn. When one of the actors present commented on the size of the attendance, his companion, another actor, quipped: "Well, if you give people what they want, they'll come out for it."

I found an empty spot in a pew on an aisle near the altar; Mary and Mort settled several rows behind me. The organist was already warming up with Bach's "Jesu, Joy of Man's Desiring," which I hope they'll play one day at my funeral, along with "Sheep May Safely Graze." Up front and not far from where I was sitting was Parker's casket, a massive mahogany affair, the white plush-lined lid back, flowers of every botanical persuasion banked around it.

Curiosity is probably my besetting vice, and of course I succumbed to it now, looking around to see who I could see. It was quite a distinguished gathering: a bevy of literary agents, a pride of literary lions, and as many editors and publishers as usually turn up at the annual Literary Guild party, which is always the industry's hottest ticket. On the other side of the center aisle I spotted Susan Markham, her hair shimmering in the light of one of the church's chandeliers. She was wearing a black silk dress, and when she turned her head to talk to a neighbor, I could see a rope of pearls around her neck. I made a mental note to call her and suggest a meeting; after all, she had offered to be of help in her note. She might know something about Parker that would help explain his murder. Just then she looked my way, and when I caught her eye, I smiled. She nodded and smiled in return.

I would have lingered after the service and spoken, but something so extraordinary happened that I missed the main event.

While I watched, several people approached the casket and looked down at Parker's remains, to pay their last respects to this paragon of editors, I supposed, or perhaps to assess the quality of the undertaker's handiwork. I myself refrained from viewing the corpse; I find the whole procedure morbid, and I wondered who had arranged for it all. Who was Parker's nearest and dearest of kin?

The last of the viewers was a woman in a bright green dress, with a flowered hat and a veil. As she stood in front of the casket, she raised the veil, leaned over, and spat in Parker's face.

Chapter 15

For a moment, I was unable to move from where I sat. Surely I couldn't have been the only person in the church to have witnessed the woman's act, but no one else showed any sign of having seen what she had done. Had I imagined the whole thing? Not bloody likely. As I watched, the woman hurried across the chancel and down the side aisle of the church. I rose and walked out of my pew after her, stepping over the legs and feet of a couple sitting next to me.

"I'm terribly sorry . . ."

"Well! Really." This from an overdressed woman in a mink stole. Mink on a summer day, of all things. There was no time for explanations; they'd have to put me down as rude and let it go at that.

When I reached the entrance at the back of the church, the woman in green had already left the building and was hurrying toward Madison Avenue. I hung a hard right and followed, although I wasn't altogether sure what I would say when I caught up with her. "Madam, I just saw you spit in Parker Foxcroft's face, would you mind telling me why?"

Before I could overtake her, she hailed a nearby cab, which

quickly engulfed her. I hailed another one right behind her and jumped in quickly when the driver braked to a stop.

Then I said the words I have longed to utter ever since I first heard them long ago, seated in a dark movie theater, watching one long-forgotten thriller or another.

"Follow that cab!"

The driver, a large black man in a short-sleeved mesh sport shirt, turned around and looked at me in bewilderment. *Don't tell me he doesn't speak English!* I glanced at the identification card on the dashboard. *Achille Belcon. A Haitian?*

"Suivez ce taxi-là," I commanded, jabbing my finger in the direction of the first cab.

"Oui, m'sieu," he said, and gunned his engine.

It was a long ride we took up Madison Avenue, through traffic thick and thin. There was no further conversation; Achille was concentrating on tailgating his quarry and I was hunched forward on my seat, impelling our cab on by sheer force of will. At 59th Street we almost lost the chase in a bedlam of trucks and vans heading for the Queensboro Bridge, but my driver recovered quickly and we picked up speed.

Somewhere in the Sixties, the driver leaned back toward me, and without taking his eyes off the street and his rear-view mirror, said: *"M'sieu. On nous suivit."*

"What?"

"We are . . . *followed? N'est-ce pas?*"

I looked out the back window. Another cab was right behind us, and as we drove on, I felt sure the driver was right; we were being followed. Somebody was sure as hell playing games with us—the same game we were playing.

At 89th Street we were still a block behind when the first

cab pulled to a stop on the northeast corner, and the Woman of Mystery, as I had begun to think of her, got out and crossed to the opposite side of Madison Avenue and headed west. I shoved a ten-dollar bill into Achille's hand, murmured *"Merci bien,"* and started after her.

As I stepped out of the cab, I looked back at the one behind us, hoping to catch a glimpse of whoever the passenger was, but as I watched, the cab swept on by, still heading north.

Meanwhile, half a block up 88th Street, my mystery lady turned right under a canopy and disappeared.

Number 19. So now I knew—or thought I knew—where she lived. All I had to do next was find out who she was.

When I reached the entrance of the apartment building, the doorman's attention was on a teenage girl holding two leashes, on the end of which was a pair of white bichons frisés, pulling at their tethers and barking out orders.

"Hi, Victor," said the girl.

The doorman raised his hand to the bill of his cap. "Hello, Miss Stacey." Looking down at the dogs, he said: "Hello, Sunshine. Hi, Snowflake." One of the dogs immediately jumped up and put its forepaws on Victor's pant legs. It was apparent from the expression on his face that he did not share the creature's enthusiasm.

Well, at least I now knew the doorman's name. That was a start, anyway.

When the two bichons had whisked Stacey off down the street, I approached Victor. He was a large, broad-chested specimen of the breed, wearing a bulky gray uniform with silver piping that made his shoulders appear even broader. He stared at me unsmiling, with hard gray eyes. His cheeks and hands were quite sunburned.

"Yes, sir?"

"Pardon me, but the lady who just entered the building—"

He stiffened. "Yes?" No *sir* this time.

"I recognized her—at least I think I recognized her, and I wonder if you could tell me—is her name Althea Frank?"

If I thought I could catch Victor the doorman off his guard, I was sadly mistaken. He gave me the kind of look I myself reserve for IRS auditors.

"We don't give out no such information," he said.

For a moment I thought I might try this gambit: *Look, I just met the woman this afternoon, and it was love at first sight, but I don't have her name, so I followed her here. You wouldn't want to interrupt the course of true love, would you?* but I decided against it.

"Look," I said, lowering my voice to a growl, "I'm a private investigator." I reached in my wallet and flashed a card that looked vaguely like an official ID; actually it was my Connecticut driver's license. "My client has asked me to find the lady in question, and I can't very well find her"— I leaned heavily on the gutturals—"unless I know her name. It's worth—" I pulled out a twenty-dollar bill and waved it at him. He just stared at me, looking like a Hollywood Storm Trooper.

I pulled out a second twenty. Still no response.

On the third twenty, he perked up; at least he permitted himself a thin smile, and on the fourth he grinned broadly, pocketed my eighty dollars, and said: "The name you want, buddy, is Judith Michaelson. Mrs. Judith Michaelson."

"Thanks."

"Apartment 3-D."

"Thanks again."

"My pleasure," said Victor. I could certainly understand

why. "Just don't tell the lady I told you," he added, with an unspoken threat as the subtext.

At the corner of Madison and 88th, I looked around to see if I could spot the taxi that had followed me up the avenue. Only one yellow cab was in sight, parked at the curb across the street. I decided to check it out. When I reached it, I looked in the back window. The passenger seat was empty. The engine was idling, however, but the overhead signal light was out. I stuck my head in the driver's right window.

"Looking for a fare?" I said.

The driver, a short, beefy man in a short-sleeved shirt, wearing a yarmulke on the back of his head, gestured toward his meter, which was still running.

"I got a fare already."

I drew away, wondering if it would be worthwhile to wait and see if the cab's passenger came back. I decided I'd better move along. Anyway, how could I be sure this was the cab that had trailed me? They all look alike, after all.

Well, now I knew a name. Enough sleuthing for the day. What next?

What was next was Jerry Hart, the sales rep with a problem. When I got back to the office, I asked Hannah if Jerry was around, and she allowed that he was somewhere on the premises and that she would be happy to track him down.

She found him in record time, and when she brought him to my office, she was glowing, and he was chuckling, so I figured he'd told one of his famous jokes. Probably the one about the traveling salesman and the private secretary.

"Jerry," I said, pumping his hand, "I'm so sorry to hear about Ellen. What a rotten goddamn break."

He waved his hand like a magician, and like magic his

smile disappeared. Jerry was short, paunchy, balding, nobody's idea of a sharp operator, but no Willy Loman, either. He was a damn good sales rep, the kind of man who, if one of the stores he serviced was burned out, would show up the next morning to help clean up the mess and restore the stock, not only our books but other publishers' books as well. At Christmastime he always volunteered to work as an unpaid salesclerk in one of his customers' shops.

At the same time, he was not one of our more literary reps. When asked what a book was about, Jerry might reply: "It's about twenty dollars." If nothing else, Jerry was honest; he wouldn't attempt to fake it with a bookseller, by pretending he'd read a book when he hadn't.

"Jerry," I once asked him, "do you ever read *anything?*"

He took a long few minutes to answer me. "I read everything you provide me, Nick. The title information sheets. The catalog. The advance reviews. The author's track record. I tell them everything they need to know except the least important thing of all—what I personally think of the book. If I read it and thought it stunk, I'd have to say so. If I loved it, it wouldn't be me being businesslike, it would be only one man's opinion."

Then he looked straight at me, and with his leprechaun's grin, said: "But I don't make too many mistakes, do I, Nick?"

He was right. Somehow he had an uncanny knack of putting the right quantities of a book—or nearly the right quantities—into the right stores. His returns were lower than anyone else's on our sales force; his sell-through was always at the top of the charts. That he loved books, I was sure; he just didn't *read* them. I could live with that.

And somehow I knew we had to keep him working for the good of the firm.

"Jerry," I said, "Mary Sunday tells me you want to come in out of the cold."

"That's right, Nick."

I opened the humidor on my desk, took out a cigar and offered it to him. He fondled it for a moment and then stuck it in his inside coat pocket.

"Thanks, Nick. I'll save it for a special occasion."

Just then the phone rang softly. Just once, before Hannah intercepted the call in the outer office, but the single ring was enough to give me an idea.

"Jerry," I said, "you're too young to retire, and too good to leave the book business—"

"Nice of you to say so, Nick."

"—so I'm going to make you a proposition."

"I'm listening."

"For some time I've thought that Barlow and Company ought to have a telemarketing department."

"Like the big boys? Simon and Schuster . . . Random House . . . Doubleday?"

"Exactly. These days personal sales calls are costing us up to two hundred fifty dollars each, and there are stores it just isn't worthwhile to send a rep to. Stores who do enough business with us, however, to rate a regular phone call."

"I see what you mean."

"Well, here's my proposition, Jerry. Give up the road, come back into the office, and set up a telemarketing department for me. I can't pay you as much as you're earning with your commissions and bonuses, but—"

Jerry waved his hand in dismissal. "I'm sure you'll be fair, Nick."

"So how about it?"

"Well . . ." He was silent for several long minutes, and then a "Have a nice day" smile creased his face. "You wouldn't do this just as a favor to me and Ellen, would you?"

"Abso*lutely* not. I'm in this business to make money, Jerry."

And sometimes, I added to myself, *sometimes we* do *make money.*

"Then I accept."

"Good."

Hart stood up, and we shook hands. At the door he turned and said: "I thank you, Nick. And my wife will thank you, too."

"The hell with the thanks, just do a good job."

When my office door had closed behind Jerry Hart, I buzzed Hannah.

"Yes, Nick?"

"Call Little, Brown for me, please, Hannah, and see if you can locate a Susan Markham. That's the New York not the Boston office."

"Will do."

A few minutes later, my call was put through, and I was listening to a voice that rose at least an octave when I said hello.

"Nick Barlow! How pleasant to hear from you."

"I've been meaning to call. I got your letter, Susan, and I would like to see you."

"Of course, Nick. What do you suggest?"

I glanced down at my desk calendar. For the balance of the week, it was a tabula rasa.

"If it's not too short notice, how about cocktails this evening?"

"I'd like that," she said, and once again her voice took a thrilling little leap. "Where?"

"Let's say . . . the St. Regis. King Cole Room. Six o'clock."

"I'll be there. And thanks for calling, Nick."

"My pleasure."

When I had replaced the phone in its cradle, these lines of Ezra Pound's occurred to me: "It rests me to be among beautiful women. Why should we lie about these things? I repeat: It rests me to converse with beautiful women, even though we talk nothing but nonsense. The purring of the invisible antennae is both stimulating and delightful."

"Nick," said Hannah a short while later, "Lieutenant Hatcher is here and would like to see you."

I groaned. *Oh shit, what now?* "Sure. Send him in."

Despite the weather—it was hot enough outside to suggest that June was somehow already pushing into July—Hatcher was wearing a wool suit; his collar and tie looked uncomfortably tight. He took out a bright red handkerchief, the kind cowboys tie around their necks, and passed it across his forehead.

"Sit down, Lieutenant. Take a load off your feet."

"Thanks, I will."

"Pretty hot out there, isn't it?"

"Yeah. Makes me glad I'm not still walking a beat."

"What can I do for you?"

He cleared his throat, paused, then cleared it a second time. Another one of his pregnant pauses—there's that cliché again—finally brought forth this: "Mr. Barlow, were you aware that you're mentioned in Parker Foxcroft's will?"

"*What?*" This was the *last* thing I'd expected Hatcher to say. I stared at him in simon-pure disbelief. If he'd counted on giving me a jolt, he'd succeeded admirably.

"Foxcroft named you his literary executor."

"Just what does that mean?"

Hatcher shrugged. "You tell me, you're the literary man."

"What I meant to say was,"—and here I cleared *my* throat—"what does that entail?"

Again, he chose not to field my question, but just looked at me with those beady eyes.

I pressed on. "How did you learn that?"

"From his attorney. Man named"—he took out his notebook and flipped it open—"Sherman Archer."

"And you think that being mentioned in Foxcroft's will gives me a motive?"

"Did I say that? I didn't say that."

I'll bet you thought it, though, you cunning bastard.

"Anything *else*, Lieutenant?" I said in my best Uriah Heep tone of voice.

He came back at me, Heep for Heep. "Not at the *moment*, thanks."

Once Hatcher had taken his leave, I asked Hannah to get me Sherman Archer on the phone. When I got through, I skipped the small talk and stated my business at once.

"Ordinarily," he said, "we wait to notify the legatees until the will is through probate. However—" Here he sounded uncertain, as though choosing whether to hem or to haw. "—however, you know what the police are like . . ." Then: silence.

"Tell me, Mr. Archer," I said. "What do you think I'll be facing as . . . literary executor for the late Parker Foxcroft?"

"There are letters, of course. Private papers. And a good many computer disks."

"When do you think I might have access to them?"

"Anytime you wish, Mr. Barlow."

"I'm wondering . . ."

"What?"

"Why Parker named *me* to deal with his literary remains."

"Well, sir," Archer said, "Parker Foxcroft was certain that a horde of scholars would descend from academia to do his literary biography once he was dead. As a result, he probably saved every note he ever committed to paper."

Lucky me, to inherit all of Parker's laundry lists! On the other hand—

"On the other hand," said Joe Scanlon, detective cum author, when I told him the news, "we may turn up something in all those files."

"Are you suggesting I turn detective myself?"

"Our chief purpose, as I understand it," he said, "is to clear you of any suspicion. If in the course of doing so, we find out who killed the man and why, so much the better."

"I don't know but—well, I suppose you're right, Joe."

"Just let me know when you're ready to start. Ready for *us* to start, that is."

By the time the cocktail hour rolled around, I was feeling more than one galvanic charge of anticipation. I thought I'd better opt for prudence as against daring, and go to the St. Regis without any amorous expectations, so that I would not be disappointed no matter what happened. After all, why should Susan Markham be interested in me romantically? There had been that hint of a flirtation in Washington, but any ardor she felt then may well have cooled down by now.

When I got to the King Cole Room, she was already there, sitting at a corner table. A good sign, I thought. I appreciate punctuality, even though I recognize, as one publisher friend of mine put it, that it's "the thief of time."

Get somewhere early enough, and you're bound to be kept waiting.

She looked and smiled as I approached the table.

"Susan."

"Hello, Nick." She held out her hand, and I gathered it into both of mine.

She was striking in a slouchy silk pajama suit, black and white stripes and cut deep, almost to the waist. She was wearing a long rope of pearls and a black beret. When she leaned forward and inched sidewise on the banquette to make room for me, the Vandyke collar of her suit opened slightly to reveal the curve of her breasts, and prudence, in my case, suffered a pronounced setback. She was one damned good-looking woman.

"I'm glad you could join me on such short notice," I said.

"Thank you for asking me." She smiled again. Her teeth, as I had earlier observed, were fine and a brilliant white, rather small but even. In short, perfect.

That did not quite complete my inventory of the Susan Markham person. Her legs were largely concealed by the table and pants of her pajama suit, but her hands, resting flat now on her lap, were quite slim and elegant, the fingers long, with bright crimson nails. She wore only one ring, a star sapphire on her right ring finger.

She laughed suddenly, a short, nervous laugh, not at anything I said, because I didn't say anything. *Satisfied?* her eyes seemed to say to me.

"I like your outfit," was the best line I could come up with.

"Thank you."

"I have a feeling it's definitely not something you wore to the office this afternoon."

"You're right, Nick. I went home and changed first. You see, I only live a few blocks from here."

"Really?"

"My apartment is on 55th and Third."

"So the St. Regis—"

"Couldn't be more convenient."

"Perhaps the place has no novelty for you?"

She shook her head. "Not at all. I have a considerable fondness for the Maxfield Parrish painting of Old King Cole."

By this time, a waiter had appeared and we'd ordered drinks: a daiquiri for her and a vodka martini straight up for me. One of these days, I ought to change drinks, just for the sake of change, to add zest to my life, perhaps, but what the hell, why give up a winning number?

We touched glasses and sipped for a few minutes. I was eager to learn more about her, but I realized that Parker Foxcroft was the proper subject of my inquiries.

"You said in your note that you'd like to help if you can."

"That's right."

"Twenty questions?"

"Fire away."

"First, do you have any idea why he was killed, or who might have done it?"

"That's two questions. No and no."

"How long had you known him?"

"A few months over a year," she said.

"I understand he was quite the Lothario."

She colored, only the slightest kind of a blush, but I found it becoming.

"Parker seldom spoke about other women, and never with any intimate details, but"—she paused, clearly searching for the mot juste—"I suspected there were other women in his life. He was a very *private* sort of person. Not at all someone who would kiss and tell."

"Did he ever mention Claire Bunter?"

"Who?"

"The writer, one of his writers. Also the wife of my sub rights director, Harry Bunter."

"The name means nothing to me, so I assume he never spoke of her."

I could not think of any way to phrase the question I wanted to ask her next, like *What did you see in that mean bastard, anyway?* so I refrained.

"Now may I ask you something, Nick?"

"Sure."

"Did you invite me here only to pick my brain?"

"Well . . ."

"I'm afraid you're only interested in my mind," Susan said.

"Unlike Parker Foxcroft?"

"Parker was never really much interested in my mind," she replied. "You're quite right about that."

"And what was *your* interest in dear dead Parker?"

"You don't sound like you cared much for him."

"I didn't."

"To answer your last question, he was a brilliant man. And I thought—"

"Yes?"

"That it might help my career to be seen with him. Does that sound crass to you? Opportunistic, perhaps? Unfeminist, as distinguished from unfeminine?"

"I can't blame you for that, Susan. But you're wrong about me."

"Oh?"

I took a deep breath. "Your mind is *not* the only thing that interests me."

"I'm so glad, Nick. That's what I hoped you'd say."

We were on our second drink by now, and I felt that pleasant sensation which comes when the first drink starts to take hold, and the inner being turns languorous and submissive. Susan Markham looked at me with the direct and wide-eyed gaze of a precocious child. A child-woman, I thought. "Mad, bad, and dangerous to know," perhaps? Her eyes were mint green in the soft light cast by the table lamp. Her lips parted in a smile—one part mocking, one part risible.

"Thinking deep thoughts, Nick?"

"Thinking," I said, taking my time with each word, "of prolonging the evening, if that's all right with you."

She leaned closer to me, and almost as though they had a will of their own, the fingers of my right hand reached out and touched the fabric of her jacket, drew slowly down over the swell of her left breast, lingering briefly at the nipple, which hardened under my fingertips.

She took a deep breath. "Certainly." And as though I hadn't heard her response: "*Certainly,* Nick."

"Well, then . . ."

"Why don't you walk me home?"

We both rose to go. If he had not suddenly appeared at my elbow, I might have forgotten the waiter altogether, and the bill as well. We sat down again, and I produced a credit card. One transaction later, we were on our way.

It was now dusk, that "enchanted metropolitan twilight," as Fitzgerald described it, "the racy, adventurous feel of New York at night." It is never quite dark, of course; there are no stars to be seen in the stone canyons, no moon; only that supernal glow of a million lights reflected in the heavens—and the constant roar of sound, an ocean of white noise.

By the time we reached Park Avenue, Susan's arm was linked in mine. At Third Avenue, she released my arm and claimed my hand.

"Here we are," she said. "Here" was an apartment building between Third and Second. 355 East 55th Street. I must remember the address.

"Come in, Nick." Her inflection made the command sound more like a question, as though she thought I might refuse her bidding. For one wild moment, I was ready to decline. *Am I really ready for something like this? Something like what, you ninny? She could just plan to serve you a drink and send you on your way.*

Instead, I followed her into the lobby, which, like myriad other specimens of Manhattan lobbies, was small, but did its best to be grand: a towering ficus tree; black and white checkerboard tile; generic oriental art; and an obsequious doorman, who obviously doted on Susan.

He undressed her with his eyes, I thought. Well, who can blame him?

We were alone in the elevator, but Susan stood close to me, as though we had to make room for other passengers. Feeling more and more like a callow youth on his first date, I leaned over and kissed her.

I cannot say the earth moved, only the elevator. Still, the taste of her lips awakened memories so old I thought they were buried for good, hungers I had almost forgotten. I shivered in anticipation.

I had no preconceived idea of what Susan Markham's apartment would be like, but I must say I was somewhat surprised at what I saw when she unlocked the door of 20-C.

If I'd made a stab at predicting the decor, I would have guessed "feminine, antiques, lots of plants, a frilly bedroom." What I found as we made the preliminary tour was a highly functional, rather austere living room with a dining ell, and a small eat-in kitchen. The furniture was Swedish modern, bright blond wood. Throw rugs on parquet floors. A bar on wheels and a wine rack. A grand piano, no less. The bookshelves were few, and from my first cursory glance, seemed to be filled entirely with popular fiction, some of the volumes, I suspected, book club selections. I found the whole effect not feminine at all, but oddly masculine.

"Drink, Nick?"

"No, not yet. You have quite a place, Susan." I could not help but wonder how she managed it on an assistant editor's salary. Family subsidy, perhaps? *None of your business, Barlow.*

"Come this way," she said, and opened the French doors at the end of the living room. I followed her out onto a wraparound terrace that overlooked both the Upper East Side and the East River. The view was a feast of lights and the silhouettes of massive towers.

"Spectacular," I murmured.

"It is impressive, isn't it?"

She was standing in front of me, looking out over the river. I put my hands on her shoulders, and she leaned quickly back into my arms, her head tilted back slightly to be kissed. I obliged her. It was no ordinary kiss; it shook me all the way down to the soles of my shoes.

When we finally broke apart, I knew there was no turning back. I felt that we were already lovers—that we had been lovers for some time and had only been waiting for the opportunity to consummate it.

"Well," I said. "Hello, Susan."

"Hello, darling," she whispered. "There's another room, you know."

"I somehow thought there would be."

No, the bedroom wasn't at all frilly. The bed was king-size, and I saw at least two full-length mirrors and a mirrored closet door. That was all the inspection I had the time to make: I took in the rest—the furniture, the television set, the computer workstation—in one sweeping glance.

It's amazing how quickly two people can shed all their clothes when there's a bed nearby.

"You are beautiful," I said, hardly trusting myself to speak at all.

"When you say that, I believe it."

Her body was before me, and then so near to me that my nostrils were full of her perfume, and then we were locked together and part of each other.

When we finally separated, she said: "Were you pleased with me?"

"Enormously. And you?"

"It did happen rather fast, Nick."

I smiled, and touched her breasts with my fingertips. "I suppose I was more than ready. However, Susan, to use a cliché I would strike from any manuscript—"

"Yes?"

"The night is young."

And so it proved to be.

Much, much later, she said: "First times are wonderful, aren't they?"

" 'The apple tree, the singing, and the gold,' " I quoted.

"What?"

"Euripides on love."

"Oh. I like that."

"There was something Rollo May wrote in his book *Love and Will* about this moment, Susan—I wish I could remember it. It had to do with the moment of entrance . . ."

"Forget books for now, darling. Forget Rollo May. We have the night ahead of us."

"I'm glad of that. And I will have that drink now."

Chapter 16

"I know how busy you are, Nick . . ."

"We'll work something out, Susan. How does Friday evening look to you?"

"Free and clear."

It was the following day. Susan had provided me with a brand-new toothbrush, a razor, also pristine, and shaving cream (clearly, overnight male guests were no rarity in the Markham flat—but what the hell, how could I complain?), and after I'd finished grooming myself, she served up a breakfast of juice, shirred eggs, bacon, a bagel, and a coffee strong in chicory. French roast, I decided. Patting my stomach in appreciation, I folded my napkin neatly, leaned over the breakfast table, and kissed her, hard.

"Thank you," I said when we'd come up for air, "for feeding me so well. I was ravenous."

"I'm not surprised. We forgot to eat any dinner."

"So we'll get together Friday evening?" She nodded. "I'm planning to go out to Connecticut on Saturday afternoon, but I hope to provide you with as good a breakfast as you've given me."

She smiled. "Call me before Friday, won't you, Nick? Let me know what you're up to."

"Of course."

It occurred to me shortly after I had walked out of her apartment building and hailed a cab that I hadn't really touched much on the subject of Parker's murder, ostensibly my reason for seeing her in the first place.

Ah well, so it goes. I haven't given up advance planning altogether, but I have certainly given up expecting those plans to work out quite as I anticipate.

When I was back in my library again, I took out the well-worn copy of *Love and Will* and quickly found the place I'd earmarked:

> The moment of greatest significance in love-making, as judged by what people remember in the experience and what patients dream about, is not the moment of orgasm. It is rather the moment of entrance, the moment of penetration. This is the moment that shakes us, that has within it the great wonder, tremendous and tremulous as it may be—or disappointing and despairing, which says the same thing from the opposite point of view. . . . This, and not the orgasm, is the moment of union and the realization that we have won the other.

I couldn't have expressed it better myself, not even if I were a psychologist.

Once settled in my office, I figured it was about time for me to huddle again with Joe Scanlon.

"Nick," he said when I called, "I've been meaning to phone you. I've picked up some interesting information."

"That makes two of us."

Within the hour, Scanlon was seated across from my desk, cradling a mug of coffee in his hands. A similar mug, bearing the profile of Mark Twain by David Levine, steamed away on my desk.

"So what have you learned, Joe?"

"First off, that Parker Foxcroft has been extremely flush lately. Dinners at the most expensive restaurants in town. Weekend trips to Atlantic City and a good deal of action at Belmont. At least one ten-day Caribbean cruise this spring. Running up sizable bills at Paul Stuart's and Ralph Lauren."

"That's nothing new," I said. "Parker has always needed a lot of money to support his lifestyle, and he was known to borrow money from every conceivable source . . ."

"That habit may have intensified in recent months, however."

"Suggesting?"

"Blackmail, perhaps," said Scanlon. "He may have been dabbling in shakedowns of one kind or another."

"Do tell."

"It's at least a strong possibility. So far, however, I haven't come up with anyone who might have been feeding his kitty."

"How about your pal Sergeant Falco? Any leads there?"

"Zip so far. But I'm working on him. We'll see what turns up."

Then I told Scanlon about Judith Michaelson. "What do you suppose I should do, Joe?"

He snorted, as though the question was just too asinine to take seriously. "Talk to the lady, by all means."

"Yeah, but by *what* means? How do I manage to meet her?"

"Want to borrow my shield, Nick?"

"Come off it, Joe. Be serious."

At once, Scanlon assumed the pose of Rodin's *Thinker*. When he finally did speak, it was hesitantly, as though he was searching hard for the right words. I had the feeling he was giving me the benefit of his subjective processes.

"You have access to Foxcroft's Rolodex, yes, Nick?"

"Yes, I do."

"She wouldn't have been at the funeral and done what she did if she didn't know him well . . . Right?"

"Right." I felt I was beginning to sound like a parrot.

"So her phone number is likely to be there. Use it. Tell her that you're getting in touch with Parker's authors and associates, and would she mind if you paid her a visit. Something like that. Okay? You're a publisher, you were Parker's boss. You have every reason to want to talk to her."

"Yes, Joe." Not for the first time, I felt cowed by Joe's professionalism. Who was I to think I am any kind of detective? Merely, after all, a publisher.

Joe was quite right; Parker's Rolodex, when flipped to the letter "M," produced a Michaelson, but not a Judith— an Alexander. Interesting. Obviously husband of Judith, and also obviously a writer.

"Hello."

"Mrs. Michaelson?"

"Yes, who's this?"

"I'm Nicholas Barlow. The publisher."

"I *know* what you are, Mr. Barlow."

Not a propitious beginning, but I soldiered bravely on. Couldn't let Joe Scanlon down at this juncture.

"I'd like to speak to your husband. A writer, I believe?

One of Parker Foxcroft's writers?" To the best of my knowledge as the publisher of Parker's books, he had never mentioned an author named Michaelson, but he might have not offered the man a contract.

Her voice suggested a temperature hovering around absolute zero. "My husband is dead, Mr. Barlow—"

"Oh, I'm so *sorry* to hear that."

"And he most definitely was *not* one of Parker Foxcroft's *writers*." No sign of a thaw in the Michaelson deep freeze.

"I'm sorry to hear *that,* too." Silence. Had I made another gaffe of some sort? This wasn't going well at *all.*

Plunging gamely on, I said: "I'm speaking to anyone who might know something about Parker's murder—and well, your husband Alexander's name was on his Rolodex, and—"

"Why bother, Mr. Barlow? Why not leave all that to the *police?*"

I was beginning to hyperventilate, so I went straight into overdrive. "I have a feeling, Mrs. Michaelson, that Parker Foxcroft may have done you and your husband an injury—"

"To say the least." *That* sounded encouraging.

"—and my firm would like to redress the injury if possible. To make amends."

"Can you raise the dead, Mr. Barlow?"

"I beg your pardon?"

"Can you bring my husband back from the grave?"

Somehow I did not feel the question required a reply. The silence that followed was tomblike—on both our parts.

Finally: "I'm sorry, Mr. Barlow. I'm sure you may not know about Parker Foxcroft's treatment of my husband . . ."

"No, madam, I did not. But I would like to find out."

"Well . . ." Now at last I felt I was reaching her. In for the kill—rather, close the sale, that sort of thing.

"May I come and see you, Mrs. Michaelson? I promise not to take too much of your time."

"Time?" She sighed, one of those soft moans that seem to come from a soul in pain. "I have a lot of that these days, Mr. Barlow. Yes, you may come and see me."

"This afternoon? Four o'clock, perhaps?"

"Why not? Let me give you the address."

I damn near told her I wouldn't need it—but thought better of that. The lady must never know that the great Barlow tailed her like some common peeper.

When I arrived at Judith Michaelson's apartment at four, give or take a few minutes, she had tea ready for us, and a tray of what appeared to be tiny cucumber sandwiches.

"Or would you prefer a drink, Mr. Barlow? Sherry, maybe?"

I raised my hand, palm out. "Tea will be fine."

Judith Michaelson was a woman in her early forties, I surmised, probably about my own age—but she appeared to be at least a decade older. Her face was almost devoid of color; there were dark circles under her eyes—but her bones were good, as they say, and her hair was perfectly composed in a style that used to be called "pageboy." She was wearing a silk housedress, green and maroon, in a flowered pattern. Altogether a woman one would call handsome.

"I'm sorry if I was so difficult on the phone, Mr. Barlow."

I dismissed this with another wave of the hand. "I can't blame you for being wary."

"It's not that so much—it's—well, it's that I don't really give a damn that Parker Foxcroft was murdered. In fact, I think whoever did it ought to be congratulated. I'm sure that sounds harsh, but—"

"Many others would agree with you, Mrs. Michaelson.

And, as you may have gathered from his obituary, others would disagree."

"Ha," she murmured. Just "ha."

"If it's not intrusive of me to ask, Mrs. Michaelson, just why did—I mean *do* you dislike Parker so much?"

"I'd be quite happy to tell you." She leaned forward and refilled my teacup. I smiled gamely. Tea is definitely not—well, not my cup of tea. "My husband was a writer, Mr. Barlow. A damn fine writer." She shook her head back and forth a few times, as though to clear it, or to shake the memories loose. I could tell she was also struggling to hold back tears.

"I'm sure he was, Mrs. Michaelson." Another fib, since I had no idea what kind of a writer the man was, but excusable in the circumstances. "Go on."

"I also write, Mr. Barlow—under the name of Judith Simon Michaelson."

"I'm afraid I don't know your work."

She made a rather poor effort to smile. "No reason why you should. I write romantic short stories for the kind of magazines women usually read under the hair dryer."

"Oh."

"My husband, on the other hand, was a literary writer. I'm told there are only two reasons for writing, Mr. Barlow—fame and money. My work paid the bills, his was going to make him famous—or so we both thought."

"Anyway," she continued, "to make a long story short—and where have I heard that before?—Alex spent twelve years working on one manuscript, writing, rewriting, polishing it until he finally deemed it ready to go out. He believed it to be a masterpiece. Having heard about Parker Foxcroft and his literary protégés, my husband sent his manuscript directly to the celebrated editor." She put a decided spin on the word "celebrated." "Foxcroft returned the book with a three-page letter that left no doubt whatever as to what he thought of Alex's effort. 'A puny piece of work,' he called it. 'Paltry in concept, and anile in execution. I suggest you put this manuscript to some useful purpose, such as starting a good blaze in your fireplace.' Those were among the *less* objectionable phrases in his letter, Mr. Barlow."

I confess I did not know what to say. I was shocked, at least mildly so. God knows there are a lot of puerile writers out there, but we usually let them down easy. Eas*ier,* anyway. What's to be gained by savaging a manuscript that already has its death warrant written all over it?

Judith Michaelson saved me the trouble of finding words that might be adequate to the situation. She went on, in a voice trembling with controlled fury: "Alex was devastated. He fell into a depression that lasted for days. I really feared for his sanity."

"I understand how you might."

"How can you *possibly* understand?" she said. "And then—"

"Yes?"

"—and then—" She bowed her head and hunched her shoulders forward. Her hands were clenched together, her eyes tightly shut. "He *killed* himself. Just a month ago, Mr. Barlow. On May the third."

Oh my God, I thought. *My God.*

"He had a gun, and—" She could not, did not, finish the sentence. There was no need.

We sat in a mutually painful silence for several moments. It was Judith Michaelson who ultimately broke it.

"So you see, Mr. Barlow, *why* I hate Parker Foxcroft. If it were not for him, my husband would still be alive. Parker

Foxcroft *drove* Alex to suicide. He said as much in the note he left behind—that his book meant everything to him, and that now he had nothing left to live for."

"But surely, Mrs. Michaelson, you don't mean—"

"Oh, but I *do* mean it. I hold Parker Foxcroft solely and completely responsible for my husband's death, as surely as if he had pulled the trigger himself. That letter—*his* letter—killed Alex."

It was clear to me that there was no way in which I could convince her that suicide is never (well, perhaps almost never) the result of a single event or an immediate cause, so I did not even make the attempt. And what if she was right, that her husband ceased to care about living after receiving Parker's letter? What if his entire self-esteem, that rickety structure most of us build out of or around our doubts, our misgivings, and our fears, depended on the praise—the recognition, at least—of a Parker Foxcroft?

At this point, sensing that her tears were "winking at the brim," quite like Keats's "beaded bubbles," I stammered out a few halfhearted (and also probably half-witted) apologies and rose to leave.

At the door, Judith Michaelson extended her hand, and I took it. "I appreciate your concern, Mr. Barlow. I wish I could have been better company."

"Don't give it another thought, Mrs. Michaelson. Thanks for the tea."

I left Judith Michaelson's apartment with mixed feelings. Doubtless, Parker was a cruel man, but it is a cruel world we live and work in, and publishing has not escaped its own homegrown cruelties. To the vast legions of wannabe authors who flood the mails with unpublishable manuscripts, which we unfailingly reject, we must seem like hanging judges, blockheads at best—disciples of the Marquis de Sade. I sighed in sympathy with Judith Simon Michaelson, and in the same gesture shrugged off any guilt I might conceivably feel for the death of her husband. And as for Parker? He's well past caring.

The doorman Victor was now on duty as I stepped out of the apartment building. He nodded and favored me with a slight smile. Well might he smile, with all those twenty-dollar bills in his pocket!

And there was this possibility to consider: could Judith Michaelson have hated Parker Foxcroft enough to kill him?

Quite possibly. In fact, quite *probably*.

Chapter 17

The following day I lunched with Joe Scanlon at The Players. I decided we'd better take a corner table in the main dining room, where we could speak in privacy, rather than going down to the Grill Room. Supplied with a vodka martini for me and a Jack Daniel's on the rocks with a splash for Scanlon, we got down to business. Police business first.

When I told him about my interview with Judith Michaelson, Scanlon nodded in what I hoped was approval.

"Her husband killed himself with a gun," he said, holding his drink poised in midair. "I wonder what kind of gun he used."

"You think it might be the same one that killed Parker? If so, perhaps it could be traced."

"No chance. According to information I got from Sergeant Falco, the murder weapon was unlicensed."

"Tough break."

"Yeah, it certainly is. No recognizable prints, either, Falco told me. Not even a latent."

"What else did you find out, Joe?"

He took a long sip from his glass and leaned forward. In

a low voice, he said: "A piece of information about one of your people, Nick. A Lester Crispin?"

"My art director. He couldn't get along with Parker."

"Lieutenant Hatcher and Falco know that. What you may not have known, Nick, is that Crispin has a record."

"What?" I knew the instant I spoke that my voice was much too loud; it wouldn't do for anyone else in the room to overhear our conversation. "Excuse me, Joe, I didn't mean to shout. It . . . comes as a shock, that's all."

"I'm sure."

"What was it?"

"Criminal assault. He was indicted but never tried, and never served any time. Apparently there were extenuating circumstances."

"Such as?"

"The party he beat the bejeesus out of had attempted to rape one of the women who worked in Crispin's office."

"Jesus, what do you know? I guess I'm not surprised, Joe. The man does have a violent temper."

"Anyway, he moves up a notch or two on the list of suspects."

"And what about me? Where do I stand?"

"You're still up there, Nick."

"I can't say I like that much. By the way, does Hatcher or Falco know of our connection?"

"Not yet, and I'm hoping we can keep it that way, at least for a while. Otherwise, he's not going to like feeding me information."

I downed my martini and signaled the waiter. "Let's move on to lunch, Joe."

After we'd ordered, I said: "To change the subject—"

"If you don't, I'll be glad to."

"Have you heard from Kay McIntire? About taking you on as a client?"

"Nothing definite yet. She's reading my stuff—said she'd let me know."

"I hope it works out."

"Nick," he said, "I'm curious about what happens after my book is out. That is—what will the launch be like?"

"Launch?" I paused. It was a long, grave pause. "Well," I said at last, "ninety percent of our books are sent out into the marketplace with a rather wistful hope that something, anything, will happen to start them selling.

"You may be thinking of a launch," I continued, "as a space shuttle roaring off into the heavens, or a new movie opening on six hundred screens. What we publishers do is—well, we kind of *push* a book out onto a huge pond, like a little toy boat. Ready to catch the wind in its sails if there *is* any wind, fortunate if it doesn't sink without a trace."

"Oh," said Scanlon.

"Let's hope, Joe," I said, not wishing to ruin his digestion altogether, "that your book is one of the other ten percent." He brightened at this.

"One other thing, Joe. How would you like to consider joining The Players?"

He whistled softly. "They've got a category for cops?"

"As an *author,* my friend. But we have had at least one cop as a member."

"How does it work? Joining, I mean."

"I nominate you for membership. Another member writes a seconding letter, and we get letters from three other members approving your nomination."

"I don't know, Nick. I'm kind of in the Groucho Marx school when it comes to private clubs."

"But you like the place, don't you?"

"Sure, it's beautiful. And it's fun being your guest here. That doesn't mean I could afford it myself."

"Then we'll just have to make you a best-selling author."

He grinned. "Barkis is willin'," he said.

I liked that. Pretty soon he'll be outquoting Nick Barlow himself.

My calendar for the day called for a meeting at three o'clock with Kay McIntire and Herbert Poole, my Great White Hope. They were right on time.

"Do you have the contract drawn up, Nick?" Kay asked.

I brought out a reasonably fat sheaf of pages, headed by the Barlow & Company logo—a capital "B" with a book superimposed on it—and starting out with the words "AGREEMENT dated June 9, 1993, and between BAR- LOW & COMPANY, INC., 18 E. 18th Street, New York, N.Y. 10003, and HERBERT E. POOLE (the "Author") c/o Kay McIntire, 175 E. 77th Street, New York, N.Y. 10020 . . ." and followed by page after page of legalese.

"Voici," I said.

"Not boilerplate, I trust," said Kay.

"I only wish," I riposted. "Boilerplate" is the standard contract we publishers offer to authors who don't know any better—a contract written entirely in our favor, and making sure the author will be fortunate even to get the book pub- lished, still less be enriched by it. "The contract has been written according to the terms we agreed on, Kay."

Instead of taking a gentleman's word for it, she insisted on reading every page and every "if," "in the event," and "notwithstanding." That took a good half hour, while Her- bert Poole and I sat sizing each other up. At least I sized *him* up in the interim.

Poole was a good-looking man—tall, lean, blond—who just escaped being an Adonis by a jaw that was too square, and strong white teeth just a shade too large. He might have made a good second lead, Horatio to Hamlet, but never the leading man or the star. He was, however, photogenic, as I'd observed at the ABA Convention when he was busy signing copies of *Pan at Twilight*.

It is not essential that an author be physically attractive, but it always helps, in publishing as elsewhere in life. The aphorism that one cannot be too rich, too thin, or too beautiful will always be true, wherever the course of history may take us. Or so I like to think.

At last Kay finished her examination of the contract. She looked up and smiled at me.

"Perfect, Nick," she said. "We've got a deal, darling." She handed the contract to Poole, open to the last page, where was written: "IN WITNESS WHEREOF, the parties hereto have duly executed this agreement on the latest day and year written below."

"Sign, please, Herbert," she said, and he did. "Now you, Nick," and I obliged her.

After I had put down my pen, I buzzed Hannah. "Bring it in," I said, and she promptly appeared with a bucket of ice, three flute glasses, and a bottle of Moët et Chandon.

"Semper paratus," I said. "Just for the occasion."

"Is this customary?" asked Poole.

Popping the cork, I said: "Only when I think we have something to celebrate."

Glasses filled with the bubbly, we clinked them, and I proposed a toast: "To the Mystery Writers of America, whose motto is 'Crime does not pay—enough.' "

"I'll drink to that," said Kay and Poole in chorus. On our way to the elevator, and out of earshot of Poole, Kay leaned over and said to me: "I've decided to take on your author Joe Scanlon as a client." I appreciated her discretion. No author cares to hear his agent discuss another author, at least not before the ink is dry on the contract.

"Good," I said sotto voce. "Joe will be pleased."

"Incidentally," said Kay, "I've heard something about Parker Foxcroft that might interest you."

"Tell me, by all means."

"I'll call you, Nick. I don't want to hold you now."

"As you wish."

"Take care of yourself, darling," she said, and blew me a kiss just before the elevator doors closed on the two of them.

The next morning Kay McIntire phoned me.

"Nick—about that information I told you I had yesterday—"

"I remember—on your way to the elevator."

"Right. You know about the Caxton Awards?"

"Sure. What about them?" The Caxton Awards were the most prestigious literary prizes of the year, even more coveted than the National Book Awards, and almost as desirable as a Pulitzer Prize. They were awarded annually to the best biography, best novel, best book of poetry—in the opinion of the judges. Each prize was worth $25,000 and a lot of publicity.

"Two years ago Parker Foxcroft was one of the judges. Remember?"

"Yeah, sort of. I knew he had served on one literary jury or another."

"Well," said Kay in a tone I could only describe as conspiratorial, if "gossipy" wasn't the better word, "the prize for fiction was awarded to a book that was definitely a dark horse. The inside story, and it was definitely kept quiet except for a few insiders—"

"Yourself among them, I suppose, Kay."

"That's between your mouth and God's ear. Would you like to hear the dirt?"

"Of course, darling. Speak."

"It would appear that Parker accepted a substantial bribe from the publisher of the winning book, and then cast the deciding vote in the competition."

"Shocking if true."

"True, I think, but not especially shocking, Nick," said Kay. "Publishing, after all, is no longer the simon-pure business it used to be, if it ever was. Some of the Hollywood glitz and shallowness have rubbed off on our industry, as well as some of Wall Street's corruption. And don't forget Washington's shady politics. We're not immune from contagion."

"I suppose so, although I'd rather give even Parker the benefit of the doubt."

"One other thing, Nick. I'd like you to do me a favor."

"Anything I can, Kay."

"Reconsider the suggestion Herbert made about spending some time in your office."

"I don't know, Kay . . ."

"Please."

"All right, if it'll make you happy. But I don't want the man underfoot."

"I promise he'll be discreet, keep a low profile. When shall I tell him to come see you?"

"Tomorrow, I suppose, will be as good a day as any."

"Thanks, Nick."

"Wait just a minute—"

"Bye, Nick. Talk to you soon."

And I was left listening to a dial tone.

Chapter 18

Herbert Poole presented himself bright and early at my office next morning. Though I still had misgivings about this little exercise, I had cleared my calendar in anticipation of his arrival, at least of any morning appointments. I could hardly expect Poole, nor want him, to spend the entire day with me. And Sidney had asked me to hold three o'clock open for our new female private-eye writer, Sarah Goodall, who was going to pay us her first visit.

"Good morning, Mr. Barlow," said Poole.

" 'Nick,' if you please. Let's drop the formalities, shall we?"

"Fine, Nick. And it's Herbert, not Herb or Herbie."

"After all, we're going to be spending a fair amount of time together."

"I do hope so," said Poole. "I know I'll want your editorial advice and the chance to see how an amateur detective operates."

"An amateur detective?" I wasn't sure I was happy about that designation.

"Haven't you been involved in at least one real murder?" Poole said.

"I can't take much credit for the solution of Jordan Walker's murder." I felt that modesty became me at the moment. After all, at times I feel that "amateur publisher" would be more appropriate to sum up my calling. "You're referring to the murder that took place here in my offices," I said.

"Yes. Your editor, Parker Foxcroft."

"Well, I'm sure the police have that one under control. At least I hope they do."

"Anyway," said Poole, "I'm looking forward to working with you."

Now that the formalities were over, I wondered where to turn next. Where did we start?

"Have you done any preliminary work on your mystery?" I said. "An outline, perhaps?"

"Is one necessary? Why not just plunge in headfirst?"

"Feetfirst, more likely," I replied. "The outline, Herbert, is a life preserver, if you will. The detective novel is essentially a puzzle, but one which must be constructed backward. First, know who your victim is, who the murderer is, and why the victim was murdered—motive, in short."

I went to one of my bookshelves and pulled out Kenneth Silverman's biography of Edgar Allan Poe. Turning to a well-thumbed page, I read aloud: " 'No other kind of fiction illustrates so clearly the writer's need to choose from the beginning some one outcome or effect, and to adapt every element of the narrative to it.'

"Right!" I said. "I think what Silverman wrote is so important that I commend it to you, too."

"Does every writer prepare such an outline?" Poole asked.

"Not every mystery writer I know does. Ed McBain, for

one, doesn't, and his mysteries are as good as any being written today. So it takes all kinds."

"I'll keep that in mind. Incidentally—"

"Yes?"

"Don't you ever get tired of the company of writers?"

"Yes, once a year."

"When is that?"

"The ABA Convention. You were there signing books. One of my favorite activities at the ABA is the Oblivion Press lunch."

"Oblivion Press? What's that?"

"Just a group of us publishing folks who get together at the ABA every year to let our hair down. Oblivion Press, of course, does not exist—that is, it's not really a press, but an imaginary publishing house, created in the spirit of buffoonery and self-mockery. When you're tired of booksellers, bookselling, publishing, and authors, you're ready for Oblivion."

"Oh," said Poole. *"Well."*

Actually what we do at Oblivion Press board meetings is to drink copiously, tell jokes, make up absurd titles and authors, and laugh uproariously at our own inside humor. A magazine writer who attended one of our sessions called us "a group of middle-aged cards." Obviously it was a mistake inviting him to our meeting, but it also clearly wasn't one of our best outings.

"So you do get tired of authors," said Poole. "Sick and tired, perhaps?"

"Let me tell you a story about that, Herbert. It seems that a young author whose first novel had just been accepted by Simon and Schuster was taken by Peter Schwed, then e-in-c, to meet one of the original partners of the firm, M. Lincoln Schuster. Schuster was rather advanced in years then, but still kept an office at Ess and Ess, which he came to regularly, though he had nothing much to do there. Said Schwed (excuse me; an unintentional rhyme): 'Mr. Schuster, I'd like you to meet Mr. So-and-So, whose first novel we'll be publishing.' The old man looked up and said: 'Author, eh? Authors . . . they're still writing books.' A pause, then: 'They'll never learn.' "

Poole laughed, but I sensed that he didn't really find the story funny. "Well, if you put it that way—" he said.

"I might tell you that some of my best friends are authors, but it wouldn't be altogether true. I'd much rather hang out with painters, actors, even musicians, the least intelligent of all the artists. And cops, especially cops. Anyone with a good story to tell.

"So," I wound up, "I'm sure you have a good story to tell. Will it make a successful mystery?"

"I hope so, Nick. You'll know when you read my outline, which I intend to start writing this very day."

"Good. What else can we talk about?"

"How about true crime?"

"Sure. Fire away."

"Parker Foxcroft," he said. "Do you have any idea who might have killed him?"

"You're not the first person to ask me that," I said. "Nor do I expect you to be the last. Anyway—"

I told Poole about my visit to Judith Michaelson. Somehow I felt she had the strongest motive I'd discovered so far. She hated Parker, and it would only have been poetic justice for her to murder him with the same gun her husband had used to kill himself. "Don't you agree, Herbert?"

"At this point, I can't say. I just don't know enough."

I ran down the list of suspects involved, winding up with

Harry Bunter—which reminded me that at some point I ought to talk to his wife.

"Now you know just about everything I know," I said to Poole. "If you get any bright ideas—"

"You'll be the first to hear them," he said.

That was the end of our conversation for that day. He left my office, promising to come back on Monday.

"I'm off to a house I have on Fire Island for the weekend."

"The wages of Pan?"

"There's nothing like a best-seller," he said. "It's a money tree for sure—as you well know."

"Until Monday, then, Herbert."

Three o'clock rolled around, and it was time for me to meet Sarah Goodall. I suspected that I would wind up editing *Icepick,* or whatever the name of her book was. Sidney Leopold, whose discovery she was, did not like to work on books in which victims were put to death in grisly and violent fashion, or in which the hero got badly beaten up, as in most P.I. mysteries; he turned that sort of thing over to me.

At any rate, promptly on the appointed hour, a knock came at my office door. It was Sidney and Sarah Goodall.

Not knowing what to expect, I cannot say that I was altogether taken by surprise by La Goodall—only a trifle taken aback.

She was of medium height, rather stocky, her hair cropped quite short. She was wearing a tee-shirt imprinted with the words "QUEER NATION." That didn't bother me particularly, but what I did find disquieting was the tiny gold earring dangling, not from her ear, but from her right eyebrow.

"Muh-meet Sarah Goodall, Nuh-Nick," said Sidney.

"Happy to meet you," she said, thrusting out her hand. Her voice was almost as deep as mine, and her handshake was strong enough to crack a few of my metacarpi. *Well,* I thought, unable to come up with anything original, *it takes all kinds.*

"My pleasure, Ms. Goodall," I said. "Have a seat, please."

Either spotting or suspecting my bewilderment at this apparition in my office, Sidney was quick to take charge of the conversation.

"Nuh-Nick has read your buh-book, Sarah," he said. "And luh-likes it, right, Nick?"

"Oh, I most certainly do."

"Surely you have some changes you'll want made," Goodall said, cocking her head while squinting her eyes, and leaning on every word.

"That's true. We editors are never completely satisfied."

"Editors? I thought you were the publisher."

"That's true—but like the general who has come up through the ranks, I still relish the heat of combat. The smoke of battle."

This time her eyes narrowed, setting the ring in her eyebrow—should I call it an eyering?—to trembling.

"You make the editorial process sound rather like the Second World War," she said.

Sidney obviously thought he'd better butt in to save my face. "Oh, Suh-Sarah, Nick is a great kuh-kidder. He doesn't muh-mean we don't get along with our authors. Nuh-not at all."

At this, she subsided. "I hope not," she muttered.

"Well," I announced, "shall we talk contract? I understand that you have no agent, Ms. Goodall?"

She shook her head. "Knowing what I know about publishers' advances," she said, "I figured I couldn't afford to give away fifteen percent. I sent the book directly to Mr. Leopold myself."

I smiled—no, I beamed. An author without an agent is easy prey for an unscrupulous publisher—even a scrupulous one, such as me.

An hour later we adjourned, and I found myself wishing Sarah Goodall *had* an agent; we might have made a better deal. She was one tough cookie, that was for sure.

"Wh-what do you thu-think, Nick?" said Sidney, when we were alone. "Doesn't she have an in-the-fuh-face *face?*" He started to giggle.

"Please, Sidney," I said. "The joke is bad enough without you laughing at it yourself."

"Suh-sorry, Nick."

"We'll do all right with this one, don't you think, Sidney?"

"Oh—" He struggled to push the word out between his lips. It was coming, coming—there it was—"absolutely!"

Dear Sidney Leopold. I don't know how I could possibly manage without him.

Chapter 19

It seemed a long time before Friday evening finally arrived, but when it did it brought Susan Markham to my doorstep.

"So this is where you live, Nick."

She was carrying a silk handbag large enough for her personal accessories. Clearly we both expected her to stay the night.

"Welcome to number 2 Gramercy Park."

I had given Oscar and Pepita the weekend off, and they had decided to spend it with Pepita's cousins in Flatbush. Pepita left behind all the ingredients I would need to whip up dinner: the veal scallopini pounded almost paper-thin and ready to be breaded, browned in oil, and garnished with melted butter, lemon slices, capers, and anchovies. Sliced potatoes for *pommes de terre sautées*. A spinach soufflé ready to warm up in the oven. Finally, a zabaglione with ladyfingers for dessert. I opened an ice-cold Connecticut varietal, half chardonnay and half Riesling, poured two glasses, removed my apron (one that resembles a full-dress dinner jacket, complete with dickey, white stiff shirt, and red bow tie), lit the candles, *et voilà!* as the French say. We ate in my wood-paneled dining room, on a refectory table set with silver and crystal.

"A sinful meal, Nick—I hate to think of the calories, not to mention the cholesterol. But delicious. Do you cook often?"

"Almost never."

"What a waste of talent."

"And when I do cook," I said, "I pick the easiest dishes I can find. Also, Susan, I have a limited repertoire."

"Well, anyhow, it was all lovely."

When we finished dinner, it was still much too early to head toward the bedroom, so I poured us each a snifter of Armagnac, and we settled down on a couch in the living room.

"I can't help thinking—" I started off.

"Isn't it better, now and then, not to?"

"Think? I suppose so. 'The pale cast of thought' and all that. Still—"

"Go ahead, Nick, spit it out."

"Spitting it out," I said, wagging my brandy snifter at her, "is not what I had in mind."

Careful, Barlow. Easy does it.

"I'm sorry. What was it you were thinking?"

"I'm not sure how to put this question so it won't sound . . . gauche."

"You'd like to know why I found Parker Foxcroft attractive."

"My God, you read minds."

"No, body language. You were fidgeting, Nick. You were embarrassed to ask me that question, because you thought it might offend me."

"Well . . . yeah."

She reached out her hand and touched my cheek with the tips of her fingers.

"I'm really not that interested in the sexual prowess of Parker Foxcroft," I said. "I'm just trying to figure out what made Parker run."

"I won't answer your question right now. But I will tell you this, Nick Barlow. Parker did not have half the style or strength of character or animal magnetism that you have. And that's just for starters."

"I wasn't fishing for compliments, really."

"I know." She leaned closer to me, so close I had little choice but to put my arms around her and kiss her.

"While I still have my wits about me," I said, "in spite of inhaling Armagnac fumes and your seductive perfume, would you answer one impersonal question? *Im*personal, yes."

"Of course."

"Do you know of any enemies Parker may have had? That is, anybody who would be happy to see him dead?"

"I don't think so."

"Yet you spent a good deal of time with him. Didn't you ever notice anything—well, odd about his behavior? Anything suspicious?"

"Such as?"

"Surely you must have known how extravagant he was. Did he ever give you any idea of where all the money came from?"

She frowned and leaned back on the couch. Apparently I had started a fruitful train of thought. "Well . . . there was one thing he said—"

"Yes?"

"We did talk about money once—just once—and Parker said something odd. He said, if I remember it right—'I've got an annuity. An Irving of my own.' "

"An Irving?"

"That's right."

"What do you suppose he meant?"

"I haven't a clue, Nick."

"Anything else, Susan?"

Again she frowned; this time the frown was directed at me.

"Why are you so curious about all this, Nick? Can't we just let the dead bury the dead?"

At this point, I stood up and began to pace. If I got any more exercised, I'd start to jingle the coins in my pants pocket.

Don't ruin the evening, dummy.

I sat down again.

Du calme, baby.

"My company has been dealt a serious blow," I said, lowering my voice to basso profundo. "Parker, a pain in the ass, if I may say so, was, according to everybody else I know, a legend in his own time, a latter-day Max Perkins. His murder leaves a void—not just in my office, but in my next spring catalog. Money is at stake. Also, my staff has been harassed and badgered by the police, who would like to know who killed that—that—"

"Don't say it, Nick."

"I know, I know. Anyway, you can see why I might be distressed, and why I might do anything I could to help find Parker's murderer. Until then, it's hard—no, it's impossible—to let the dead bury the dead. So, Susan, if you can help me—please do. Please. Think about it, anyway."

"The only thing I can think of—"

"Yes?" Her hand was in mine now; I stared deep into those blue-green eyes. *Give, darling, give.*

"One night," Susan said, "I was in his apartment. You're

sure you want to hear this, Nick? Absolutely sure?" Her speech was beginning to sound slurred. So, I suppose, was mine.

"Go ahead. I can take it, for Christ's sake."

"He thought I was asleep, only I wasn't. He had gone into the other room, his office, to have a cigarette, I thought, or whatever. You know?"

"Go ahead, my dear."

"The computer screen was lit up, and he was punching things into the keyboard. I was standing behind him, looking at the screen. There were names on it, and numbers, I think."

"Did you recognize any of the names?"

"Not really, Nick. Before I could, he turned around and saw me. He was *furious.*"

"Really?"

" 'What the hell are you doing here?' he said in a nasty tone of voice—well, I tell you, I was shocked. Shocked, Nick. He'd never spoken to me that way before. Never.

" 'I came looking for you,' I said to him. 'Why don't you come back to bed?' You're still sure you want to hear this, Nick? Darling?"

"Well, if that's all there is . . ."

"That's all there is."

"It's—not so bad," I said, but in truth I felt slightly nauseous. The picture of Susan in Parker's bed was a disquieting one.

The picture of her in *my* bed, on the other hand, was quite attractive, as I realized when my stomach stopped churning. Let the dead bury the dead applied to love affairs as well. And here she was, Susan Markham, intensely alive, like a lovely surprise, an unexpected gift.

"Shall we get ready for bed?" she said. A mind reader as well as an authentic beauty.

"Let's. You first," and I led the way to my bedroom.

Dropping her silk handbag on the bed, she looked around, appraising the room and its contents—my mahogany chest of drawers, the Chippendale secretary, the light blue velvet chaise near my emperor-size bed—nodding in approval.

"You live well, Nick."

"Thanks."

She crossed the room to my clothes closet, which took up almost the length of one wall. Opening it, she ran her hands along my suits, which hung all along the closet.

"So many suits," she murmured, rather like Daisy Buchanan admiring Jay Gatsby's shirts.

"There's a reason for the quantity," I said.

"Oh?"

"There are really three sizes of suit in this closet," I said. "Those on this end are worn when I'm a middleweight. Those in the middle when I'm a light heavyweight. And those on the far end—"

She laughed. "I can guess. I do have one suggestion, though, Nick."

"What's that?"

"If I were you, I'd switch from Brooks Brothers to Giorgio Armani."

I sniffed somewhat haughtily. "Actually, some of them are made for me in London, by a tailor on Savile Row. He bespoke suited my father, and he bespoke suits me as well. Occasionally."

"I stand corrected," she said with a smile.

"Now, why don't you get ready while I fix us a nightcap?"

When I came back from the living room with a snifter of brandy, she was waiting for me, stretched out on the chaise. She was wearing a black lace body stocking, which brought out every detail of her body and yet remained quite beautiful in itself.

I'm sure she could read the admiration in my eyes. "Daring enough for you, Nick?" she said.

"A dare I gladly accept."

It was time for me to prepare for what I hoped would be, like our first rendezvous, a night to remember. In my dressing room, which is also my bath, I quickly undressed, shaved, and rubbed lotion on my face. Then I slipped into a robe and returned to the bedroom.

Susan was still lying back on the chaise, sipping brandy.

"Nick," she said, "I wasn't going to mention Parker ever again, but I just know there's one thing you're curious about. If I tell you, will you promise not to ask me about him again?"

"Well—"

"Promise, Nick."

"I promise."

"You want to know what made him so attractive to women."

"That's right. I found him singularly *un*attractive."

"It's quite simple. His body smelled of honey."

My mouth fell open, and for a moment I was altogether speechless. When I found my voice, I croaked: *"Honey?"*

"That's right. Now you know. And now it's time to keep your promise. And also time for you to come over here and kiss me—before I run out of patience."

Although I'm not at all used to being ordered about, I found this command only too easy to obey. What ensued was only to be expected. The bed was near at hand. Off came the body stocking. Slowly, inch by inch, with many delicious pauses along the way. Then off came my robe, and on came the night.

Much later, just before dawn, I lay awake thinking, while Susan breathed softly at my side, one hand resting on my chest as she slept.

What she had told me was, clearly, all she intended to tell me, that much I knew for sure. Still, had she told me everything she knew? Suppose she even knew the identity of Parker's murderer and was afraid to tell me. Afraid—or reluctant?

It wouldn't take a genius to surmise that I was smitten with Susan Markham. Smitten—or about to be, I wasn't quite sure which myself. Sex always confuses the mind, even as it sweeps away any indecision. "The awful daring of a moment's surrender," as Eliot wrote, "which a lifetime of prudence can never retract." Of course, he might also have been speaking of murder.

It occurred to me—just as a second sleep, deep and restful, overcame me—that I was probably . . . falling in love . . . with Susan Markham . . .

. . . but . . . could I trust her?

Chapter 20

Much as I wanted to take Susan with me to Connecticut on Saturday, I decided it was much too soon to spring her on my mother. Although she claims to be a broad-minded party, Mother is in actual fact rather old-fashioned, and I could not visualize her permitting Susan and me to occupy the same four-poster. Moreover, she is forever accusing me of "getting involved with another woman." The truth is, she cleaves to Margo, heart and soul, and wishes that we two were together again. I didn't want Susan to have to compete with an idealized Margo Richmond.

I did, however, tell Tim about Susan, sparing only the graphic details.

"So she was keeping company with Parker as a career move," said Tim.

"That's right."

"And how do you know that's not her motive in sleeping with you?"

I tensed up a bit. The implication that ambition not lust was what burned in Susan's breast put me on my guard.

Suppose it was true that she only had advancement in mind—and not romance?

"I admit that might be the case," I said, "but I'm in no position to help her career, and I wouldn't if I could."

"No?" Ever the skeptic, my brother.

"No—most emphatically not. There's enough nepotism in this family as it is."

Tim grinned. "I can see you're a little touchy on the matter, so we won't pursue the subject any further. In any case, Nick, I hope it all ends well."

Relieved, I punched him lightly on the shoulder. "I can only say that so far, so good."

We then got on the subject of what Susan had told me about Parker.

"Irving," murmured Tim. "*Irving.*" He scratched his head. "Let's think publishing first. Who are the Irvings? Irving Stone?"

"Irving Wallace," I chimed in.

"Clifford Irving?"

"How about the Irving Trust?"

Tim brightened. "That may well be it. The Irving Trust Company . . ."

"Parker mentioned an annuity."

"The two could be connected," said Tim, spinning his wheelchair around until he faced the wall, something he frequently did when he was into hard thinking.

"Do you suppose," he went on, "that Joe Scanlon or one of the cops on the case could find out if Parker had an account at the Irving Trust?"

"More likely a safe-deposit box, don't you think?"

He nodded. "Yeah—and to get into one of those—"

"You need a court order, which, Parker having shuffled off this mortal coil, shouldn't be a problem to get."

"It's worth a phone call on your part, anyway, Nick."

We turned next to the problem of the Widow Michaelson.

"I have a suggestion," said Tim.

"Shoot."

"I gather you're pretty upset about that letter of Parker's . . ."

Upset? Too mild a word. Goddamned angry about it.

"Parker ticked me off enough when he was alive," I said, "but now that he's dead I'm finding even more reasons to hate his guts. Virtually every day brings a new indictment of his character."

"My suggestion, then, is that you talk to Judith Michaelson and offer, in her husband's memory, to publish his novel posthumously. Remember *A Confederacy of Dunces?*"

"The O'Toole novel? Of course. Like Michaelson, he killed himself because no one would publish it. At least that's the conventional wisdom."

"But," I added, "suppose the book isn't worth publishing?"

"That was only Parker Foxcroft's opinion, Nick. Why don't you ask the lady for a copy of the manuscript so you can read it for yourself?"

Which is exactly what I did on Monday morning, when I got back to New York.

Judith Michaelson was hesitant when I asked her if I might drop by for another talk, but I persisted, and she finally relented. I had the feeling that she didn't have too many visitors—not just because she had lost her husband or was antisocial, but because most writers, as I well know, are often lonely when they're not writing—and even when they are.

It seemed to me that when she greeted me at the door of

her apartment, she was wearing the same housedress she'd had on the first time I called on her. Not that I expected her to get gussied up just for me—but she had made *one* concession to vanity today: she'd put on makeup.

When we were settled, once again with the tea things out and in service, I explained to her what I had in mind.

"So if you would let me have a copy of your husband's book, Mrs. Michaelson—"

"Oh, but that's not possible, Mr. Barlow."

"Oh?"

"I don't mean to sound as though I don't appreciate your kind offer, and if I had a copy of Alex's manuscript, I'd be glad to let you read it. But, Mr. Barlow, there aren't any copies."

"No copies, Mrs. Michaelson?

"None."

"No computer disks, perhaps?"

"My husband didn't use a computer. He wouldn't even use an electric typewriter, only the old Olivetti portable he got as a present from his family when he graduated from college."

An Olivetti portable, no less.

I sighed, deep inside my being. If only *all* authors worked on computers, how much easier the preservation of the written word would be! No, no, there are some writers who even write with pens or pencils—or in longhand, for God's sake. And only too often manuscripts are lost. Remember Hemingway's suitcase?

Not that we publishers are much better. I have had more than one author ask me if I'd rather deal with his floppies than hard copy—and I have always had to smile sadly, bow my head in shame, and admit that Barlow & Company is only just creeping into the electronic age. All over America, enterprising authors are composing their books on computer terminals, running off type for them on their laser printers, and shipping the pages off to a printer; five weeks later they have bound books, while we supposedly "mainstream" publishers take anywhere from nine to eighteen months to bring a book to market. It is to laugh. So why aren't we au courant? Why are we dragging our feet? Force of habit, I suppose; *that's the way it has always been done. Ever since Gutenberg.*

It must have been evident that I was in a state of reverie, for Judith Michaelson cleared her throat and said: "Mr. Barlow?"

"Yes?"

"Are you all right?"

"Perfectly. I was just thinking . . . your husband did leave a manuscript behind—somewhere?"

"Yes. I did have a copy."

"What became of it?"

She paused and held out a plate of cookies for my inspection. I declined to take one, toothsome as they looked.

"I gave it to a mutual friend of Alex and mine," she said. "Another writer."

"Oh? And what did this friend say?"

"He told me that while it was undeserving of Parker's destructive criticism, the book was essentially mediocre at best; he recommended that it be destroyed."

"Destroyed? Surely you didn't . . ."

"Not exactly," Michaelson said. "I thought we ought to have a second opinion. My friend agreed. He suggested Peter Jensen, the critic."

I nodded. "A sensible idea. I know Jensen—not well, but I respect his judgment."

"At any rate," she continued, "my friend said he would

send the book to Jensen by messenger. But the messenger never arrived at Jensen's office; he was hit by a car on the way—and somehow the manuscript disappeared. At least it was never found."

"What a pity," I murmured. "You didn't read it first? Before sending it to your friend?"

"Oh no." She gave a fleeting grimace. "Alex and I made a practice of never reading each other's work. He felt it might threaten our marriage."

"I don't follow."

"Either we might be too critical, and wound the other, or we might praise poor writing for fear of hurting the other person's feelings. And you see, Mr. Barlow, we didn't write at *all* alike."

So that was that: a washout.

When Herbert Poole showed up at my office that afternoon, I told him about my two meetings with Judith Michaelson and how disappointed I was at the outcome.

"Would you really have published the man's book?" Poole asked. Once again, I was struck by how he drawled out his question.

"Almost certainly. Even though the lady *is*, in my opinion, a suspect in our murder."

"Do you really think so?" Poole—who was sitting on the visitor's chair in my office—rose, walked over to one of my mahogany bookcases, took out a volume, and began idly leafing through it. I saw that the book was *Bloody Murder*, by Julian Symons.

"My view," he continued, "now that I've given it some thought, is that the lady has probably suffered enough. She did lose a husband, after all, and in the most brutal fashion imaginable. Self-murder is always shocking. Hard for the survivor to bear."

I considered this for a moment. "You're probably right about the suffering—"

"As for killing Parker Foxcroft, do you suppose she would turn up at his funeral if she was responsible for his death?"

"Well—no, I guess not."

"Hardly," said Poole emphatically.

That seemed to end the matter, at least for now. Changing the subject, I said to Poole: "Have you finished your outline yet?"

"Not quite. However, it's coming along." He replaced the Symons in its proper niche on the shelf.

"One thing I'd like you to remember, Herbert," I said, assuming my professional mien. "When you write a mystery, you are essentially writing a fantasy."

"How so?"

"A realistic detective story is probably a contradiction in terms. Private eyes in the real world do not get mixed up in murder cases. They collect evidence for lawyers, they do marital surveillance, insurance fraud, or missing-person cases. Amateur sleuths do not solve murders where the police cannot. And even police procedurals rely on strong fictional elements. If they didn't, they'd make damn dull reading. Mystery depends on the bizarre to be convincing. On the fantastic, in short. End of lecture."

"I see what you mean," Poole said. "Go off the wall."

"Exactly."

"By the way," I said, "Parker's office has now been unsealed by the police. Tomorrow you and I might start going through the Foxcroft legacy—his papers and computer disks. If you'd like to do it, that is. What do you say?"

"Are you sure I can be helpful?"

"Let's say you can provide a useful second opinion."

"Then I'll be happy to lend a hand. What are we looking for?"

"I wish I could say we're looking for his murderer, but I doubt it. This is the real world, not fiction. I suspect we're looking to see if we can tell what made Parker tick."

Poole started toward the door and then turned, his hand on the doorknob. "Oh, Nick—" he said. "There's something else I meant to tell you. About Foxcroft."

"What is it?"

"Something my former agent—before Kay—told me. You know Finlay Norton, don't you?"

"We all do," I said. "I'm glad you switched agents." Finlay Norton was notorious along Publishers Row for forcing the prices he put on books unreasonably high.

"He as much as accused Parker of blackmail," said Poole.

"Isn't *that* interesting," I said. "How so?"

"Apparently Parker caught Finlay out in a shady deal of some kind—he wouldn't say what it was for sure, but that's what I suspect it was. Unethical behavior in an auction, I believe. Anyway, Parker was forcing Norton into giving him exceptionally favorable terms with his clients."

"If you ask me," I said, "they deserved each other."

Poole smiled and opened the office door. "Quite so. Which is one reason why I changed agents. See you tomorrow, Nick."

Chapter 21

The following morning, Tuesday, found Herbert Poole and me ensconced in Parker Foxcroft's office, glumly going through reams of paper.

The Foxcroft correspondence consisted largely of letters to agents, letters to authors, letters to would-be authors, and an occasional letter to a reviewer, complaining about an unfavorable notice of one of Parker's books.

"Hardly the sort of stuff to interest the National Archives," I said to Poole. "Or even Parker's alma mater, which I believe was Duke."

As we dug deeper, however, and particularly when we tackled the computer files, a picture of Parker Foxcroft as an editorial Vlad the Impaler began to emerge.

"You have shown the unparalleled effrontery to attempt a life of James Joyce," he wrote one scholar, "when you ought to know, if you have read the literature, that Richard Ellmann's biography is monumental, and will not be superseded in our lifetime, not by plodding academic hackwork such as you have produced. It's not even a creditable rip-off of Ellmann."

And:

"Do not have the audacity to dream that I would put my imprint on a shoddy piece of keyhole-peeping such as this one," he scolded an impertinent journalist who had turned out an exposé of Hollywood flimflam. "I suggest you try a vanity press."

"That one became a modest best-seller," I remarked, rather glumly.

"Here's another dilly," said Poole, and he read: "There are at least five hundred and ninety-nine different writing courses in America, and your unfortunate prose would indicate that you have taken all of them and learned from none. I would respectfully suggest that, if you have a paying trade of some kind, you stick to it with all the undoubted energy it took you to scribble these interminable pages."

Or:

"Dear Sir: Because you have enclosed a stamped, self-addressed return envelope, I am returning your manuscript, although, if lost in my office or in the mail, it would be no loss whatever. The device of enclosing a ten-dollar bill in the second chapter to see if the reader has really read it is so hoary that it is beneath contempt. I had only to shake the manuscript and the bill fell out. The bill I am keeping."

To be completely fair, Parker's acceptance letters were as effusive as his rejections were withering. To one poet he wrote: "As a moth may not venture too close to a flame, so might a reader be wary of approaching so much brilliance as you display in your work. Talent such as you possess is granted to only a few writers in any generation. Welcome to that pantheon."

"Had to have been a woman," I muttered.

"What?"

"Forget it."

On and on we read, until my eyes began to swell in their sockets.

"I think I've had enough for one day," I said to Poole.

He looked up and winked at me. "I don't blame you," he said. "Let me go on reading them. I'm sure you have other things to do."

"Okay, but don't strain your eyes."

"I'll read for just a while longer and then take off," he said. "See you tomorrow?"

I nodded, and returned to my own office.

The picture I had now of Parker Foxcroft was essentially complete. I did not believe we would find any other pieces to fit into the jigsaw puzzle—except one: who hated him enough to want him dead? Here was a man whose brilliance was equaled only by his savagery and, as it turned out, by his mendacity. I found it rather amazing that none of these rejected authors thought to sue him for libel—but what would they gain, and how could they expect to win, given Parker's impeccable editorial credentials? No third person can possibly evaluate or second-guess an editor's judgments. The editor is judge and jury all in one.

Conceivably one of these hapless victims of Parker's spleen might like to do him in; more likely they might follow Alexander Michaelson and turn their guns on themselves.

Anyhow, it was time to get back to work. I had an important call to make.

"Claire Bunter speaking."

"Oh good, I found you in. It's Nick Barlow, Claire."

"Nick." Her voice fell off perceptibly. Apprehension? Suspicion, perhaps?

I had already prepared my script.

"If you're calling for Harry—"

"No."

"—or about Harry—"

"Neither, Claire. I'm calling about you. *Your* work."

"Okay. Go ahead, Nick."

"Look," I said, "your personal life is really none of my business, but you were one of Parker Foxcroft's authors, after all, which makes you one of Barlow and Company's authors."

"And?"

"Parker wasn't our only editor. I have at least three people on staff, starting with Sidney Leopold, who would love to do your next book. Won't you at least talk with me about it?"

"Well?" I could detect a gradual warming of the atmosphere at her end of the phone.

"Have you," I asked, with just a touch of wistfulness, "signed with any other publisher?"

"No, not yet. Though I've been thinking—"

"So you do have a new book?"

"Or will—soon, Nick."

"I'm delighted to hear that. We did well with" (what the hell was the name of that book?) *"Newport Nights"* (that was it!).

"I know."

"So would you let me lunch you, Claire, so we can talk about your next book?"

"I don't do lunch much, Nick. Not when I'm writing."

"I understand. The work always comes first. But you must break at the end of the day . . ."

"Usually."

"So," I said, not one to take no for an answer—or even maybe—"would you meet me for a drink at The Players?"

"When?"

"Just a moment, Claire." I ran down my appointment calendar. No parties, no dates. Even Susan wasn't on the calendar. We had agreed to hold off a few days before meeting again. "Anything wrong with tomorrow?"

"That's Wednesday?"

"Right."

"Well . . ." The word trailed off into a sigh. "All right, Nick. But please don't try the hard sell, okay?"

"I? The hard sell?"

"Don't try the soft sell, either. Let's just have a pleasant drink."

"My pleasure, too. Six o'clock?"

"Six-fifteen," she said, and rang off.

Quite some time later, I looked at my watch and saw that it was well after closing hour.

Walking down the hall, I saw no one, not even Sidney, who almost always works late. I peeked into Foxcroft's office. It was dark. Poole, too, had left.

Some people, I believe, find an empty office ominous. I rather like the peace and quiet. All those computers sleeping soundly in their stations; the phones and fax machines gone silent; the occasional squawk as our night answering machine kicks in to tell some importune caller what our business hours are; these things impart a sense of shutting down, like the ceremony of tattoo in the military service, or as nature shuts down when twilight slides almost imperceptibly into darkness.

It was getting dark. I was about to switch on a light when I heard the click of a lock snapping open. *Crack.* The lock I had installed after Parker Foxcroft's murder. The lock that was supposed to keep anybody out there *out.*

"Jesus," I whispered. I backed up, ever so slowly, seeking the darkest corner of the hallway.

Suddenly the hall was flooded with light, almost blinding me, and I was looking into the mean black mouths of a double-barreled shotgun—and above it a hulking figure in a fatigue jacket and a black ski mask.

Chapter 22

"Freeze! Police!"

Ski Mask's command was quite unnecessary; I was already as good as paralyzed. I am as brave as the next man in a fair fight, but a shotgun pointed at my midsection makes the odds against me unfairly high. I obeyed.

"Put your hands against the wall and bend over."

I didn't have much choice but to carry out that order as well. I did think, however, that I might be permitted to speak.

"What's going on?" I said.

"Shut up."

In as much time as it takes to recall the moment, I was patted down and relieved of my wallet. *What was this, anyway?*

"Nicholas Barlow," said the voice behind me, obviously reciting from one of my IDs.

"I am."

"We had a report this office was being burglarized."

"Not as far as *I* know."

I heard a second, muffled voice in the background; obviously Ski Mask had been joined by somebody else. I gathered from the little I could make out that they—whoever *they* were—were deciding what to do with me. It was clear to me by this time that they were not cops, but baddies.

"Lie down on the floor, Barlow."

"The floor?"

"You heard me. Lie down on the fucking floor. Face-down."

This was beginning to get undignified, but I did as I was told.

"Now," said my bogus policeman, prodding me in the back with the barrel of his gun, "just stay right there until I tell you not to."

He placed the gun barrel against the back of my neck, and I thought: *Is this the way it happens? Is he going to kill me?* Images of violent death flooded my mind: bodies lying on bloodstained floors just like this one. Victims of bank robberies and gas station stickups, their flesh mangled and covered with blood. I fought off fear and nausea as best I could. Should I pray? Prayer didn't seem appropriate in the circumstances; only weddings and funerals ever got me into church, and then, like King Claudius, "my words fly up, my thoughts remain below. Words without thoughts never to heaven go."

Shakespeare. My comfort on any occasion. How did those lines go? "I care not; a man can die but once; we owe God a death. He that dies this year is quit for the next." *Henry IV, Part II*. Oh God, I'd still rather stick around—and not just for another year, either . . .

It was a short while later that I realized I no longer felt the pressure of cold metal on my neck; and sometime after that I had the feeling that I was alone in the room. Still, I couldn't be sure, so I waited perhaps five or six minutes longer, and then, very slowly, turned my head so that my left cheek rested on the floor, and by craning my neck, I could see a small part of the room. No one in sight.

Feeling as foolish as I'm sure I looked, I put my hands flat on the floor and pushed myself up to a kneeling position. Nothing happened, so I got to my feet and looked around. I was alone. My face was damp with sweat, and I could feel my shirt sticking to my back. I leaned against a nearby desk for a moment to clear my head, which was still beset by a morbid band of fancies.

It occurred to me that the police ought to be notified, and I had picked up the phone to call the Thirteenth Precinct station and report a holdup, when I heard a commotion out in the hallway: footsteps pounding down the hall, the sound of male voices, and then, moments later, someone was pounding on my office door.

"Come in," I shouted.

The door flew open and two uniformed officers appeared, both of them holding police specials aimed at me.

"There's been a burglary on this floor," one of them said.

"Oh no—not again."

"Oh yes, there sure has."

"You two?" I said. I recognized them at once: the two cops who had been in my office once before, and in my front parlor; it was during my first brush with crime: the Jordan Walker murder. The pair were Artie, a good-looking black patrolman, and his partner Buster, a pint-size patrolwoman.

"Never a dull moment, right, Mr. Barlow?" said Buster.

"Not in this office, I'm afraid."

I told them what had happened, and they clucked sympathetically during my recital.

"You should have known they weren't cops," was Artie's first comment.

"Don't you guys sometimes go undercover and dress like hoods?"

"Even so, we have to flash a badge," said Artie.

"He flashed a shotgun, and that was enough for me."

"What kind of shotgun?"

"How would I know?"

"Well," said Artie, "what did it look like?"

"It had a short barrel. That's about all I remember."

"How was the guy holding it?"

"In his right hand."

"A pistol grip? Probably a Remington 870," said Artie.

I shrugged. "It's all the same to me—just a shotgun. No matter what it was, I wasn't about to question it."

Artie was persistent, just as I remembered him. "Can you describe the perp for me?"

"All I saw was a black ski mask. I don't even remember the color of his eyes. I believe he was a white male. Sorry. That's all I can give you."

Artie put his notebook away, and shrugged.

It was Buster who filled me in on what had happened. Down the hall was the office of a jewelry importer. Burglars had broken in, cracked the safe, and when they got at the jewels and cash that were there, they set off an alarm at police headquarters.

"They didn't get all that much," said Buster. "Apparently they grabbed what they could and took off like big-ass birds. There was still quite a bit of stuff in the safe."

"But why did they break in here?" I asked.

"Probably they saw a light in your office, and thought you might figure out what was going on, so it was best to keep you quiet."

"You might have been killed," Artie said. "You run lucky, don't you, Mr. Barlow?"

Yeah. A murder and a holdup in my office—all in a space of two weeks. What next?

"Anyway, thanks for dropping by, guys. I feel much safer knowing you're on the job."

Artie gave me a raised-eyebrows, "Are you kidding me?" look.

"No, I'm serious, really." I spread out my hands. "Look, no irony."

"Good night, Mr. Barlow," said Buster. "See you around."

And so to bed, to an uneasy sleep, punctuated with bad dreams and ghostly thoughts.

The next morning I felt more like staying in bed, nibbling on chocolate candy and watching daytime game shows, instead of going in to the office, but a sense of having been reprieved somehow, or, putting it another way, of having been offered another chance to redeem myself, gave me the impetus I needed to get up and get on with the day.

As usual, I first read through both the *Times* and the *Daily News*. Both had brief squibs about the burglary in my office building; neither, thank heaven, made any mention of me. My public relations person, one Georgia Nussbaum, is hired, not to get me in the news, but to keep me out of it if at all possible.

At the office, Hannah beckoned me over to her desk.

"You got a call from the manager at The Players."

"Oh?"

"She said it was quite urgent, Nick."

Evelyn Randall is the manager of the Club. She is the very nerve center of the place—also its generator, the engine that runs it, and also its chief communicator. She flutters over the members like a benevolent mother hen.

I rang her up immediately. Randy, as we call her, is always busier than any two or three of us publisher-members, and it is difficult enough sometimes to reach her on the phone; consequently one does not ignore one of *her* calls.

"What is it, Randy?"

"Fred Drew is in jail, Mr. Barlow."

"What?"

"He's in the Tombs. He told me they arrested him on suspicion of murdering your editor—Parker Foxcroft, wasn't it? He wants you to come and see him—to help him if you can."

"Good God—Fred Drew?"

"He didn't sound all that happy about it on the phone, either."

"Why do you suppose he didn't call his lawyer?"

"I don't think he has one."

"Well—I'll see what I can do. Thanks for calling me, Randy."

"Anytime."

Two hours and a mess of red tape later I was seated at a conference table in the Tombs, facing Frederick Drew, perhaps America's unluckiest poet. He was too old for the Yale Younger Series of Poets Award, too idiosyncratic for the Pulitzer Prize or National Book Award people; neither Jewish, nor gay, nor a feminist, and thus left out of every poetic cult. And now he was in jail, accused of murder. One thing I felt sure of: he was not François Villon reincarnate.

I had been passed through a metal detector machine, frisked, and subjected to a barrage of questions as to why I was there. I insisted that I was Drew's publisher, which didn't seem to mean much to the guardians of the Tombs, who would have preferred that I be a lawyer, God forbid, until I added that Drew and I were also distant relatives, second cousins twice removed. It could be possible; everybody is related somehow to virtually everybody else, in my opinion. Anyhow, I was finally allowed to talk to the prisoner, in the company of a strapping big guard, who hovered near us.

Drew's head was bowed when I entered; his shoulders hunched. When he saw me, he straightened up and attempted a smile, which somehow fell short of its intention.

"Ah," he said in a somber voice, " 'Stately, plump Buck Mulligan,' I presume."

" 'Kinch,' " I replied, " 'you fearful Jesuit.' Happy Bloomsday."

"The same to you, brother."

It was Bloomsday, all right—June 16. On that day in 1904, as the historians tell us, James Joyce met his Nora Barnacle, and when he wrote *Ulysses,* the saga of a single day in Dublin, that is the day he re-created in the book. It is celebrated in New York literary circles by a marathon reading of the novel at Symphony Space on upper Broadway—a reading by dozens of actors, writers, and assorted publishing folk that lasts all of twenty-four hours or more. I myself read a section of it one year. However . . .

"What are you doing in here, Fred?" I asked Drew.

"What are you doing out there, Nick?" he said in reply.

"I suggest we skip the small talk, Fred. Also the literary allusions. Let's talk seriously."

"Whatever you say."

"Why do the police suspect you of murdering Parker Foxcroft?"

"I had the motive—which you know—and the opportunity."

"I understand."

Drew pulled out a rumpled pack of cigarettes and lit one, then held the pack out to me. I shook my head.

"No thanks."

He inhaled deeply, blew a perfect blue smoke ring, then put the cigarette down in an ashtray, where it smoked away by itself for the rest of our conversation.

"It was Juan," he said at last.

"The bartender at The Players?"

He nodded. "The police questioned the staff of the Club. About you apparently, Nick. They wanted to know who you'd spoken to and whether you'd had any phone calls. The concierge told them that Foxcroft had called, and Juan told them that when you went into the phone booth to take your call, I picked up the extension on the bar and listened to your call."

"And did you?" *Had I been right after all?*

"Sure. I knew Foxcroft would be waiting for you in his office. I decided to go there and confront him. Tell him off."

"To murder him?"

"No, *no*."

"And?"

"I got as far as your office building but I didn't go in. Lost my nerve, I guess. Or maybe it was fear. Fear that I hated his guts so much I might do him an injury."

He sighed, pinched the bridge of his nose, and shut his eyes. "Lost my nerve," he repeated. "I wish I had killed him, but I didn't."

"And the police—"

"Learned from Juan that I left the bar as soon as Parker's phone call was over. Opportunity, you see, Nick."

"Yeah, I see."

"But I didn't do it, Nick. You believe me, don't you?"

"Sure, I believe you." And I did—purely a matter of faith. "I still don't see why the police are holding you. What evidence could they possibly have?"

"It wasn't evidence, it was what I said when they questioned me. I was drunk, I suppose. Confused—you know how it is. I wasn't sure what I was saying. I . . . oh shit, I . . ."

His voice trailed off. I could picture the scene. Hatcher and Falco probably badgered the poor bastard until he got angry. Frederick Drew in a drunken, inchoate rage would say almost anything. He would contradict himself right and left.

"Why did you say anything at all?" I demanded. "Why answer any questions? Didn't they read you your rights?"

Again he nodded. "They read me my rights. Fuck 'em. Fuck their rights. So they booked me." Then he smiled, but it was an odd smile, almost sly, crafty, as though he'd put a fast one over on the cops. *They'd* be sorry, all right. *I'll* show 'em.

I made a face which I hope was commiserative.

"Okay, Fred," I said, "I'll do what I can to help. The first thing is to find you a lawyer."

"I don't have much money, Nick." He started coughing, rather violently, and wiping his eyes. The smoke from his festering cigarette was beginning to sting my eyes, too. "Rewrite that line. I don't have *any* money to speak of."

"We'll work something out, Fred. You're a member of the Authors Guild, aren't you?"

"Yes."

"I believe they have a fund of some kind to lend out. So does The Players. The John Drew Fund, appropriately enough. Anyway, let me worry about that for now. Is there anything you need here, Fred?"

"Yeah, but I don't think you'll be able to provide it for me."

"What is it?"

He pantomimed lifting a glass to his lips and chugalugging. Typical. It was the sauce that had done him in, and still he wanted more of it. Once an alcoholic . . .

I knew there was no way I could or even would bring him liquor, but I've always thought that if I were in prison, or in a hospital, I would be grateful if some Good Samaritan were to supply me with a martini or two. On that score, I remember visiting a colleague once in North Shore Hospital on Long Island. I brought along a small thermos of martinis, and in turn was given a hospital lunch at the same time my colleague was served—one of the best lunches I have ever enjoyed, in a hospital or out: a small, rare filet mignon, with tiny roasted new potatoes, and asparagus in butter and garlic sauce. Only the proper red wine was lacking.

"I'll be back when I have news for you, Fred," I said, and got up. The guard stiffened to attention. "It's okay," I told him. "I'm just leaving."

"Thanks for coming, Nick," said the poet.

Poet indeed. *Un poète maudit,* the French would call him. A poet cursed.

That same day I called my attorney for all seasons, Alex Margolies, and told him about Drew's plight.

"Sure you want to get involved in this, Nick?"

"Why not? I believe he's being jobbed. Frederick Drew didn't kill anybody."

"I'm only sugge*st*ing," Margolies continued, "that it's like the Chinese thing—you know, if you save a man's life in China, you become responsible for him. You want to be responsible for that lush?"

"Not particularly. Anyway, this is not China. I just want to get him out of jail."

"Well, he needs a lawyer, all right, but not me. I don't do criminal work myself, or windows. Give me a juicy tax problem to unsnarl, and I'm blissed out."

"Got any suggestions?"

"I understand that Andrew Svenson is probably available. At least I haven't seen his name in the papers recently. You remember Svenson—the guy who tied you in knots when you testified at that hood's trial?"

"He didn't exactly tie me in *knots,* Alex. Actually—"

"Made a monkey out of you, no?"

Yes. Svenson had made me appear foolish in court on the occasion of the hearing of one Salvatore Marco, whom I had accused of attempting to mug me—but I wouldn't hold that against the lawyer; he was only doing his job. If he was the best man around when habeas corpus was the issue, bring him on, by all means.

Which is what I instructed Alex Margolies to do. Posthaste.

Watching Claire Bunter enter the Grill Room of The Players at exactly six-fifteen, not a minute more or less, I understood immediately why Parker Foxcroft had taken her under his capacious wing. If she didn't exactly walk in beauty like the night, she did shine in her own way. She was exceptionally tall, but her proportions would have pleased any sculptor from Praxiteles to Rodin. Auburn hair caught back in a barrette, and high, finely cut cheekbones. Kirghiz eyes, the kind Hans Castorp found in Frau Chauchat in Thomas Mann's *The Magic Mountain.* The only flaw in an otherwise cinematic face was her nose, which was a shade too long and too thin.

I had told Claire that dress in the Club between Memorial Day and Labor Day was always casual. She was wearing a skirt short enough to advertise her splendid brown legs and part of her equally well-tanned thighs, and a light cotton vee-neck sweater, blue and white stripes, with short sleeves.

I set my martini glass down on the table and rose from my banquette to greet her.

"Claire, your latest jacket photograph doesn't do you justice."

She smiled and sat down in the armchair facing me. "Maybe next time you ought to hire Annie Leibovitz."

"Ouch."

"Never mind, Nick. I'm much more concerned with what's inside my books than how they're packaged."

"You don't believe that a book can be judged by its cover?"

"I only know that your books never look cheap."

"Thank you."

"Even if they are."

Zing. We were sparring with each other, but to what purpose I could not tell. I decided I'd better ease off. "What are you drinking, Claire?"

"Rum and Diet Coke."

Cuba Libre. I wonder if anyone calls it that anymore. Only in Miami, perhaps.

After I fetched her drink and a small plate of crackers and cheese, I raised my glass, touched hers lightly, and said: "Confusion to the enemy."

"I'll drink to that."

"Claire," I said, "I appreciate your coming down here on such short notice—"

"I'm not exactly fighting off engagements, Nick."

"That isn't what I meant."

"I know, I know. Don't look so injured. Like a little boy whose game is going badly."

"Well, I'm sorry as hell about that. However, now that you're here, I'd like to talk book. As in your next one."

"Talking business? Here in these sacred precincts?"

I pursed my lips but said nothing. She took several rapid swallows of her drink and then brought it down on the table with an audible *clunk*.

"I know how you men adore this place. Your playpen, your little nineteenth-century hideaway."

"We have women members now, too," I protested. "Quite a few of them, and they also seem to enjoy these sacred precincts, as you put it."

"Nick, Nick . . . let's not argue the point. I'm too tired to argue. I've been slaving over a hot computer all day."

"I have no desire to argue, Claire, really. I mean it. Look, let's clear the air if we can. You were Parker's author—"

She looked as though I had struck her. Her face turned an angry red, her eyes glittered, her jaws tightened, and I thought for a moment she was going to hiss at me like a snake.

"—but he wasn't the only editor in town," I said, plowing on anyway, against all odds.

"There's something you ought to know, Nick." Her voice was not exactly filled with venom, but there was a frightening calmness about her manner, a deadly sincerity.

"I decided several months ago that I would never—never in this lifetime—ever publish another book with Parker Foxcroft, or any company he worked for. Even if it meant I would never be in print again."

"You disliked him that much?"

"I loathed him, I detested him, I'm glad he's dead. Is that strong enough for you?"

"Yeah—more than strong enough." Then I fell silent. Where was I going to go from here? How in hell was I going to turn *this* conversation around? "Claire," I said, "I ran into Harry last weekend on a Metro North train."

"How did he look?" Her voice, which had been harsh before, in an intense and quiet way, softened.

"Terrible."

Drawing a deep breath, she leaned back in her chair and shook her head back and forth slowly.

"It was his idea to move out, not mine," she said, speaking as though I wasn't there at all. "I didn't kick him out. He could have stayed. It was over. All over . . ."

"I'm sorry," was all I could think to say.

She brightened, or at least she managed to manufacture a smile of sorts. "Anyhow, I'm discovering what it's like to be alone again in the big bad city."

"And how is it? In the big bad city?"

"Not so big—and not so bad. Do you believe that?"

"Not really."

"Good. Because it ain't so. I rather miss Harry, the lovable slob. Would you tell him that?"

"Sure. Another rum and Coke?"

"I'll pass. No, I'll take a rain check."

"Good. And, Claire—"

"Yes?"

"I'll get in touch with your agent. Is it still Bruno Wiley?"

"Still. And thanks for the drink, Nick."

After she had left, I sat there thinking. Thinking—and drinking. More thinking than drinking. What had Harry Bunter said on the train about his wife? *Claire is capable of anything.* "Anything" was the word he stressed. Did that

include murder? One thing was clear: she hated Parker
Foxcroft with a crystal-pure passion.

And I thought I knew why. He had dumped her. Frankie
and Johnny all over again? It could well be.

Chapter 23

On Friday Herbert Poole and I were back in Parker Foxcroft's office for the third day, plowing through what seemed to be every scrap of paper the man ever covered, some pages with bile, others with syrup. As his "literary executor," I was uncertain what to do with the stuff, as we read and then tossed it aside. Would anyone want to buy it? I wondered. Could I even give it away? Somehow Parker had overestimated the value of his notes and letters, at least that's how it seemed to me. I decided to beg the question by packing it all away in cardboard book cartons from our shipping room, that portion of it which hadn't drifted to the floor, where even now a mound of it had gathered. I would decide later what to do with it.

Still, even the most Herculean task must come to an end sometime, and this one was wound up around the cocktail hour.

"Thank God," I said.

"Amen," said Poole. "Do we have it all?"

"I devoutly hope so."

"And what do we have?"

"As far as I can tell, nothing. When it comes to the rejection letters, we're left with a good zillion potential suspects but no clues. Too bad he didn't keep a journal of some kind."

"Well," said Poole, "at least we haven't *lost* any ground."

"By the way," I said, "we've been so busy burrowing into Parker's verbiage that we haven't discussed your book."

"*Pan at Twilight?*"

"Not that book—your mystery. The one you're going to write for me, remember?"

He laughed, more a chuckle than a laugh, but I've never cared for the expression "He chuckled." It doesn't sound serious enough.

"I'd be happy to talk about it," Poole said. "I've only got the idea for the book now, but it's taking shape in my mind."

"Good. Let's hear about it."

For a variety of reasons, I no longer felt comfortable in Parker's office, if I ever had, so I motioned Poole to follow me, and led the way back to my own office. It isn't exactly that I felt Parker's presence in his office, nothing like that; he didn't *haunt* the place, thank God, because it was expensive real estate and I couldn't afford to let it stand vacant much longer. Nevertheless, I couldn't forget that I'd found his body there. The blood may have been washed away, but the memory of that moment was still powerful. Violent death can't just be forgotten or brushed aside—Susan Markham's injunction to let the dead bury the dead notwithstanding.

"So tell me," I said to Poole, when we were at ease on leather chairs in my familiar wood-paneled and book-lined nest. "What do you plan to do?"

"I respect what you said about the mystery genre," he

said. "About it being fantasy? And I think you're probably right—for the most part."

"No generality holds up against every particular, as we know."

Poole got up and began to pace back and forth as he spoke. "Do you remember the Casolaro case?"

I thought for a moment. "Vaguely. A writer, wasn't he?"

"It happened several years ago," Poole continued. "Joseph Casolaro was a freelance writer working on an article about a suspected government conspiracy. He had been investigating a case in which the owners of a computer software company accused the Justice Department of stealing programs the company had designed to track criminal cases worldwide. Justice denied all the allegations and resisted the computer company's challenges in court."

"I do remember reading about it. Casolaro may have been close to uncovering some kind of huge, Watergate-like conspiracy, right? And he was found dead in a West Virginia motel room."

"That's it. The authorities considered it suicide because it looked like suicide. But he told his brother two months before his death that if he died in an accident, 'don't believe it.' Also, the guy had received death threats, and, although he was a conscientious reporter, none of his investigative notes were found in his motel room."

"You believe he was murdered."

Poole stopped pacing and rested his hands on my desk, looking straight into my eyes. "I do," he said. "And because I can't really prove anything, and I'm not a journalist, I intend to fictionalize the story. And if I can, solve it. What do you think, Nick?"

I crossed the room to the low bookcase where the bronze

bust of my father stood on its wooden pedestal, reached down, and pulled out a Library of America volume of Edgar Allan Poe.

"The Mystery of Marie Roget," I said. "Based on the murder of a young New York woman named Mary Rogers. Poe wrote the novel in an attempt to solve the case through pure ratiocination."

"And did he succeed?" asked Poole.

"No. He claimed to have solved it, but he was fudging the issue. Actually no one ever found a solution to the case."

"Maybe I'll have better luck," said Poole. He smiled. "Worth a try, anyway."

"I agree, I definitely agree. Go ahead with it. And let me know how you're doing."

After Poole had left, I turned to the phone messages, notes, and correspondence I'd ignored in favor of combing through Parker Foxcroft's Mount Rushmore of paper.

One envelope stood out: mint green and lightly perfumed. It bore the monogram "SSM." I tore it open.

"Nick, darling," the note read, "6 little words: Call, if ever you need me. Love, Susan."

I picked up the phone and dialed her number. Four rings and then the answering machine kicked in. "This is Susan speaking. I can't come to the phone just now, but if you'll leave your name and number, I'll return your call as soon as I can." *Beep.*

"Hello, Susan," I said. "I would recognize your notepaper anywhere; it's the color of your eyes. I would recognize your perfume anywhere, too; its scent still clings to a pillow in my bedroom. As for your voice, it makes me think of cocktail piano music played softly in a dimly lit bar. Three little words: I miss you." I had barely finished when I was cut off.

I returned to the tasks at hand, most of which required signing correspondence and initialing memos I had dictated earlier, between sessions with Poole.

Shortly before five, a call came from Alex Margolies.

"We've got Frederick Drew out of durance vile," he said. "That is, Svenson has. He's going to be arraigned on Tuesday, however, and we may require bail. Are you willing to post the bond?"

I swallowed hard and said yes. Mortimer Mandelbaum wouldn't like this. *Mother* wouldn't like this, either. Tim would probably think I was getting softheaded as well as softhearted. So why was I doing it? I believed I knew my man. He wouldn't skip, and he wasn't guilty. At least *I* thought so.

"I'll keep you posted," said Alex. "By the way, he's most grateful. I believe he means to dedicate a sonnet sequence to you."

"That's wonderful."

"Have a pleasant weekend, Nick."

"The same to you. *Shalom aleichem.*"

I had decided that maybe it wasn't all that safe to stick around the Barlow & Company offices after darkness had set in, so I stuck several chapters of Sarah Goodall's private-eye novel in my briefcase and left.

It was five-thirty when I stepped out of the building, and the heat was stifling. New York in summer can be like Calcutta, but that's usually in July or August, not in mid-June. Anyway, it was hot hot hot and so humid I began to sweat the instant I hit the outside air. I walked out to the curb and paused, waiting for the traffic light to turn green.

I hardly noticed the man who approached from the right; I was only aware of him when suddenly he seized the sleeve of my jacket and pulled me roughly away from the spot where I was standing. At the same time, I could sense that something had come hurtling down alongside me, brushing close by but not touching me. When whatever it was shattered on the sidewalk, a chip flew up and hit my cheek.

"My *God*," I said. I had probably meant to say something about the rudeness of strangers, but I realized in time that this particular stranger had undoubtedly saved my life. "What the hell happened?"

"Are you all right, sir?" asked my benefactor.

"Sure, just a scratch, I think." I put my hand up to my cheek, and when I drew it away, there was blood on one of my fingers.

We both then looked down at what had fallen, from God knows how many flights up. It was a heavy stone urn, such as one puts funerary ashes in—but it was empty. That was a relief; I'd hate to have been brained by somebody's last remains.

I turned to the man who had pulled me away from the path of the urn. He was short, stout, almost pear-shaped. Behind his Coke-bottle glasses, his eyes blinked incessantly. Despite the heat, he wore a felt hat—to cover his baldness, I suspected.

"I don't know how to thank you," I said. "Jesus, that was close."

"No need for thanks, no need at all." He reached out and touched my arm, a light, solicitous touch this time. "Sure you're all right?"

"Quite sure."

"Well, then—" He nodded, touched the brim of his hat, and started to move off.

"Wait a minute, sir," I said. "Won't you tell me who I must be grateful to?"

"Certainly." He pulled a small leather case out of his pocket and extracted a business card, which he handed to me. "My name is Flitcraft, Homer B. Flitcraft. I'm from Spokane, Washington State. I'm in real estate out there."

"Mr. Flitcraft," I said, "I can't tell you how much I appreciate this. But how—"

I was going to say, "How can I thank you?" or something of the sort, but he finished the sentence for me.

"How did it happen? It was just good fortune that I came along when I did, and that I happened to be looking up while you were looking down. I saw this object falling, and grabbed you. Anyone else would have done the same, don't you think? Good evening."

And he walked off. I looked more closely at his card. "Homer B. Flitcraft, Real Estate Broker," followed by his address, phone number, and fax number. Odd little man, but a godsend.

What could I do to thank him? Send him one of my books? Perhaps he didn't read. Well, if I ever got to Spokane . . .

But why on earth would I want to go to Spokane?

And why in the world did an urn just happen to drop precisely where I had been standing?

I dabbed my cheek with my handkerchief and started walking.

If it was an accident, it was certainly freaky. Just suppose it wasn't an accident at all. What was I to make of that? Nick Barlow, still running lucky—as Artie the cop had observed.

*   *   *

When I got out to Connecticut that weekend, I brought Mother and Tim up to speed on recent events, doing my best to downplay the shotgun incident and the falling urn.

Of the former, Mother, as usual, had a theory.

"But surely the burglars intended to rob *our* firm, Nicholas, not the jeweler."

"I don't follow that, Mother."

"The break-in at the jeweler's must have been a cover for the one at Barlow and Company. Undoubtedly they wanted to steal something in one of our offices. Yes, that's it. Possibly something in Mr. Foxcroft's office, something that has to do with his murder."

"Like what?"

"*Humph.* You can't expect me to work out every detail, now can you?" She snorted again. "You or the police will have to find the rest of the answers."

Mother's theory seemed to me as full of holes as one of her lace doilies, but, as always, I forbore to challenge her. Domestic harmony meant more to me in Connecticut than scoring points—unlike New York City, where I usually find myself as aggressive as the next man, unless the next man is lurking in a darkened doorway with a switchblade.

Of the urn, Tim's first question: "Was it Grecian?"

I didn't think that worthy of a response, either.

When I was closeted with Tim in his upstairs apartment, I admitted that the shotgun and the urn had both unnerved me.

"When it comes to the shotgun," I said, "I suspect I just happened to be in the right place at the wrong time. The urn, however, seemed aimed at me and no one else. Or so I think, though I could be mistaken—maybe that, too, was an accident. What's your opinion, Tim?"

"Whether it was blind chance that the urn fell, or someone's intention to kill you, I figure you ought to be grateful that Mr. Flitcraft was there."

"Oh, I am."

"His presence," said Tim, "was probably the real accident."

"So you think I was targeted."

He nodded. "You may represent a threat to somebody in this investigation, Nick."

"I prefer just being a suspect."

When I then told Tim about how thorough a search Poole and I had made through Parker's files, he smiled in approval and said: "Of course you checked his computer hard drive, too."

I must have looked dumbstruck, because Tim shook his head sadly, as though thinking: *my idiot brother, as usual.*

"You didn't?"

"Not yet."

"But you intend to."

"Oh sure, Tim. As soon as I get back to the office."

Leave it to Tim to puncture any show of smugness on my part. Before leaving, I asked Tim what he was reading these days. He pointed to a stack of books on his night table. "You see there the complete works of your latest acquisition."

"Poole?"

"Right. His first three novels. *Time Lock. The Edge of the Precipice. Cody Appleton.* And his best-seller, *Pan at Twilight.*"

Tim picked up one of the novels, opened it to the back flap, and said, "He's a Virginian."

"Yes, I recognized the accent."

"Herbert Poole, Jr., was born in Newport News, Virginia," Tim read, "the son of a naval officer. He attended elementary school at Hilton Village, Virginia, and completed his high school training at Christ Church School, Virginia. He attended Davidson College and the University of Virginia." Tim broke off, and closed the book. "I guess that makes him a Virginian, all right."

"And what do you think of his books?"

"I'm barely into them," replied Tim, "and I'm really reading them to see what kind of writer he is—what sort of mystery he might do for us. That's the point of the exercise."

"Well, let me know if you think I ought to read them, too."

"So far as I can tell, he's good. He's damn good. I think you've got a winner."

"Hallelujah."

On that Sunday, Mother as much as dragged me down Kellogg Hill Road to the neighborhood Episcopal church, whether to give thanks for my deliverance from evil, or just to improve my character, I can't be sure.

The Emmanuel Episcopal church is as unlike the Little Church Around the Corner as two such houses of worship could be. To begin with, Emmanuel ought to be the one called "the Little Church." It was built in the style of an early New England meeting house, and could easily be a Congregational or Presbyterian parish. Plain, down-to-earth architecture; no frills. The walls painted white, the only decoration a large wooden cross hung above an unpretentious altar. However, there is a cleanliness, a sparse beauty in that style, which I find enormously soothing, even if I'm just sitting there and not paying too close attention to the service itself. A rather Low Church service—no incense or chanting, such as you'll find in the Church of the Transfiguration. The sun was streaming through the windows on my left, setting the chandeliers aglitter, and a breeze blew across the pews from the open windows. I found life, the world, mankind even, to be passing fair, or at least not as bad as they might be. The choir sang with gusto, the minister did not make too much of an ass of himself by preaching about original sin or man's wickedness to man—I'd had enough of that lately. And I was making my mother happy.

When we stepped out into the bright sunshine, I took a deep breath and drew in the splendors of a Connecticut summer: flowers of every color in full bloom, the trees leafed out, and the scent of pine in the air.

Turning to my mother, I said: "One of those June days that Will Shakespeare found so rare, isn't it?"

"It surely is," she said, and took my arm as we followed the other members of the congregation down the sidewalk to our car.

Once again, the countryside had worked its restorative magic on my troubled spirit, and I could go back to the city much strengthened.

Chapter 24

I called Herbert Poole as soon as I reached the office next morning and told him what Tim had recommended.

"The hard drive? I ought to have thought of that."

"Do you know anything about computers, Herbert?" Somehow I didn't feel equal to the task ahead, not alone, anyway.

"I sure do," he said. "I have had quite a bit of experience with them. I've already run through two computers and I'm putting a lot of mileage on the third."

"Then if you don't mind—"

"Absolutely not, Nick. I'll be right there."

Poole was a man of his word, as I would expect a Virginian to be. ("When you say that, *smile*.") He was beginning to become a familiar figure around the office, so the receptionist did not bother to notify me that he was here, but must have waved him on through, because the next thing I knew he was knocking softly on my door. I led him immediately down the hall to Parker's office.

At the computer terminal, he sat down, flexed his fingers

as though he was about to play a Chopin étude, and while I stood looking over his shoulder, he booted the operating system. The screen lit up, and we saw four sectors on the screen—INFORMATION, YOUR SOFTWARE, MICROSOFT WORKS, and IBM DOS. He moved the cursor to YOUR SOFTWARE and clicked the mouse. We saw the following menu on the screen:

THE PROGRAM DIRECTOR

1. WORDPERFECT 5.1
2. UTILITIES
3. LOTUS 1-2-3
4. ACT
5. JEOPARDY
6. MOVIE MASTER

SELECTION: _____

"I believe this is what we want," said Poole, and typed in the number 4. The screen told us it was loading for a few seconds, and this appeared:

AUTOMATED CONTACT TRACKING
Enter password for database C:\ACTZ\ACT.CCD:

Below that on the left was a box with eight compartments and a flashing cursor.

"This is where it gets tricky," said Poole. "We need Parker's personal password to get into the program."

I clucked my tongue against my teeth. I hadn't counted on this particular roadblock; I supposed Poole had. "How do we find that?"

"Guesswork is all we can go on," he said. "He's not likely to have written it down. Most people use something easy to remember. Like the month of their birth or their astrological sign. Their own name, maybe. Why don't we start with that?" He went to work on the keyboard and the box, and promptly typed in PARKER. No go. FOXCROFT brought the same results.

"Let's try words that can be formed from the letters of his name," said Poole. And he ran through PARK, PEAK, REAP, RAKE, and PERK, without hitting the jackpot. Then he typed FOX, COOP, FOOT, FORT, and TOX, to no avail.

"Do you suppose you can find out the month of Parker's birth?" asked Poole.

"Just a phone call away," I said, and buzzed Hannah. I told her what we wanted, and to get Parker's file from personnel. While we were waiting, Poole explained to me what the ACT software was—a way of keeping a database of all one's contacts, with the necessary information about them. Would Parker need such a database? I wondered. Conceivably, Poole told me.

The phone rang. It was Hannah.

"April eighteenth," she reported.

Poole tried APRIL and APRIL18. Nothing. Then ARIES. Still no luck.

"We haven't thought of one other possibility," said Poole. "Did the man have a middle name?"

As it turned out when we posed the question to Hannah, Parker, like many another WASP, had not one but *two* middle names: Henry and Edgar.

Poole put HENRY in the frustrating little box first, and we struck out again.

But when he typed EDGAR—success! We got this:

FILE   EDIT   LOOK UP   VIEW   REPORTS

CONTACT _____   Address _____

Name _____   City _____

Title _____   State _____

Phone _____   Zip _____

LAST CONTACT _____

CALL _____

STATUS _____

USER DEFINED:

NOTES:

"What do we do now?" I asked.

Poole moved the cursor to FILE and clicked it. A "pull down" window appeared in the upper right-hand part of the screen, with this list:

OPEN

NEW

DELETE

EXIT

"We go to OPEN," said Poole.

He did so, and another window appeared just below the first one.

_____ DATABASES LIST
_____ AUTHORS
_____ PUBLISHING HOUSES
_____ AGENTS
_____ PERSONAL

Now we were off and running. We went to AUTHORS first.

"See if you can find 'Michaelson, Alexander,' " I said. He was not on the list.

"PERSONAL?" Poole suggested. I nodded.

And that was where we hit pay dirt—emphasis on dirt. For PERSONAL was nothing more nor less than the amorous history, "the sexual conquests" if you will, of the late Parker Foxcroft. Disgusting. As a man about town, I've certainly enjoyed my sexual encounters—though I never thought of them as conquests, just various successes—but to write them down, and in a database at that, I find utterly disgusting.

"How many names are there in this database?" I asked.

"One hundred fifty," said Poole.

I considered this figure. Not enough to get Parker into the *Guinness Book of Records,* by far, but a substantial achievement for one not yet forty. I remembered, however, that there are star basketball players who number their so-called victories in the thousands—though it seems to me that unless they can recall the names of every bed partner and the precise details of each gratification, the numbers are inconsequential.

"It's possible, of course, that Parker kept other records," I said.

"Of course," said Poole.

It might have been squeamishness on my part, but I just didn't want to confront the data on one Susan Markham, who was most assuredly in Parker's files, so I asked Poole if he would mind combing through the files by himself, paying particular attention to anyone who might have even the faintest connection with Parker's murder.

"One file I'd like to read myself," I said. "Would you print out whatever Parker entered on Claire Bunter?"

"Glad to."

And I left him to explore the libidinous exploits of Parker Foxcroft.

Chapter 25

The call I had been waiting for came the following morning.

"Nick, darling," said the voice I had last heard on an answering machine, "it's Susan. How are you?"

"Susan," I said, "you know, you can make the most threadbare phrase in the language, 'How are you?' sound like you just thought it up."

"That's sweet, Nick—but altogether exaggerated. Anyway, I meant it—how *are* you?"

"The better for hearing from you, my dear."

"I'd have called before," she said, "except I've been out of town briefly. Now that I'm back—"

"Let's get together?"

"Right." I heard a *click* in the telephone receiver. "Oh damn," she said, "it's another call. D'you mind, Nick? I'll just find out who it is and be back in two secs. Don't go away, promise? Are you sure you don't mind?"

"No, I don't mind," I said, but I did mind. Damn call interruptus, anyhow, and cursed be he or she who invented it in the first place. Perhaps I oughtn't to complain, though;

I don't have it because I don't need it—but what if I were without someone to answer my phone?

"I'm back, Nick. It was nothing important—just the office."

"Stupid of me," I said. "That's where I thought you were."

"No, I'm at home."

"At ten o'clock on a Tuesday workday?"

"My trip was business, darling, including the weekend, so I decided to give myself a day off. Anything wrong with that?"

"Not so far as I'm concerned."

"Moreover, I want you to spend it with me—part of it, anyway."

"Which part is that?"

"Come to my place for lunch, Nick—I've got a surprise for you."

"Oh? What is it?"

"Typical reaction. It's a surprise, that's what it is."

I looked down at my calendar. Mirabile dictu, no lunch date; already a pleasant surprise. I'd had lunches booked solidly every day for almost two weeks.

"What do you know," I said, "I'm free."

"I'll expect you around one," Susan said.

"Okay—"

"And be sure to cancel any afternoon appointments you might have on your calendar. Bye, dear."

What, I wondered, was I getting myself into? *An assignation, that's all, dummy,* said my inner demon. *A seductive trap,* said my guardian angel. *You're getting yourself entangled. Think of Margo.*

But does Margo think of me? Besides, it's a lovely way to spend an afternoon.

It is the essence, the special savor, of a love affair, to be secretive, clandestine, if you will, even if there is no reason for concealment—another spouse, perhaps. Marriage is so open, so public—everybody *knows* what you're up to on Saturday night or Sunday morning—but a love affair! There you have the possibility of brief encounters, eyes across the table, legs touching on the banquette, kisses in the backseats of cars, and heart-pounding synergies—how's that for a euphemism?—in parked cars on moonlight nights. And best of all—*nobody* knows!

All this ran through my mind after my phone call with Susan, until I was interrupted—not by another phone call—but by Herbert Poole.

"Morning, Nick," he said, closing the door softly behind him. "I hope I'm not interrupting anything."

"Not at all, Herbert. Come on in."

He crossed the room and put two sheets of paper on my desk blotter.

"This is the Claire Bunter file you asked for," he said.

"Oh good," I said, lifting the sheets and holding them up at arm's length. "Can't wait to read this." I stared at Poole, who was smiling at some private joke of his own. "Is it gamey, Herbert?"

"It's"—he allowed himself another one of his chuckles—"titillating, I would say."

"Are you still working on the hard drive?"

"Still. There's some way to go to get to the end of this database, hear? I'm only up to number sixty-five of one hundred fifty."

Not up to Susan yet, I thought grimly.

"Well, carry on. I do appreciate your help, Herbert."

"Glad to be of use, Nick." And he took his leave.

I picked up the first sheet of Claire Bunter's file from Parker's database.

It started with her name, address, and phone number, and then listed these entries:

LAST CONTACT: May 4, this year
CALL: Don't call
STATUS: Limbo
USER DEFINED: Former lover

It was the NOTES, however, that engaged my full attention. The entries were short and always explicit. The first one was dated over a year ago and described the beginning of the affair. They had just had a vinous lunch at The Four Seasons, and Parker drove her home in a cab through Central Park. On the journey, he kissed her, shyly, as he reported it, but when she responded by opening her mouth and tonguing him, he drew back and whispered, "Not yet. But soon," and drew her hand down to touch his erection. This gambit apparently inflamed her latent passion, or so he remarked. Not long afterward, Parker's editorial conferences with Claire ripened into meetings at his apartment, where he seduced her with dreams of glory and his intuitive awareness that Claire was ready, after years of marriage, to embark on a liaison with her brilliant and charming editor. "Your books have just not been properly edited, Claire dear," he told her. "Your talent has not been properly appreciated."

"To win a woman over," Parker wrote in his notes on Claire, "you must always tell her what she most wants to hear, whatever it is."

They met, I read on, in his apartment mainly, but also at a summer writers' conference they both attended in Vermont where, Parker noted, "we ran all the changes on 'the beast with two backs'—both in the cabins where we were housed

and in the deep sun-dappled woods, on thick beds of leaves
and pine boughs. Also in the lake, late at night, skinny-
dipping." Parker seemed quite proud of his ability to mount
his lady love, or to sustain her while she mounted him,
several times a night . . .

I felt, reading this stuff, knowing I had no business
reading it, that I was invading Claire Bunter's privacy, and
that I had no excuse for such an intrusion except that I had
good reason to suspect her of murdering Parker. If I could
establish motive and opportunity, all this would be worthwhile, however unpleasant.

I skipped to the end of Parker's entries, where he remarked: "Claire is pressing me to 'do something' about our
situation, as though there was anything I could do. She is
becoming a nag, wants more of me and my attention than
I can give her, threatens to tell her husband about us and
ask for a divorce so that we can marry. Not possible, I tell
her, I wouldn't marry you even if you were free. Of course
I don't blame her for being angry . . ."

There followed a series of transcripts of phone messages
Claire had left on his answering machine, messages I found
particularly weird:

You don't know what you're doing, walking out on
me like this. You don't know what you're giving up.
Why haven't you called me? (Click)

Where are you? Where the hell are you? I can't stand
this, it's disgusting. How can you do this to me, you
pig? (Click)

It's four o'clock in the morning and I just woke up.

Four o'clock—about time to reach over and grab a breast. Who are you with this time? Is it the woman I saw you leaving your office with yesterday? (Click)

I just have to add one more comment on this whole situation 'cause if what I think is going on, you're really . . . you're sick! I hope you have a coronary! (Click)

Last call, darling. I think you're one of the biggest assholes I've ever known. You just threw it away. You just threw something good so easily away. (Sigh . . . click)

Really the last call, DAMN YOU! You know you're lucky I didn't have a knife handy when you walked out on me last week. I wanted to kill you! I still do, you bastard! (Click)

I put the file aside, leaned back in my chair, and made a steeple out of my fingertips. I had not thought that Claire Bunter, on the surface a poised, sophisticated woman, could nurture so much anger and resentment. I had read enough of her work to know that she saw life, as they say, steadily and whole. Surely she must have known that an adulterous affair, however exciting, must end sometime, and often badly. However, if I have one cardinal virtue, it is this: I am, where human emotions are concerned, completely nonjudgmental.

But not where murder is concerned. I probably ought to tell Lieutenant Hatcher about Parker's files. First, though, I thought I'd better seek Joe Scanlon's advice.

* * *

After my deep immersion in the erotic legacy of Parker Foxcroft, I felt I needed a bath. The next best thing, I decided, was to be with Susan Markham. I told Hannah that I would not be returning after lunch and that she should field all calls and inquiries.

"What about Herbert Poole?" she asked.

"He's to have complete access to Foxcroft's office," I said, "and anything he might need."

Stepping out on the street to head for East 55th Street, I hailed a cab, and miracle of miracles, it turned out to be a Checker. I climbed in gratefully; it looked as though it was going to turn out to be a memorable day, after all.

"How many of these beauties are still left?" I asked the driver, a somewhat wizened middle-aged man. *Angelo Martelli. 45703.* I don't know why, but I always make a mental note of a cabdriver's name and usually the number. You never know when you might need it.

"Ten, I think," he said.

Only ten. The last time I snared a Checker there were twelve of them. Think of the odds against running across one. Where, I wondered, had they gone; and why had the cab companies ever given them up in favor of those grungy little Dodges? In my salad days, there were dozens of Checkers on the city streets, roomy enough so that even a disabled person could get into them, all with jump seats and a wealth of legroom. Now—well, I have never subscribed to any belief in the progress of mankind or its ultimate improvement.

The ride, as I expected, was a happy one, and when we pulled up in front of Susan's apartment building, I gladly overtipped the driver. "Don't let this baby go," I told him.

He hadn't spoken during the ride, and now he only grunted his thanks, but I could tell he was pleased.

Susan greeted me at the door of her apartment by kissing me sweetly, then drawing me inside with both hands.

"You're early," she said.

"Couldn't wait, could you?"

"Absolutely not."

She was wearing a white satin robe, belted, trimmed at the cuffs and the hem with lace. And, as far as I could tell, nothing else.

"The first thing," she said, struggling with my jacket, "is to get *this* off, and then"—tugging at my necktie—*"this."*

"What's the third thing?"

"I'm sure you don't need any help finding the bedroom, do you, Nick?"

By now we had begun to learn the secrets of each other's bodies, and their hidden rhythms, so it was some long time before we drew apart, still clasping hands, but spent and silent. There was no need for either of us to ask if it had been good.

When I started to get out of bed, Susan pushed me back down. "Stay right there, sir," she said, "for your first surprise."

It was a linen robe, periwinkle blue, with a shawl collar.

"Hey," I said. "Where did this come from?"

"Saks. I dropped in there this morning."

"Well, I thank you kindly."

"Now you know that you can stop by anytime and you'll always be decent."

I kissed her, just a touch of the lips. "Are you, or are you not, the best thing that's happened to me since I can't remember when?" I hugged her again. "You are."

"I think," she said, drawing back but at the same time

running her hand down the side of my face, "that I'd better see to lunch."

"I hope you haven't gone to too much trouble . . ."

"I've made a quiche and a salad," she said, "and I promise you won't gain any weight. But first, the wine. It's my other surprise."

I followed her into the kitchen, where she opened the refrigerator and took out a bottle.

"I hope it's chilled enough," she said, holding the bottle up for my inspection. It was a rosé, God forbid.

"It's special," Susan said.

"Oh?" *How on earth could that wine be special?* I hoped my disappointment wouldn't be too plain to see. I put on my best smile, even though it was more painful to produce than my worst frown. "How so, Susan?"

"Well," she said, clearly pleased, "it arrived at my office with a card that read, 'From a grateful author.' Isn't that neat, Nick?"

"I'll say," I said. "Any idea who the author is?"

"No, but I hope it is who I think it is—one of Little, Brown's most difficult authors."

"Susan dear, they're *all* difficult, aren't they?"

"Now, don't be cynical, darling. Here, let's drink a toast."

She brought out two stemware glasses and poured the wine into them, almost to the brim.

"To us," she said.

"To us," I echoed, and took a sip. Somehow a sip seemed to be enough. I know it is snobbish, but I have never been able to appreciate rosé. I consider it an adulterated wine, neither white nor red. You might as well drink that carbonated stuff from Portugal—I forget its name. I hoped I could get away with just another sip or two.

Meanwhile, Susan was emptying her glass with obvious relish, chatting away and fussing around with her salad. Suddenly it seemed to me that the most important thing in the world was for Susan to be happy, even if I had to drink a glass of rosé to achieve it.

I was about to have another swallow, shutting down my olfactory sense as I did so, when something odd happened. Susan belched.

"Oh my," she said. "Oh my Lord." And then she hiccuped. "Excuse . . . excuse . . ." I put my wineglass down and turned to her. She was swaying, ever so slightly.

"Are you all right?" I asked.

"I don't feel so good, Nick," she said, almost inaudibly. "Excuse me . . . okay . . . I think I'll—" And with that, she bolted for the bathroom.

"Need any help?" I called. There was no answer, but shortly afterward I heard the sound of retching from behind the bathroom door.

What the hell? I hadn't thought the wine was *that* bad, just ordinarily unappetizing. I picked up the bottle and looked at it. *Armand de Jacquin Gamay Rosé.* So who are you, Armand de Jacquin?

The cork was lying beside the bottle. It was dry, usually a bad sign. When the wine steward brings you the cork, you're supposed to feel if it's slightly damp, as it ought to be, not smell it, as some people do.

Then I noticed something strange. Several tiny holes in the top and bottom of the cork.

I picked it up and called out: "Are you okay? Susan?"

My only answer was a soft moan from the bathroom.

And by now I was beginning to feel . . . nauseous. Dizzy, in fact. The wine—something wrong with the wine.

Holy shit, I thought, have we been poisoned? But who? Why?

"Susan!" I cried out, but I don't think she heard me, for there was no answer. I made my way to the bathroom, step by step, hoping that I wouldn't vomit before I got there.

"Susan . . ." This time I could barely croak her name. "Oh my God . . ."

She was lying on the bathroom floor, her head resting against the base of the toilet.

Somehow I managed to get back to the living room. The phone . . . pick up the phone . . . dial 911 . . .

Three numbers to dial. They took forever. And then I remembered nothing. Nothing at all.

Chapter 26

The voice came from a long, long way off. *"Niiick,"* the voice said. *"Can . . . you . . . hear me . . . Nick?"* So faint, so far away, it might have been disembodied, celestial even.

I attempted to speak, but could only utter a strangled croak, an unearthly, subhuman sound. My eyes were still tightly closed; I struggled to open the lids.

Then the sense of touch came back, and by groping around with my hands, I could tell that I was lying on a bed, that my head was on a pillow.

At last my eyes came open, and I saw, looming over me, a figure in white, eyes behind gleaming lenses, blinking at me. Again I opened my mouth to speak, but the same gurgling *aggh!* was all I could manage. It was then I realized that I could not speak because there was a tube of some kind stuck down my throat, choking me, blocking my vocal cords. For a moment I thought I was going to vomit, but the nausea passed and left me limp, sweating from what seemed to be every pore in my body.

"Mr. Barlow," said a voice, not the one I had heard at first, "you must not try to talk just now." The voice was calm, measured, soothing. It belonged to the figure in white with the glittering eyeglasses. A doctor, I thought, and with a bedside manner at that. Which meant that I—

"You're in a hospital," said the doctor, still hovering over me.

Which one? I wondered.

"Doctors."

Reassuring—a hospital full of doctors, of all things.

"We'll be taking that drain in your stomach out shortly, and then you'll be able to talk."

Thank God. Nick Barlow unable to talk is Nick Barlow disarmed.

It was something like an hour later when the drain was finally removed, and I was able to sit up. Shortly after that, I was assisted out of bed, seated in front of a table of some kind, and fed what tasted like mashed potatoes and creamed corn, although neither dish would ever pass muster even at a truck stop. Nevertheless, I ate greedily. Not only was I ravenous, but I was so relieved to be alive that I would have gobbled down anything at all.

Once again, I was assisted back into bed, by a nurse on one side and Joe Scanlon on the other.

"Joe," I said, "I'm glad you're here. I think I was poisoned."

He nodded. "You certainly were."

"But Susan," I said, sitting bolt upright in bed. "How is she, Joe? Tell me."

"She didn't make it," he said in the flat, unaccented way with which he probably delivered that sort of bad news to more than one survivor of a tragedy. "DOA, Nick."

"Oh *no!* Goddamn it, *why?* Why her, for God's sake?"

"I'm sorry, Nick, believe me," Scanlon said. "I gather she meant something to you."

"That, yes, and the damned unfairness of it. She was just too young, Joe."

Scanlon hunched his shoulders and sighed. Too many deaths, I thought. He's seen so many, and every last one of them probably unfair. And what is too young, anyhow?

"That's not all of it, Nick," he said. "There's more, I'm sorry to say."

"More what?"

"The police think you did it. That you poisoned the wine, Nick."

"But why in hell would I do that?"

"They'll do their best to figure that out."

Of course. It made perfect sense. If I had wanted to poison the wine, I'd have given a full glass to Susan, confident that she'd drink it, and only sip from my glass. Just enough to make me sick, not enough to kill me—but more than enough, probably, to kill *her*. Well, I'll be a son of a bitch . . .

I told Scanlon about the cork of the wine bottle.

"Hatcher and Falco will be paying you a visit shortly, Nick. Be sure to tell them about the cork. I beat them here only by posing as the investigating officer. I told the medics this was a homicide matter, and I'd have to question you as soon as you were conscious."

"But how did you find out I was here?"

He coughed and turned a light shade of red. "You were, shall I say, not dressed in your usual style, but there was a pocket diary in your jacket. Margo Richmond was listed as the one to call in an emergency. The ERS guys called her, and she called me. I hightailed over here as soon as I could."

"I'm certainly glad of that, Joe."

"And I suspect Margo will be here soon, too, Nick."

I leaned back, suddenly aware that my eyes were full of tears. Was I crying for Susan's death? Gratitude to be alive?

To have friends like Margo . . . like Joe Scanlon? All of the above, probably. *Thank you, Your Ineluctableness, whoever and whatever you are* . . .

After Scanlon had left, I slid into a dreary torpor, an immense lassitude that ultimately deepened into sleep. I don't know how long my nap lasted, but when I awoke in due course, Lieutenant Hatcher and Sergeant Falco were seated on either side of my bed.

"Do you feel up to answering a few questions, Mr. Barlow?" asked Hatcher.

"Sure," I said. "Fire away."

"Just tell us everything that happened, exactly as it happened."

Falco took out his faithful notebook and a stub of a pencil, which he gripped tightly in his left hand, poised for action.

After I had finished my recital, Hatcher was silent for a moment; leaning back in his chair, he stroked his chin and said: "You're sure about the punctures in the cork?"

"Positive."

"We'll send someone around to check on that. One other thing: the victim did not tell you who had sent the bottle of wine to her?"

"She didn't know who it was. The card was just signed, 'a grateful author.' "

"Did you see the card?"

"No, I didn't."

Addressing Falco, Hatcher said: "We'll look for the card, too. Meanwhile—"

"Yes, Lieutenant?"

"Don't plan on leaving town for a few days."

"I was thinking of going to Connecticut for the weekend. Once I get out of here, that is."

"Don't even go to Connecticut, okay?"

"Okay," I said, but my tone was anything but gracious. I have never liked being told where I may or may not go. *Some bloody nerve.*

Hatcher and Falco slipped out as quietly as they had come. A nurse appeared in their wake and asked if I needed anything. "Juice?" she suggested, and when I shook my head, "Ice water?"

"Ice water would be fine, thank you."

It was not the nurse, however, who brought the glass of ice water to me, it was Margo. She was a welcome sight, raven-black hair, jet-green eyes, and all.

"My ministering angel," I murmured.

Margo laughed, showing her tiny white teeth. "Not quite," she said. "When I was a little girl, though, I wanted to be a nurse when I grew up."

"And why didn't you?"

"Same reason you didn't become a doctor or a lawyer or an arctic explorer, I suppose. What might have been."

"Instead you became Mrs. Nicholas Barlow."

"Not at all, Nick. I became Margo Richmond Barlow."

"You know, Margo, if we'd stayed married—" She put her finger to my lips.

"No, don't say it."

"I was merely going to remark that if we'd stayed married, I'd have gotten into a lot less trouble."

She smiled, and I felt the blood rising to my face, for hers was a smile that never ceased to bring me pleasure.

"You have been misbehaving, haven't you?" she said.

I winced, but managed a weak, rather crestfallen smile of my own.

"The doctor said you were lucky to be alive, that if you had drunk much more of that poisoned wine, you probably wouldn't have survived. Even so, it was close, and they pumped your stomach out just in time."

"What was in that wine, anyhow?" I asked.

"Potassium chlorate, probably. At least that's what the doctor suspects it was."

"How long will I be here, Margo, did he tell you that?"

"You ought to be discharged tomorrow, but, darling—"

How sweet that word sounded in my ears. Did it mean that I was back in Margo's favor again? Perhaps not, but it did give me hope . . .

"—I'm going to be here to take you home," she continued. "What's more, I'm going to stay with you in the house for a few days—at least until you feel completely well. Is that understood?"

I muttered something like "I'm no invalid," but there was obviously no conviction in my voice. In fact, the conversation had altogether exhausted me. I slumped down in bed and closed my eyes.

"When you feel up to it, darling, I want you to call your man Oscar and tell him and Pepita to get the spare room ready for me. Nick? . . . Nick?" And on that faint, rising note, Margo's voice faded away as darkness closed in again.

Chapter 27

My release from the hospital went off smoothly, although I stoutly resisted being pushed out of the place in a wheelchair. I was woozy, but still able, with Margo's assistance, to navigate under my own power.

Margo helped trundle me into a cab, and we headed downtown.

"I've saved all the newspaper reports for you," she said as we bucketed along, hitting one pothole after another.

"I'll bet they're juicy," I said.

"They are that," she admitted. " 'Publisher in Deadly Tryst' was the headline in the *Daily News*."

"Oh great. Just *great*."

"Or this one—'Beautiful Young Editor Drinks Fatal Toast.' "

"I can't wait to read all about it."

"The television news showed the scene of the crime—or should I say, of the fatal tryst?"

"Please, Margo—I'd rather not talk about it just now."

"As you wish, darling."

I had been grateful that, since her arrival at the hospital

yesterday, Margo had not once mentioned Susan's name in any of our conversations, which I thought showed admirable restraint on her part. I had no doubt, however, that the subject would come up sooner or later, and at that time I would have to define my relationship with Susan honestly and fully. But not yet. I was still sorting things out in my own mind. Who had sent that poisoned wine—and why? Was it meant for Susan? For me? Or for both of us, perhaps?

One thing I knew for sure—I wouldn't be able to rest until I had the answers to these questions, and quite a few others.

Oscar and Pepita both met us at the door of number 2 Gramercy Park, greeting Margo warmly (I remembered how fond they had been of her in the old days), and me with the proper note of solicitude, not quite clucking over me, but showing a marked concern that went just a shade beyond their customary reserve.

"Would you like a cold drink, sir?" Oscar inquired in his thick Latvian accent.

"Iced tea would be perfect," I said. The ideal summer tipple in my view, fresh-brewed with a slice of lemon and a sprig of mint, but no sugar—and certainly never anything out of a bottle or a can. On hot summer days, I drink as much as a quart of the stuff—at least up to cocktail time.

"I want you to go lie down, Nick," said Margo in a tone that brooked no discussion, least of all any dispute.

"Can't I have my iced tea first?"

"All right," she said. "After your tea, bed."

I knew then I was in for a certain amount of bossing around, which, odd as it may seem, I didn't mind at all. I must be mellowing, like it or not.

*   *   *

So began My Three Days With Margo. She had been quite
emphatic on that point. "I don't intend to move in with
you, Nick," she said, "so don't get any ideas."

"Can't blame me for hoping, can you?"

"Just be good, darling. I intend to stay in the spare room
while I'm here. And I'm not sure I trust you even there."

The newspapers carried a mention of a memorial service
for Susan at a funeral home in Bronxville, where Susan's
parents lived and where she had grown up. I wasn't in any
condition to attend, though I would have wanted to; I
sent flowers and a condolence card, which I knew was an
inadequate gesture in the circumstances, but it was all I
could do. Poor Susan; what rotten luck I'd brought her. I
thought that I ought to call her parents and tell them how
bad I felt . . .

A man answered the phone. "Mr. Markham?" I said.

"Who's this?" His voice was gruff, a bit daunting.

"Nicholas Barlow." A longish silence followed. "Mr.
Markham? I want you to know—"

"I have nothing to say to you, Mr. Barlow."

"Perhaps if I spoke with Mrs. Markham—"

"That will not be possible, sir."

"But—"

The phone went dead. So much for good intentions. Oh
well, I can't say I blamed them. Not only was their daughter
murdered, she was found in flagrante delicto. Hell of a
situation.

That was the first day. On the second day Scanlon called
with the Bad News.

"The police checked out Susan Markham's apartment,"
he said. "But they were too late."

"How so?"

"Susan's housecleaner had been there first. She got rid of the bottle and the cork—"

"Oh no."

"But for some unaccountable reason, maybe because she hadn't heard the news, and thought Susan might be coming back to finish it off, she left the two wineglasses. One, Susan's, we presume, was empty. The other, yours, was almost full."

"She got rid of the bottle, Joe?"

"From the looks of things, it fell, or was dropped, by you or Susan, and broke on the floor. So she cleaned it up."

"And the poison?"

"Potassium chlorate was found in your wineglass, and traces of it in Susan's glass. The wonder is that the maid didn't destroy that evidence, too."

"So why don't they arrest me?"

"So far," Scanlon said, "they can't find a motive, although they're doing their best to tie it to Parker Foxcroft's murder somehow. And you're a solid citizen, Nick. A personage, if I may put it that way. They're not going to fuck around with you, unless they've got a steel-belted case against you."

"I see. Well, they're going to have one hell of a time finding a motive. I feel rotten about this, Joe, and worst of all because I think I might have inadvertently been responsible for Susan's death."

"Watch that conscience of yours, Nick. It's gotten you into trouble before, you know."

"We've got to do something about this mess, Joe."

"Stick to publishing, Nick. Writers like me need guys like you to get their books out. Leave the detecting to the pros."

I knew what he was saying and why, yet I was still determined to do something. But what?

It was Margo who came up with the idea. When I bemoaned my lack of progress in what I liked to think of as "my murder investigation," a slipshod, amateurish affair at best (but no less successful, apparently, than the official one), Margo reminded me of Mohonk.

"Remember our Mystery Weekend at Mohonk?" she said.

I did indeed. A few years back, a large band of us putative crime-solvers gathered for a long weekend at Mohonk Mountain House in New Paltz, New York. It's an annual affair, and great fun, though Margo and I only made it there once. At the beginning of the weekend, the attendees are assigned to various groups of twelve to fifteen people, each group with an identifying name, and they then watch a video of a fictional murder committed in one locale or another—it was an English manor house the year we attended. During the following few days, the groups have the opportunity to question various suspects, all of them mystery writers costumed as the characters they play. The year Margo and I went, Ed McBain, Simon Brett, and Mary Higgins Clark were among the authors present. After the questioning periods, and another simulated murder or two, each group huddles in one of the myriad nooks and crannies with which Mohonk Mountain House, a rambling castle of a hotel perched on a mountainside, is amply supplied.

"When the group we were in met to compare notes and devise a solution to the mystery," Margo said, "you remember what we did, Nick?"

"Sure. We used a blackboard—no, actually, it was a large pad on an easel—"

"And we divided the top sheet into three categories: motive, opportunity, and alibi, I believe it was—"

"And then proceeded to list the various suspects," I concluded, "according to those categories."

"After which," Margo said triumphantly, "we decided who the likeliest suspect was, and then we wrote a five-minute skit exposing our chosen murderer."

And got it all wrong. However, it was still a lot of fun.

"What I'm suggesting now, darling," Margo continued, "is that we get together in Connecticut the first weekend that's available—"

"This one's out," I reminded her. *Thanks to Lieutenant Hatcher.*

"—and form a group, just as we did at Mohonk, and go through the same procedure. Let's see. There'll be you, me, Tim, and Joe Scanlon, if he'll come—"

"I suppose we'd better include my mother," I said, "and Herbert Poole."

"Poole by all means, and Gertrude if she's game."

"She'll be game, all right," I muttered. Aloud: "It's a brilliant idea, Margo."

She beamed. "I thought you'd like it."

On the third day of Margo's stay with me, I made all the arrangements. Phone calls to Joe Scanlon, who said he'd always wanted to see where a wealthy publisher spent his weekends, and to Herbert Poole, who was willing to give up Fire Island for one weekend in order to play detective. My family was more than willing to cooperate, as was Margo.

That third night, I awoke in the middle of the night, screaming and moaning, to find Margo lying on the bed, her arms around me, saying, "There, there, Nicky—it's all right, I'm here," and wiping the perspiration from my forehead with the edge of the sheet.

"I must have had a nightmare," I said, "though I can't for the life of me remember what it was . . . oh my God, I only know it was awful."

"It's all right now, darling," said Margo, and kissed me on the lips, as she had on several occasions since we left the hospital, but always lightly, to let me know that she had no serious intentions whatsoever.

This time, however, the kiss was more intense, and she did not take her arms from around me, but nestled closer. I could feel the warmth and comforting fullness and strength of her splendid body through the thin silk nightgown she was wearing. I sighed, kissed her back, and took her into my arms.

She did not leave my bed for the rest of the night. And the next morning, there was no mention of her returning to her own apartment.

She did, however, bring up the subject of Susan Markham, while we were having breakfast, and I was rather relieved she did, because I didn't want anything from the recent past to cloud our new beginning, as I looked upon it.

"Darling," she said, "I suppose it's insecurity on my part to ask this, but—she was *younger* than I am, of course, but were you—well, were you in love with her? You know what I mean, Nick."

Yes, I knew what Margo meant. She wanted to know if I found Susan *better* than I found her.

"No, I don't think I was in love with her," I said. "There wasn't time for that. We didn't share a life together, as you and I did. I was infatuated with her, certainly. I found her *different*— in the way that every woman is different from every other woman. 'Comparison,' as Soren Kierkegaard wrote, 'is the source of all unhappiness.' "

That answer seemed to satisfy her. I have often considered that it is the "difference" between one woman and another that makes sexual fidelity—monogamy, if you will—so hard for some men to achieve. It's the *difference* that attracts. If all women looked exactly alike, dressed in the same drab clothing (as the women in Red China did for so long, in those unattractive blue jackets and pants), how easy it would be to be faithful to one woman all one's life!

Still, one makes every effort—especially if the woman in question is Margo Richmond.

Chapter 28

The following weekend included the Fourth of July, which meant the usual round of pomp and ceremony: parades, patriotic oratory, grand firework displays, and all the trimmings—as unavoidable in Connecticut as anywhere else in America. I can't say I find any of this foofaraw thrilling enough to clear away all the blemishes on our national escutcheon—but it's relatively harmless, and almost certain to bring out the small boy in more than one otherwise mature male.

Margo, Herbert Poole, Joe Scanlon, and I rode out to Weston in the Mercedes, with Oscar at the wheel. We didn't talk much on the way out—groused a bit about the weather; the thermometer had reached 98 degrees by noon that Saturday, with enough humidity to turn the entire tri-state area into the country's largest tropical rain forest. For the most part, we settled back in air-conditioned comfort and listened to Mozart on the stereo; the Piano Concerto Number 26 ("Coronation"), and the Rondo for Piano and Orchestra in D Major, both played by Murray Perahia with the English Chamber Orchestra. Nobody complained about that, al-

though I did notice that Scanlon fidgeted a bit at the beginning. However, he ultimately succumbed to Mozart's
celestial genius, and was nodding his head in tempo with
the rest of us. Afterward, he said the Rondo reminded him
"of the movie *Hopscotch*."

"Quite right, Joe," I said. "That was the movie's score."

When we arrived at the Kellogg Hill Road house, Mother
was waiting for us in the conservatory, busy watering her
plants and flowers. She pulled off her work gloves and the
floppy straw hat she wore whenever attending to her garden-
ing chores, and patted her coils of faintly blue hair back in
place. She was especially pleased to see Margo. I knew she
would be; Margo was a particular favorite.

"How good to see you two children together again," she
said, embracing us both in word and gesture. With Scanlon
and Poole she was her regal self: gracious and imposing,
with just a touch of coquettishness for Scanlon ("Lieutenant,
I've wanted Nicholas to bring you out to the country for the
longest time." Untrue, but I wasn't about to correct her.),
and properly respectful of Poole, who was, after all, a Best-
selling Author. To Mother, in retirement as well as in the
days when she played an active role in Barlow & Company,
authors were privileged beings.

I remembered how much she enjoyed playing a card game
called Authors with Father, Tim, and me. It was the only
card game my father ever played. He thought bridge was a
game for idlers and poker a pastime for the dissolute, but
Authors he enjoyed. I can still remember the pleasure both
he and Mother took in matching up mustachioed Robert
Louis Stevenson and Nathaniel Hawthorne with their four
respective books. And there was Dickens with his chin
whiskers, Thackeray with his tiny round spectacles, and, of
course, James Fenimore Cooper and Washington Irving—

and the token female author, Louisa May Alcott. All the old masters that nobody reads anymore unless compelled to do so by a school teacher. Today, if we were to re-create the game for the 1990s, it would have to include rock stars, serial killers, minor statesmen and stateswomen, unindicted coconspirators, and aged movie icons. Still, to Mother, Herbert Poole was the Real Thing.

"How shall we go about this sleuthing game of ours?" Margo asked when we had all gathered in the living room. Though none of us had forgotten the purpose of our trip to Connecticut, it had after all been her suggestion, and I had pretty well decided to let her play the leading role in our mystery weekend.

"I suggest," I said, "that we enjoy our cocktails and dinner without taxing our little gray cells, get a good night's sleep, and then, when our brains are revved up, that we tackle 'The Case of the Fair-Haired Editor.' "

"I second the motion," said Tim. He was always ready for a good game of Trivial Pursuit, Clue, or 221B Baker Street.

The rest of the party murmured their agreement to my proposal—and the evening passed in a pleasant flow of food, drink, and conversation.

When bedtime rolled around, Margo and I headed for the room we had always occupied during our married life. Mother had made no objection to this, and had, in fact, arranged it before we even arrived. In matters of this kind, she was quite Catholic in her opinions. Once married, always married—in her eyes, as well as God's.

Nothing arouses my amorous inclinations more than the cool night air of Connecticut, which did not let us down that night, I'm happy to say. When we had reached that point where smokers light up their cigarettes, and nonsmokers roll over and sink into their pillows, we decided to get out of bed and go out on our balcony. There, hand in hand, we watched a vivid display of heat lightning overhead, vast yellow flashes which made their own lovely works of fire in the cavernous sky. We were happy just to stand there and breathe in the perfume of a New England summer in full bloom.

"We're getting to be a habit again, aren't we," said Margo. "That's not in any way a complaint, darling."

"Have you thought at all," I said, "that perhaps it's our destiny?"

"Destiny." She considered this for a moment or two. "That's a rather large word, isn't it?"

"Well, we do seem to be Elected Affinities, don't we?"

"Elected Affinities. Whose term is that?"

"I don't know," I said. "It just . . . floated into my mind. It's from one philosopher or another, but damned if I can remember which one just now."

"For my part," said Margo, "I'm just going to take it day by day, see what happens. You understand, Nick?"

"Of course," I said. "It's the only way to live." That's one thing, I thought, that Alcoholics Anonymous got absolutely right.

"And you won't rush me, will you?"

"Certainly not. I shall backpedal my way straight into your heart."

"Idiot," she said, and after giving me a kiss that awakened any lust I might have sacrificed to the night air, she steered me back into the bedroom.

Before we had all separated the night before, I'd laid down one inflexible rule: "No work without nourishment first."

When we gathered downstairs again next morning, we found the buffet table laden with platters of cold ham and turkey; both of them I'd smoked myself on my last visit to Connecticut (a minor talent, but one I take pride in). The sauce was a mayonnaise and Dijon mustard. Alongside the meats was a huge serving of *pasta e pesto* on a bed of romaine, and a bowl of mixed fruit on ice. Bottles of Taittinger champagne, and pitchers of fresh orange juice—for anyone who wanted a mimosa—completed the feast. I stuck to straight champagne myself, as did most of the others. Poole alone drank only the juice.

"The champagne might make it hard for me to concentrate," he said, "and I'm really looking forward to—what'd you call it, Margo—the sleuthing game?"

"That's right."

It took Joe Scanlon to remind us that "murder was a serious business. Not a game," he said. "And there are two murders here, or aren't we planning to tackle the second one?"

"Wouldn't you all agree," Tim interjected, "that the two are connected—that the second one is simply a sequel to the first—committed by the original murderer to cover up the first crime in some way?"

As the fortunate survivor of what might have been a double murder (thank God I can't abide pink wine), I could only agree. Susan must have known something—or the murderer *thought* she knew something, that would somehow be incriminating.

"Shall we begin?" said Margo.

We had finished our brunch and were now in the solarium, like the conservatory, banked with so many of Mother's flowers and plants that it suggested southern Florida. But it was cool, with all that oxygen pumped into the air, and with stone tile underfoot, and comfortable wicker furniture.

Margo stood at the entrance to the room with an easel and a large pad of white paper; the rest of us sat in a semicircle around her. Each time she finished filling out a sheet, she tore it from the pad and fixed it to the back wall with scotch tape. In the end the wall was festooned with sheets, each one a suspect.

"We're looking for motive, opportunity, and alibi," she announced. "Facts first, from whoever has them, and then speculations. Our first suspect . . ."

She turned to me, leaving me no choice but to splutter "But . . . but . . ." and rise half out of my chair. Then I fell back. Of course Margo was right. Didn't the police still have me on their shortlist?

"Nick," said Margo, "you can tell us what your motive might have been."

I could hardly refuse to play along. "Well, I wanted to get rid of Parker, but I didn't want to buy out his contract. I'm a well-known tightwad, you see." If I'd hoped to provoke a laugh with this line, or even a titter, I was disappointed. "Also," I added, "Parker was a disruptive force in my company. People were quitting, or threatening to quit, because of his antics."

"Opportunity," said Margo. "You found the body."

"He was already dead when I did," I pointed out.

"If you'd killed him, it would have been natural for you to *pretend* you'd just found the body," said Tim.

My own brother, for Christ's sake. "Whose side are you on?" I muttered, too softly to be heard.

"But I saw someone leaving the office, someone who almost knocked me down," I protested.

"You're the only one who did see anyone else—and," said Margo, scribbling furiously on the pad with a magic marker, "you have no alibi. You were also the last one to talk to Parker."

"The phone call I got at The Players was from Parker, but the calls I made to him in the office—well, the voice could have been anyone's, even a woman's."

"Don't you think we've taken this one far enough?" It was Joe Scanlon. *Thanks, Joe, heartfelt thanks.*

"I agree," I said. "Unless you're hoping I'll confess, so we can end the exercise."

Next Margo ran through the people in the office, one by one.

"Harry Bunter," she said. "Motive: his wife was having an affair with Parker."

"He also disliked Parker on general principles." My contribution. "As did many another."

"Opportunity?" said Margo. "I assume he had a key to the office." I nodded. "But," I pointed out, "the office was unlocked, at least when I got there."

"We don't know who unlocked it," said Tim. "Could have been Foxcroft, could have been the murderer."

"As for alibi . . ." Margo was determined to keep us on track.

It was Joe Scanlon's move. "I have gotten enough information from my friend Falco to fill in those blanks," he said. "Bunter's alibi was that he was in a gin mill on the Lower East Side, drowning his sorrows. He had never been in this particular joint before, no one there knew him, and nobody, not even the bartender, remembered seeing him."

Under Margo's expert direction, we rapidly ran through the other members of the staff. Lester Crispin was a prime suspect; he had the opportunity—a key to the office. A motive of sorts: an intense dislike of Parker, who threatened his career. As for alibi?

"None," said Scanlon. "Said he was at home. No one to back up his alibi—or to deny it."

Having exhausted the insiders, myself and the two other likely Barlow & Company staff, we turned to the outsiders. Claire Bunter was first.

I reported what I knew about her motives. We had no specific facts about her opportunity to kill Parker, and Scanlon again came up empty. "She claims she was home alone, writing," he said.

"And her husband at the time was in a gin mill somewhere on the Lower East Side, drowning his sorrows, you said."

"Right."

"Too bad they can't even alibi each other," said Poole.

Next came Frederick Drew. We spent some time on his motive and opportunity, which were strong, or the police would not have hauled him in.

"But he's out on bail now," I said, "and I suspect that when he gets to the A.P., he'll be turned loose."

"The A.P.," said Margo. "And what is that? Not the Associated Press, certainly."

"It's called 'the All-Purpose part,' " I said. "From what Drew's attorney told my attorney, I gather it's where Drew appears with his lawyer before a judge, to determine if there's enough evidence against him to bring up before the grand jury for indictment. At that time, his bail could be renewed or revoked. Or he could be freed."

"Mighty complicated, the judicial system," Margo remarked in passing.

Finally we took up the case against Judith Michaelson. Her motive was perhaps the strongest of all: she had nursed a hatred of Parker for more than a year, a hatred that might well have driven her beyond the edge of sanity. As for her alibi—we knew nothing. Zip.

Mother, who had been uncharacteristically silent through the proceedings, spoke up at last.

"I think the Michaelson woman is our best prospect," she announced. "And the Bunter woman is second best."

Tim chimed in. "Oh? Do you mind telling us why you think so, Mother?"

"I don't see any of the other motives as being at all strong enough," she said. "Hatred and revenge—what motives could be stronger? And a woman scorned—"

"I can't speak about Mrs. Bunter," said Poole, "but I'll repeat what I said to Nick about Mrs. Michaelson. I don't think she'd have showed up at Foxcroft's funeral if she'd murdered him. I doubt that any woman would have the stomach for that."

"But she spat in his face," Margo protested.

"Revenge taken too late," was Poole's answer to that. "Her last chance to make a gesture, to strike back at the man who had driven her husband to suicide."

"But where are we now?" Margo spoke almost in a wail, as though ready to throw up her hands in despair. "Who do we accuse?"

"No one yet," I said. "Somehow we still don't know enough."

It was Tim who brought us around again. "Nick, you and Poole researched Parker's hard drive and went through his papers, right?"

"Yes."

"And you didn't find the solution there. So there must still be something else. Computer disks, probably. Disks on which he recorded even more private matters."

"It's possible," I said. "Wait just a minute."

"What?"

"I was thinking of something Susan told me. About Parker? How she surprised him working at his computer terminal one day and he snapped at her as though she'd caught him doing something shifty. So there must be other disks."

"If you could find those—" said Tim.

"*If* we knew where to look," I said.

At that point, the gathering broke up. Margo was still keenly disappointed, and I did my best to cheer her up.

"It was a good idea, darling. We did make some progress."

"Not enough, Nick. Not as much as we did at Mohonk."

"Mohonk was for laughs, Margo. And we lost the game there, too, if you'll recall."

Later that day, I took Scanlon and Poole aside.

"Joe," I said, "did Sergeant Falco tell you if they found any records of any kind—computer disks, maybe—in Parker's apartment when they searched it?"

"Nope. And I'm sure they searched down to the last dust bunny under the bed."

"So why don't we make the same kind of search of Parker's office?"

"I'm sure the detective squad already did," said Scanlon.

"But they wouldn't have known what to look for."

"Maybe," Scanlon said. "Anyhow, what's this 'we' business?"

"You primarily," I said. "You're the cop, you know how it's done. Down to the last dust bunny, no?"

"Well, it's not in my line of duty just now," said Scanlon, "but I'm willing to give it a whirl."

"Herbert?"

"I'll be glad to help," said Poole.

"Good. So let's the three of us tackle the job first thing Monday morning."

"Not likely," said Scanlon.

"And why not?"

"You're forgetting something, Nick. Monday is the Fourth of July holiday. Everything's shut down, and I for one didn't come out to Connecticut just to schmooze. I want a swim, at least, before heading back to town."

Chapter 29

Tuesday morning found the three of us, Poole, Scanlon, and myself, in Parker Foxcroft's office. Scanlon set to work searching the room, with what I considered remarkable speed and efficiency. He removed every drawer from Parker's desk, looked at their undersides and backs, and searched under and at the back of the desk itself. He did the same thing with each individual drawer in the file cabinets. Taking down all the paintings and photographs in the room, he turned them around as well, "for anything Foxcroft may have taped on the backs." Where one corner of the wall-to-wall carpet had come suspiciously loose, he pulled it back and looked underneath it.

After giving the room a thorough going-over, he turned to the bookcase. With the help of Poole and me, he swung the bookcase around so that he could run his hand over the back of it; he applied the same procedure to the underside of the shelves.

"Now we have only the books to go through," he said. "But it's a hell of a job if we have to look at every one of them; there must be several hundred. It would save time if—" He paused to wipe off his hands, which were black with dust.

"If what, Joe?" I said.

"If we could read Parker's mind—so to speak. He'd probably pick a book that neither he nor anyone else would be likely to read."

"The Holy Bible," suggested Poole. I couldn't help smiling at that.

"My choice," I said, "would be *Finnegans Wake*. Joyce said, you may recall, that he expected anyone who wanted to understand the book to spend his entire life reading and rereading it."

"Is there one here?" asked Scanlon. I pointed the book out; he removed it from the shelf and opened it.

"Eureka," he said, and held it open for me and Poole to see. There, taped to the inside of the front cover, was a floppy disk. A second floppy was taped to the inside of the back cover.

"Now," I said, "all we have to do is run these through a computer. But again, it's a hell of a long job."

"I'll be glad to tackle it," said Poole.

I was about to hand him the disks when it occurred to me that, after our abortive attempt in Connecticut to find the murderer, I had seen Tim's spirits decline quite precipitously.

"Thank you, Herbert," I said, "but my brother, Tim, has been looking a bit out of sorts lately, and working on these disks may cheer him up."

"As you think best," said Poole. "But if you change your mind, just let me know."

"Congratulations, Joe," I said to Scanlon. "You've both earned an expense-account lunch."

And I took them to the Colombe d'Or, where the words

"prix fixe" are not in the maître d's vocabulary, not even in the deepest recession.

I was much too impatient to wait until the weekend to get Parker's disks to Tim, so I had them sent to him by overnight mail, after first asking Hannah to copy them, just in case. When I called Tim to tell him to be on the lookout for them, I said: "If you find something, just give me a call, and I'll drop everything and come right out to Weston."

He called me the next day. All the energy and high spirits I found so inspiring in Tim were back in his voice again, stronger than ever.

"But you just got the bloody things," I said. "You couldn't possibly have had time to go through them."

"Didn't need to, buddy," he fairly chirped.

"So what did you find?"

"I think in order to save time that you'd better come out here pronto, Nick."

"If you say so." I really didn't need the invitation; I was already primed to bolt for Grand Central Station.

"I think you'll be happy," said Tim, as we were about to hang up, "with what I've found."

Hallelujah. Could the game at last be afoot?

"What I did," Tim told me when I got to Connecticut, "was print out the menus of the two disks you sent me." He pulled out a single sheet from a sheaf of computer printouts.

"This is the one you'll find interesting."

I picked up the sheet and looked at it. This is what I saw:

ENVELOPE		8093	09/28/92	15:57	ENVELOPE	.BK!	8093	09/28/92	15:50
FAIRE	.LET	1550	10/16/92	08:41	FC	.DOC	1953	07/28/88	11:39
FC	.EXE	23552	07/28/88	11:39	FINALED	.BAK	14827	08/15/92	09:00

Name	Ext	Size	Date	Time	Name	Ext	Size	Date	Time
FINAS		23708	09/17/92	18:59	FIXBIOS	.COM	50	07/28/88	11:39
FLAG	.WPG	730	07/01/88	14:50	FRIENDS	.BK!	9065	03/29/93	14:54
FRIENDS	.TLK	9065	03/29/93	14:55	GARLAND	.	40718	02/01/93	17:11
GARLAND	.BK!	40718	02/01/93	17:10	GAVEL	.WPG	856	07/01/88	14:50
GENE	.BK!	3881	03/08/93	17:11	GENE	.LET	3881	04/26/93	15:11
GENIUS1	.WPD	4692	07/01/88	14:50	GENIUS2	.WPD	4735	07/01/88	14:50
GOODNEWS	.WPG	4242	07/01/88	14:50	GRAB	.COM	15161	07/01/88	14:50
GRAPHCNV	.EXE	77312	07/28/88	11:39	H-LINE	.STY	279	09/29/88	10:28
HAND	.WPG	1054	07/01/88	14:50	HEADINGS	.STY	916	09/21/88	03:17
HOLT	.BK!	4235	05/20/92	14:12	HOLT	.LST	4289	05/27/93	10:53
HOURGLAS	.WPG	1834	07/01/88	14:50	HOWTO	.ART	8812	10/21/92	18:13
HPLASEII	.PRS	41529	11/30/88	15:47	HRF12	.FRS	49152	07/01/88	14:50
HRF6	.FRS	49152	07/01/88	14:50	IBQUIII	.PRS	3396	11/16/88	15:25
IBQUIIII	.PRS	3406	11/16/88	10:48	INS	.BK!	1471	09/27/92	18:17
INS	.LET	1928	09/27/92	18:33	IRVING	.	8254	03/13/92	15:31
JACKLET	.	4666	03/30/92	10:39	JACKLET	.BK!	3932	03/27/93	17:28
JELIAS	.LET	731	01/13/91	19:24	JUSTINE	.	708	01/13/91	19:23
KAREN	.	70257	08/05/92	18:22	KAREN	.2	78679	08/17/92	20:31
KAREN	.BK!	76256	08/17/91	20:08	KERN	.TST	3222	07/28/88	11:39
KEY	.WPG	1578	07/01/88	14:50	KEYS	.MRS	4800	06/12/89	12:16
KOREA	.318	52613	03/18/93	11:09	KOREA	.RJ	50257	03/02/93	18:14
KOREAN	.BK	57033	02/18/93	17:07	KOREAN	.BK!	60059	02/16/93	10:57
LABEL	.STY	416	06/15/89	15:49	LIBRARY	.STY	670	07/28/88	11:39
MACROCNV	.EXE	23957	07/28/88	11:39	MACROS	.WPK	14656	07/28/88	11:39
MAILBOOK	.	16602	10/28/92	18:31	MALLOY	.BK!	3072	01/08/92	09:52
MALLOY	.LET	3072	01/08/93	10:02	MAPSYMBL	.WPG	2450	07/01/88	14:50
MASSMKT	.BKS	39121	10/26/91	15:31	MEMO2	.	12412	12/02/88	16:35
MIKE1010	.	3463	10/11/92	22:36	MM1	.	2259	10/03/88	10:33
MOVING	.	3907	10/04/92	19:48	MULTISNC	.WPD	4010	07/01/88	14:50
NEWSPAPR	.WPG	1388	07/01/88	14:50	NO1	.WPG	3234	07/01/88	14:50
ORDERWPG	.DOC	6155	07/01/88	14:50	PACHTER	.BK!	4106	02/18/93	15:33
PACHTER	.LET	2728	08/03/92	15:46	PC	.WPG	2586	07/01/88	14:50
PENCIL	.WPG	3510	07/01/88	14:50	PHONE	.WPG	4180	07/01/88	14:50

"I'm not sure what I'm looking for, Tim," I said, after quickly glancing at the printout.

"You must look more closely, Nick," he said, and put his finger on the entry IRVING.

"Irving," I said. "What d'you know? The mysterious Irving that Parker mentioned to Susan Markham."

"Precisely," said Tim. "And what this file contains is the rejection letter Parker wrote to Judith Michaelson's husband, the letter she claims drove him to suicide."

"Well, I'll be damned," I said. "It did mean something after all—*Irving*."

"Here you are." Tim handed me several more sheets. "The letter itself, which I printed out. I suggest you read it."

The letter opened with "Dear Mr. Michaelson" and then this opening paragraph:

> You have apparently sent this manuscript to me to read because I have a reputation as a literary editor, as distinguished from one of the commercial hacks who ply our editorial waters. At least one of your assumptions is far off the mark. Literary I may well be; literary your book is most assuredly not; nor do I believe it ever can be, with the most assiduous rewriting. I strongly advise you to consign this abortive piece of rubbish to the flames, or the trash can, whichever may be most convenient.

"Ordinarily," Parker's letter continued, "I would not waste my valuable time criticizing your work in any detail, but because you mentioned the name of a good friend of mine in your submission letter, I have decided to take a few pains at least and point out to you where your manuscript is lacking both coherence and literary merit."

And there followed, as far as I could tell from a hasty reading, a page and a half of comments on the plot of Michaelson's novel, and what Parker found to be "its manifest weaknesses of style and structure."

Shaking my head, I handed the transcript of the letter back to Tim. "Leaving aside the brutality of Parker's rejection," I said, "and we already know what he is capable of in that department, what am I to make of this?"

"Patience, and all will become clear," said Tim. "First, I want you to call Judith Michaelson and ask her one question."

"Okay, I'll do it."

He told me the question I was to ask. I called Judith Michaelson and asked the question. She answered me without hesitation.

And shortly after that, Tim came through, as I had instinctively known he would.

All became brilliantly clear.

Chapter 30

When I told Joe Scanlon what I planned to do, he was convinced that the shock of Susan's death and my close call had driven me right off the deep end.

"I believe it's the only way, Joe," I said.

"In my opinion, you've read at least one too many mysteries, and I'd be happy to tell you which one."

"Do you have a better idea?"

"Go straight to Hatcher with what information you have, and let him handle it."

"I'm not saying he'd bungle it—possibly not. But I think I have a proprietary interest in this case, and I want to see it through."

I had asked Scanlon to come to my office as soon as I returned from Connecticut. Instead of sitting in his usual chair, he was pacing back and forth in a state of extreme agitation, such as I had never seen him in before—not even when I had broken one of his cherished police rules.

"Indulge me, Joe."

"Okay, Nick, okay. It's your funeral. I'll do what I can."

My plan was quite simple, as well as time-worn. I had

decided to gather all the principals in the case together in the Barlow & Company conference room, and I needed Joe's help to round up Hatcher and Falco (on the premise that I had "new information" on the murder to give them); nothing was to be said about the rest of the cast of characters. I would also need Joe to make sure that the two women, Claire Bunter and Judith Michaelson, would be there. This he could do by throwing his weight around. It would be an easy matter to flash his shield; they would hardly be aware that he was on leave and had no jurisdiction in the matter.

"The brass'll have my head if they find out about this," he grumbled.

"You're not arresting anyone, Joe, which it would be quite within your duty to do if you saw a crime occurring, leave or no leave."

"Yes, but—oh well, what the hell—in for a penny—"

And he left to carry out his assignment. I myself could account for Poole, Margo, and the two suspects in my office: Harry Bunter and Lester Crispin. We could do without Frederick Drew, I had decided; he was still somewhere in the judicial machinery of New York City, but I was confident he would be exonerated in short order. As early, perhaps, as this afternoon.

The meeting was scheduled for four o'clock, which I thought would allow plenty of time to round everybody up.

And promptly at four, there they all were, seated around the conference table, with the exception of Hatcher, Falco, and Joe Scanlon, who hovered in the background. Hatcher was beet-red and silent; Falco grim-faced and equally silent. I had the feeling that it would not take much for either or both of them to stop smoldering and erupt.

On one side of the long oak table, to the left of my chair, sat Herbert Poole, Margo, and Claire Bunter, who apparently chose that chair because she thought Margo might be sympathetic—and because it was as far away as possible from her husband. Harry Bunter was in the seat next to mine on the right side of the table, and next to him were Lester Crispin and Judith Michaelson, across from Claire Bunter. Of all the people there, Judith Michaelson appeared the most ill at ease; she gazed around the room with a vague, distracted expression on her face.

Nobody said a word, either on entering the conference room or after sitting down. They all simply stared at me, as though, like Scanlon, they were convinced I had taken leave of my senses. I had the strange sensation that I was either going to enjoy the biggest triumph of my career or lay the biggest egg.

Well, here goes, Nick. I took a deep breath.

"The time-honored line in a situation like this," I began, "is 'I suppose you're all wondering why I brought you here.' "

"Oh no," said Harry Bunter sotto voce.

"I'm only sorry my brother, Tim, isn't here," I said, ignoring Harry, "or I'd let him run the meeting. But he doesn't travel easily, and I do, so you'll have to put up with me. I want it known, however, that Tim is responsible for unraveling this mess.

"A word or two of summary to set the scene," I continued. "As you all know, Parker Foxcroft was killed in his office on this floor on the evening of June first. A number of us here were—make that *are*—suspects in that murder."

"Speak for yourself, Nick." It was Claire Bunter.

"I just did. And if you don't think you're still a suspect, Claire, ask Lieutenant Hatcher here." She did not reply to this, and Hatcher only grunted something unintelligible.

"Nick, why don't you just cut to the chase?" said Scanlon.

"Patience, and I will. Most of our efforts—and I presume most of the police's efforts as well—have been directed toward looking for motives, checking alibis, and inquiring into Parker Foxcroft's past. One of the suspects, Frederick Drew, was arrested and is, I believe, now out on bail—"

"That's correct, Mr. Barlow." It was Lieutenant Hatcher, finally heard from. "But—"

I didn't give him a chance to offer any disclaimers.

"What we have learned about Parker Foxcroft has not been pleasant," I said. "The likelihood is that he was practicing blackmail on a small, possibly a large, scale. But who was he blackmailing, and why? What did he know that gave him so much power over the person we'll call 'X' for now?

"The identity of X lay concealed somewhere in Parker's files, we were convinced of that. A search of his office yielded nothing—until we found two computer disks that he had hidden away. My brother was able to track down the file that led us to X's identity, thanks to a clue Susan Markham had given us."

"And what might that have been?" demanded Hatcher in a loud voice—too loud for the size of the room. "And why weren't the police told about this 'clue' of yours?"

"We might have told you, I agree," I said, "but it wouldn't have meant any more to you than it did to us— at first. It was a literary clue that Parker left, and I'll explain it later. What is important is that Parker had used it as the name of a file on one of his disks. When Tim read the file and printed it out for me to read, we knew immediately what had taken place—and why."

At last I detected a stir of interest, if not excitement, in the room, so I plowed on.

"The file was named IRVING, and it contained the letter Parker Foxcroft wrote rejecting Alexander Michaelson's novel, a letter that Mrs. Michaelson, unfortunately, destroyed."

"What else would you expect me to do?" Judith Michaelson cried out. "My husband was dead!"

"No one is blaming you, Mrs. Michaelson," I said. "If you had saved that letter, we'd have known the identity of the murderer sooner, it is true, but anyone else would have acted just as you did.

"The manuscript, by the way," I continued, "was lost and also probably destroyed. What we learned from that letter—correction, what *Tim* learned from that letter—is that it described a novel now riding high on the fiction bestseller lists. A novel called *Pan at Twilight*."

I had to hand it to Herbert Poole; he barely blinked an eye. A slight smile was the only reaction he gave to the title of his book. He leaned back in his chair, crossing his arms in front of his chest. *Show me. Cool.*

"Tim, fortunately for us, had read *Pan at Twilight,* and Parker Foxcroft, of course, had read it when the book was in manuscript. The so-called author of the book"—and here I made no effort to conceal my contempt—"was sent the manuscript by Alexander Michaelson's widow, because he was a knowledgeable friend, and she wanted his opinion on her husband's work. Knowledgeable, yes; friend, hardly. This 'friend' told her that the book was probably unpublishable, and he recommended that she destroy it. He arranged for a messenger to pick it up, presumably to deliver it to the critic Peter Jensen. He then copied it and submitted it to his publisher under his own name, as a 'daring' and 'different' new turn in his career. The rest you know; the book was an immediate success. What we didn't know is that Parker Foxcroft recognized the book as one he had rejected, and, possibly smarting over the realization that he had passed up a best-seller himself, and seizing the opportunity to blackmail the author"—here I made quote marks in the air—"he threatened to expose a flagrant case of plagiarism. If not a crime, by the way, plagiarism is certainly more than just a breach of good taste."

"You!" Judith Michaelson rose and pointed at Herbert Poole. "How could you?"

Poole raised his hands in the air as though to disavow any acquaintance with this peculiar creature across the table from him. His smile now was so disingenuous I felt like picking him up and shaking him like a rat. *Who, me?* that smile said.

"Let me explain why Parker chose the code name IRVING for his blackmail. There are a number of Irvings in publishing history, but the one Parker chose was *John* Irving. Why him? Because John Irving, like our murderous author, had published three unsuccessful novels before he achieved what we call his 'breakout' or 'breakthrough' book, the one that brought him fame and fortune. In Irving's case it was *The World According to Garp;* so successful was it that we sometimes speak of a book being 'Garped,' meaning that it has broken its author out of obscurity and into the limelight. For Herbert Poole, the 'Garping' was *Pan at Twilight.* That was Parker Foxcroft's little literary conceit—his joke, if you will."

I could tell from the expression on their faces, and the way they shifted about, that I had finally reached Hatcher and Falco; they were paying attention; and certainly Joe was with me. The others reacted with a mixture of dismay and, understandably, relief. Not I, but he, is the guilty one.

"Beautiful, Nick," said Margo. "Well done."

Poole was no longer smiling, but as cool in demeanor as ever.

"There's no proof there," he said. "No evidence. You can't prove anything. It's all supposition."

"The plagiarism will be hard to prove, perhaps, but if you photocopied Michaelson's original manuscript and just put your name on it," I said, "that copy will be in the publisher's office. There will be no problem tracking it back to Michaelson's manual typewriter.

"Also," I continued, "you remember that line in *All the President's Men*? Deep Throat says to Woodward and Bernstein: 'Follow the money.' I think that if we look at your bank account and Parker's bank account, we will probably find a pattern of withdrawals from your account and deposits in his. 'Follow the money.' "

"I've put up with enough of this nonsense," said Poole. He got up and rested his hands on the table. "You'll be hearing from my attorney, Barlow. I consider that I've been libeled."

"Slandered, Herbert, not libeled. And I believe you'll probably be hearing from the police."

Hatcher, Falco, and Scanlon moved toward Poole.

Then Judith Michaelson rose and said: *"Herbert."*

He turned to her; she held a pistol in one hand and the purse she'd taken it from in the other.

"No, no, Judith," said Poole, but she had fired even as he spoke—two shots before Hatcher was able to wrest the gun out of her hand. Poole slumped back in his chair, head falling forward onto the table.

He looked, I thought, exactly as Parker had looked when I found his body.

Chapter 31

Herbert Poole did not die of the gunshot wounds he suffered at the hands of Judith Michaelson. Like so many people, she was not altogether sure where in the chest cavity the heart is located, or perhaps she was just a poor shot; consequently, one of her shots nicked Poole's right lung and the other struck him in the right shoulder. He survived to face murder charges. The police were able to link Poole with Parker Foxcroft's blackmailing activities, and a creditable witness placed him in the neighborhood of our offices when Parker was shot. Poole, however—rather than stand trial on a murder charge, where the verdict might have gone either way—elected to plea-bargain with the district attorney, accepting a charge of manslaughter. The D.A. recommended a sentence of seven to ten years, which the judge, in keeping with the quality of mercy, ultimately suspended. He walks the streets a free man. I do not, however, expect to publish a mystery under his name, or any other kind of book.

Judith Michaelson deserved punishment far less than Poole, but wound up with a sentence for aggravated assault of a year in a correctional facility. She served only six months, but in my view, as much as I deplore people taking vigilante action, she ought not to have served jail time at all. However, we know that fairness and justice are almost as elusive as that will-o'-the-wisp we all talk about, but which nobody has ever seen. Poetic justice was served when it was revealed that the gun she shot Poole with was the very one her husband used to take his own life.

Vindication of a sort, however, was rendered by Herbert Poole's publisher, who made a substantial cash settlement on Judith Michaelson, taking the money from Poole's royalties. He fought this in court subsequently, but lost. I assume that Judith made a much more persuasive witness on the stand than he. Furthermore, Tim submitted a computer analysis of Poole's books, demonstrating that the first three were the work of one writer, and the fourth, his best-seller, the work of another.

All this happened not at once, but as the summer passed into fall and then winter. Meanwhile, the fortunes of Barlow & Company began to prosper, not because of anything I did, but in part because the Book-of-the-Month Club decided to start a Prudence Henderson Harte Library, bringing all her earlier books back into print, with a vengeance. Moreover, a movie made from a novel by another of my authors, Warren Dallas, sparked a new and phenomenally successful movie tie-in paperback. Backlist, in the publishing business, is what makes the mare go, now and always. As for frontlist, Sarah Goodall's female P.I. novel, *Iceman,* has been delivered and will be published next spring. Will it be a success? Who ever knows?

Margo and I did not exactly decide to live together, but "to be together as long as it seems to be working out," a loose but mutually satisfactory arrangement. While she still maintains her own apartment, "for breathing room"—that is, the occasional solitude everyone needs—we are together every weekend from Friday through Monday, either at my house or in Connecticut, and we have planned a two-week Caribbean cruise in December, which I think is the closest we will come to a second honeymoon.

I believe it was Balzac, in his *Physiologie de Mariage,* who recommended that a married couple not only not share the same bedroom, but that they not share the same house. Impractical these days—but Honoré had a point all the same.

On one of those weekends I invited Joe Scanlon to dinner.

"I'm not pressing you for that revised manuscript, Joe. You understand that, don't you?"

"It's almost ready, Nick, I swear."

"Anyway, come to dinner with Margo and me. We haven't seen enough of you lately."

"Can I . . . that is, may I bring a friend?" I would have sworn that he sounded almost bashful.

"Of course, Joe—please do."

The friend he brought turned out to be his agent, Kay McIntire, whose beauty and intelligence I have already praised enough. I had only to observe the two of them together—the way they looked at each other, and those secret smiles—to know that they were prime candidates for Liz Smith's column.

"Makes me feel almost like a matchmaker," I told Margo after Joe and Kay had left.

"You're mellowing, Nicky," she said. "No more the grumpy, somewhat misogynous middle-aged bachelor?"

"I am happy for both Joe and Kay McIntire as two people I like and wish well. But I retain the privilege of lashing out at whatever in this life I find offensive."

Only one thing in my thoughts did I keep private even from Margo, and that was the memory of Susan Markham. Her death remained a constant reproach, more powerful at some moments than at others, but always there, just beneath the surface of my contentment. Despite the best efforts of the police, no way had been found to link Herbert Poole to her murder, and so the crime remained on the books, still open. How I wished I could find a way to prove his guilt. Without physical evidence, there was nothing to tie Susan's death with Parker's, only my suspicion—no, my conviction—that Poole had done it. Take the bottle of wine, for just one example. Only an abstainer like Poole, a wine illiterate, if you will, would choose a rosé as a special gift. He was also probably the one who dropped the urn off the roof, but I couldn't prove that either.

I was glad that I had not run into Poole after he was carried out of my conference room on a stretcher. I don't know what I might have done or said. I only hope I could have controlled my natural instincts, which would have been to squash him like some nasty little insect.

Shortly after Labor Day, I received the following letter, which read, in its entirety:

Dear Mr. Barlow:

I am a graduate student in English at your alma mater, Princeton. I plan to do my doctoral thesis on the editor Parker Foxcroft, who, I know, had a prestigious imprint at your firm. I understand also that you are his literary executor.

My request is this: would it be possible for me to examine all the letters, papers, and memorabilia relating to Mr. Foxcroft's distinguished career?

If it would be convenient, I should appreciate the opportunity to meet with you and discuss this project in more detail.

Eagerly awaiting your reply, I remain
                              Sincerely yours,

The signature was that of a T. Wyndham Prescott III. I dictated the following reply:

Dear Mr. Prescott III:

Of course you may have access to the files and personal papers of the late Parker Foxcroft. I know he would have been pleased at your request to do your doctoral thesis on his career. In fact, I'm convinced his entire working life was planned so that some scholar, such as yourself, would wish to delve into his literary remains.

Just call my secretary, Ms. Hannah Stein, and she'll be happy to set up an appointment.

                              Sincerely yours, etc.

P.S. I haven't had much contact with Princeton lately, except the usual fund-raising letters from the Alumni Association, but I gather that the Tiger is alive and still roaring.

It was time, it seemed to me, to exorcise the ghost of Parker Foxcroft. After all, like a much, much better man, he now belonged to the ages.